THE CARVER

A THOMAS SHEPHERD MYSTERY
BOOK 6

DAN PADAVONA

GET A FREE BOOK!

I'm a pretty nice guy once you look past the grisly images in my head. Most of all, I love connecting with awesome readers like you.

Join my VIP Reader Group and get a FREE serial killer thriller for your Kindle.

Get My Free Book

www.danpadavona.com/thriller-readers-vip-group/

1

An oppressive darkness smothered every corner of the room. A single light bulb hung from a frayed wire in the center of the ceiling, spilling a sickly glow over the walls and floor below. The blood-red hue coloring the room seemed to emanate from a rusted metal table, slick with a crimson mixture of filth. Shadows danced and contorted on the stained walls.

Bound to a steel chair, Gresham Thompson could do little more than squint against the darkness as he tried to make out his surroundings. His heart hammered against his ribs, a cacophony of dread echoing within him as his ears strained to pick up any sound other than his own labored breathing. Clammy sweat trickled down the sides of his face, his shirt sticking to his back like a second skin. As the footsteps approached, each thud sending tremors through the floor, icy tendrils of terror snaked through his veins.

"Please," he whispered, his throat raw from screaming and pleading, but his voice fell flat in the unforgiving chamber.

The footsteps grew louder, closer, until they paused outside the door. Gresham's breath hitched, every muscle in his body coiled with desperation. But the restraints binding him to the chair dug into his wrists and ankles, leaving angry welts where they bit into his skin.

As the door creaked open, revealing the hulking figure of his tormentor, his eyes widened in fear. He knew this man—or rather, this monster—held his fate in those hands. And as the room closed in around him, he could only hope for a miracle that would never come.

The sound of metal against metal filled the air as the man rummaged through a collection of surgical equipment. The chilling clink and scrape intensified Gresham's dread, each note a harrowing reminder of what awaited him.

"Ah, there it is," the madman muttered to himself, his voice cold and devoid of emotion.

Gresham strained to see what instrument he'd chosen, but the man's frame obscured his view. Desperation took hold, and he struggled against the restraints. They were thick leather straps with heavy-duty buckles, secured around his wrists and ankles. He pulled and struggled, feeling the unforgiving material dig deeper into his flesh.

"Struggle all you want. It won't do you any good."

"Please," Gresham whispered, the word barely escaping his cracked lips. "You don't have to do this."

"Ah, Gresham," the madman clucked, like a teacher chastising a wayward student. "I thought we'd established that begging won't work with me."

Gresham fell silent, knowing the futility of his words. As the seconds ticked by, his hope dwindled, until it was nothing more than a dying ember.

"Very well." In the man's hand was an ominous-looking scalpel, its blade gleaming in the blood-red glow of the room. "Let's begin, shall we?"

A single thought echoed through Gresham's head: why? He

couldn't fathom who would do this to him or what he had done to deserve such treatment. No face came to mind, no enemies surfaced from the depths of his past. But there must have been something—some reason for his torment.

"Who are you?"

"Ah, the million-dollar question." With that, the man turned away, leaving Gresham in tortured silence. His captor's identity remained a mystery.

As Gresham's thoughts turned back to his predicament, flashes of his last memory before this nightmare replayed in his mind. He remembered walking down the quiet street, the sun dipping below the horizon as the day gave way to twilight. He recalled stopping at the corner store, the bell above the door jingling as he entered, the smell of fresh bread and brewing coffee filling his nostrils. A friendly exchange with the cashier, a few dollar bills passed back and forth, and he was on his way.

Then the chilly trek back to his car, which he never reached before something struck the back of his skull.

"Just tell me why."

"Does knowing why change anything? Will it make the pain any less real?" The madman was right—the reason didn't matter in the end. All that mattered was holding on to hope, finding some way out of this hell. "Your determination is admirable, but I wonder . . . how long will it last?"

Gresham tasted blood in his mouth. It mixed with the salty dampness of his sweat and tears. The throbbing in his head intensified as memories of the impact resurfaced—the violent blow that had shattered his world and rendered him unconscious.

He hadn't seen the attacker coming. One moment, he was searching for his keys, and the next, a crack echoed through his brain, followed by searing pain.

How had he wound up here? Where was his wife? At the

thought of her, his hands clenched as he prayed she was safe. The man was tall and broad-shouldered, his face a grotesque mask that resembled a rotting skull.

"Do I know you?"

"No, I don't believe so. I'm an admirer of sorts. You see, I've been watching you for quite some time. You and your lovely wife."

"Please, she has nothing to do with this."

"Ah, but that's where you're wrong," the madman said, stopping in front of him. He kneeled, bringing his face inches from Gresham's. "I've devised a little game to test your devotion to one another."

The madman leaned closer, his breath hot and foul.

"Tell me," he whispered, his words crawling like spiders over the farmer's skin. "Would you give an arm or a leg to save your wife's life?"

Gresham's chest tightened.

"Would you?" the madman demanded.

The room seemed to close in, the shadows creeping closer. He thought of his wife, her beautiful smile, and the life they'd built together.

"Yes. She's my wife."

"I realize it's just a saying, but I'm glad to see you're willing to sacrifice for love."

"Please, I'll do anything. Just don't hurt her."

The madman tilted his head to one side, considering for a moment before a sinister chuckle escaped his lungs. "Very well, Gresham. But I want you to remember that it was your choice to make this sacrifice. Which limb would you prefer to give up? Your arm, perhaps? Or maybe one of your legs?"

He stepped closer, the sound of metal scraping against metal cutting through the air as he brandished a bone saw, its serrated edge glinting.

"Choose wisely, Gresham."

"No, I didn't mean it literally. I'd do anything for my wife, but—"

"So you lied." The man tutted. "Such a shame you refuse to prove your love, especially after you cheated on her."

"What? I would never cheat on my wife."

Except he had. And somehow this man knew.

"Choose. If you don't, I will choose for you. What will it be? An arm or a leg?"

"It doesn't matter what I say. You'll kill me anyway."

The madman circled the room. Gresham's eyes remained fixed on the serrated edge, the cold steel reflecting the unholy light. His pulse pounded in his ears as the madman stopped, planting himself at the foot of the makeshift operating table.

"Your leg," the madman said, his voice devoid of empathy.

Gresham squeezed his eyes shut. This was just a game, a threat. The man wouldn't do really remove his leg.

"You're sick."

"Sick? No, I crave justice." Anger flashed in the man's eyes. "Isn't it ironic that a man named after justice received none?"

This man was insane. Gresham didn't know what he was raving about.

"Let's begin."

The madman positioned the bone saw over Gresham's thigh. He pressed down, the serrated teeth digging into flesh and drawing a thin line of blood.

"God, no!" Gresham screamed, convulsing against his restraints as the blade cut through skin and muscle. The pain was unlike anything he'd ever experienced, a searing, white-hot agony that obliterated all other thoughts.

His mind retreated inward, desperate to escape the gruesome reality unfolding before him. He imagined himself running through a field with his wife, hand in hand, the warm sun shining down on them. But like a relentless tide, the pain washed away his fantasies and dragged him back to the present.

"Please, stop!"

The madman ignored his pleas, working the bone saw with slow, deliberate strokes. Gresham's vision blurred as the pain intensified.

"Your love is truly commendable, Gresham, but your journey has only just begun."

As the blade sliced deeper into Gresham's leg, the last threads of hope unraveled within him, leaving only despair.

And agony.

2

The February wind swept over the frozen lake, casting a chill upon Thomas Shepherd and Chelsey Byrd as they worked outside their lakeside A-frame. They were repairing the roof and windows damaged by last December's storm, which had left the house vulnerable to the harsh winter elements. Thomas climbed up the ladder, hammer in hand, while Chelsey stood on the ground below, passing him the necessary supplies. Though the work was demanding, Thomas found solace in the distraction; it kept his mind from wandering to dark places.

"Hand me another shingle, will you?" Thomas called down to Chelsey, his breath visible in the air as he spoke. She nodded, picking one up from the stack beside her and handing it to him.

"Here you go," she said, watching him secure it into place. As they continued to work, the rhythm of their labor became almost meditative, the sound of the hammer echoing through the quiet lakeside landscape.

"Hey, Thomas?" Chelsey asked after a while, breaking the silence. "How did your appointment with Dr. Mandal go yesterday?"

Thomas paused mid-swing, the question catching him off guard. He hadn't expected her to ask about the appointment, but he supposed it was only natural for her to be curious. The Victor Bacchus attack on Laurel Mountain had left him with emotional scars that refused to heal overnight. Climbing down the ladder, he dry-washed his hands before responding.

"Uh, it went well. Dr. Mandal said I'm making progress and that the therapy sessions are helping."

Chelsey offered him a smile, pleased with the news. "That's great, Thomas. I'm really glad to hear you're doing better." She hesitated for a moment, considering her next words. "Do you think you'll ever be able to move past what happened on Laurel Mountain? I still dream about Victor Bacchus."

Thomas looked out over the lake, its frozen surface reflecting the pale winter sun. He knew he would never forget the horror of that day, but he couldn't let it define him forever. With Dr. Mandal's help, he was learning to compartmentalize and move forward.

"Not entirely," he said. "But I'm working on it."

She placed a reassuring hand on his arm, her touch grounding him in the present moment. "You're doing great, Thomas. Just take it one day at a time. But I know one thing for sure: You're stronger than you think, and you're not alone."

The wind whispered through the bare branches of the trees as he balanced on the ladder. She remained nearby, handing him tools and supplies. The frigid air nipped at their exposed skin, but despite the chill, Thomas couldn't help but feel a sense of peace in this setting.

"Even with therapy, the snowstorm and the attack will always be a part of me," he said, concentrating on driving a nail into the shingles. "But I've learned to compartmentalize and move forward."

Chelsey applied a bead of caulk along the edge of a

windowpane, sealing it against the cold. "That's all any of us can do: take our experiences, learn from them, and continue living."

He paused for a moment, hammer in hand, and looked at his fiancée. Her face was set in concentration, but the understanding in her eyes never failed to comfort him. She understood the weight of his words, having faced her own demons in the past.

Thomas resumed hammering nails into place. The sound of metal striking metal echoed around them, punctuating the stillness of the winter air. As he worked, his mind churned with thoughts of the future. The uncertainties, the dangers, and the unspoken fears that lay just beneath the surface.

Through the pain and uncertainty, one thing remained clear. His connection with Chelsey was unwavering, a beacon of hope amid the shadows of doubt. With each swing of the hammer, each sealed window, he reminded himself that they were a team. They could conquer anything.

"Let's finish up before it gets too cold," he said. "I'm sure Jack and Tigger want dinner."

"Almost done with this window."

"The roof is in much better shape with the new shingles." As they worked, Thomas reflected on his therapy sessions. "Dr. Mandal thinks I'm ready to take on more challenging investigations. Even murders."

"Really?" She looked up from the window. "That's great news, isn't it?"

"Maybe." He hesitated. "I just wonder if she's right . . . if I'm really ready for that."

"You've come so far since the attack. I love the way you delegate responsibility at the office."

"If I don't, Aguilar will smack me in the head."

"Stop."

"At least the nightmares aren't as frequent," he said. "I can finally sleep soundly again."

"See? That's progress. And you know I'll be here to support you every step of the way."

"Your support means everything to me. Heck, I think I might even marry you."

She laughed and swatted his shin.

As the last of the light faded, they stepped back to admire their handiwork.

"Looks like we're done here," she said, a satisfied smile playing on her lips.

"Amazing work. Let's head inside and warm up."

As they entered the warmth of the A-frame, leaving the cold and wind behind, Jack rushed over to greet them. The dog stood on his hind legs and licked their faces. Tigger padded across the floor and glared at them. Had the cat owned a watch, he would have tapped it to show they were late in feeding him.

Thomas got to work on dinner while Chelsey fed the pets. They worked in a companionable silence only broken by the water boiling as Thomas removed a box of pasta from the pantry.

After dinner, they settled into the living room with cups of hot chocolate. The fire crackled and popped, and they daydreamed about a vacation in the tropics. They discussed what to pack, where to go, and the many activities they could enjoy. No blizzards, just sunburns. Picturing the vacation made his doubts recede.

He stole looks at Chelsey, drawing strength from her presence. Despite his concerns, he knew that with her support, he would put the December blizzard and murders behind him.

This moment, right here with his future wife by his side, was worth fighting for. And he would do whatever it took to hold on to it.

3

Scout Mourning gripped the steering wheel of LeVar's black Chrysler Limited, her eyes locked on the way forward as they traveled the treacherous, ice-covered roads. She had received her learner's permit a few months prior, but her mother, Naomi, refused to let her take the driver's test until her seventeenth birthday—a source of great frustration for her.

"LeVar," she said, hoping the heater would warm the car's interior, "I can't wait to graduate high school and join you at Kane Grove University. I just want to get a head start on my future, you know?"

He looked over at her, his dreadlocks framing his face. "I understand your eagerness, but you need to slow down and enjoy your time in high school. You only get to experience it once."

"Easy for you to say," she muttered under her breath, her eyes darting between the rearview mirror and the road ahead. An SUV tailgated her.

"Ignore him."

"I'm trying, but he's riding my butt."

LeVar laughed until he coughed. "Yo, another choice of words, *aight*?"

The SUV blew past. Snow-covered trees lined the streets, their branches weighed down with the heavy burden of winter.

"Trust me," he said. "You'll look back on these days and wish they'd never ended. Don't be in such a rush to grow up."

LeVar leaned back in his seat. If he was comfortable with her driving on snow and ice, that made one of them. But she had to learn.

She sighed, her grip loosening on the wheel as she considered his words. They had been friends long enough for her to trust his opinion, but it was difficult to see past her own ambitions. She knew her abilities went beyond high school.

"I guess you're right. It's just hard to stay patient when I feel like I'm ready for something more."

"Believe me, I get you. But you've got time. You'll accomplish great things; just don't forget to live in the present."

Snowflakes danced outside the windows, their intricate patterns forming a mesmerizing display as they fell in slow motion.

"Speaking of high school," she said, breaking the silence, "have you noticed how Liz has been acting around you lately?"

LeVar's face flushed, his attention shifting towards the window. "Uh, I've noticed she's been . . . friendlier, I guess."

"Friendlier? She has a major crush on you." Scout chuckled. "She talks about you all the time."

"I don't wanna hear this." LeVar squirmed in his seat. "I mean, I'm flattered, but damn. She's sixteen."

"Relax. I told her you have a girlfriend." She realized how her words sounded and wanted to reclaim them. "I didn't say *me*. We're just friends, right?"

"Hundred percent. Thanks for telling her, though. It would've been awkward if she asked for a date."

"No problem."

Inside, she experienced a pang of envy, wondering when someone would take notice of her the way Liz had of LeVar. She lost herself in thought, picturing the qualities she admired in him: his kindness, his trustworthiness, his loyalty.

"Keep your eyes on the road," LeVar reminded her as she drifted too close to the edge of the lane. She nodded, refocusing her eyes on the path ahead.

"Sorry."

Her hands tightened around the wheel as she silently chastised herself for letting her thoughts wander. She couldn't wait to graduate high school and escape the drama. The boys still saw her as the nerdy girl with glasses, never giving her a second glance. She remembered overhearing them call her "Velma" after the Scooby Doo character. It stung more than she cared to admit.

"LeVar, do you think I'll ever fit in? At school?"

"Whatchu mean?" he asked, his eyes on the road but his attention focused on her words.

"Well, it's just that I'm still an outsider, you know? The boys treat me differently than other girls. They don't see me as someone they could date or even be friends with."

"Listen to me: High school can be rough. But trust me when I say that you're better than stupid guys who don't see your worth. You're smart, talented, and strong. You shouldn't have to change who you are just to fit in."

She wished someone would see her the way LeVar saw her, someone who would appreciate her for who she was.

"In the meantime," he said, "you've got me as a friend, right? And I've got your back no matter what."

A sharp curve appeared ahead, demanding unwavering focus from an inexperienced driver.

"Be careful on these turns," he said, scanning the icy path ahead. "Remember, slow and steady wins the race."

"Got it."

"Don't strangle the steering wheel. Chill, sis."

"Doing my best."

"No need to sweat it. These snow tires are banging."

She did her best not to chuckle and spin off the road. An accident wasn't something she wished to explain to Mom.

The surrounding landscape seemed almost magical, like something straight out of a storybook. Each flake of snow that fell added to the thick white blanket over the ground, muffling the sounds of the world and creating a calming stillness. She lost herself in the beauty of nature. While paying attention to the road, she took in the sight of the frosted evergreens and the way the icicles hung from the eaves of houses. When she earned her license, she'd drive all the time during the winter. Or at least she felt that way now.

"Wow, it's really beautiful out here. I've always loved winter."

"It's all right. Me? I like a hot summer day with the air rippling off the pavement. That's my kind of weather."

"And cool plunges into the lake."

"Damn straight."

She hoped for someone to share these moments with. Someone who got her like LeVar.

"Coming up on a stop sign," he said as he guided her through the drive.

"Right." She eased her foot onto the brake pedal. The car rolled to a halt, its engine humming in the stillness of the snowy world.

"Good job. Just remember to signal when you turn."

"I won't forget," she said, flicking the turn signal. The car moved forward, tires crunching over the compacted snow.

As they drove, she thought about graduating from high

school and joining LeVar at Kane Grove University. He might still be there when she arrived as a freshman. She wondered what life would be like away from the familiar comforts of home, surrounded by fresh faces and experiences. It both excited and terrified her, leaving her with a knot of uncertainty twisting in her stomach.

"Did you ever feel scared when you started college?" Her words came out in a nervous rush, betraying her own fears.

"Hell, yeah. It's natural to feel that way. But once I met my professors and started making friends, it became easier. You'll adapt, too."

"I hope so."

"Life's full of uncertainties. But that's what makes it interesting. Just take it slowly."

"Right," she agreed, finding solace in his wisdom.

One step at a time, she thought. That was all she could do.

And as the car moved forward through the wintry world outside, Scout journeyed into an unknown future.

4

Thomas approached the entrance to the Nightshade County Sheriff's Department with a sense of accomplishment. Repairing the A-frame with Chelsey had been akin to closing the door on the December blizzard and Victor Bacchus. Salt covered the walkway and melted the inch of snow that had fallen overnight.

He pushed open the door and strode into the operations area, which was nothing more than a gloomy hallway with desks taking up most of the space. The heating system was on the fritz again. They needed a modern building.

"Morning, Thomas." Aguilar greeted him with a smile, her short hair accentuating her no-nonsense attitude. She held out a cup filled with a green liquid. "I made you a smoothie. Thought you could use something fresh to start your day."

Thomas looked down at the concoction. In the back of his mind, he appreciated Aguilar's attempt to get him to break out of his comfort zone, but he liked his usual smoothie with berries and spinach.

"Thanks, Aguilar," he said, taking the smoothie reluctantly. "What's in it?"

"Kale, spinach, ginger. Trust me," she assured him. "Give it a try."

Setting his hat on the desk, Thomas took a tentative sip of the smoothie. The sharp tastes of ginger and earthy greens surprised him, and he enjoyed the taste.

"This is different."

"I know you're not big on trying new things, but I thought it might be good for you."

Thomas hesitated, his fingers fidgeting with the edge of the cup. His Asperger's syndrome made him resistant to change, and he often stuck to familiar routines and foods. But here was Aguilar attempting to help him expand his horizons and help him grow beyond his self-imposed restrictions. He took another sip.

"I kinda like it."

The flavors were strong and carried a punch, and while it wasn't something he would have chosen for himself, he found it more than palatable.

"See? It's not so bad, is it?" Aguilar said, grinning. Thomas took another sip.

The front door opened. Maggie, the administrative assistant, walked into the office. Thomas stood up from his chair and approached. Now that Aguilar had him trying her latest recipe, he kept the ball rolling by engaging in conversation.

"Morning, Maggie," he said, nodding at her. "How was your weekend?"

Maggie smiled, always appreciative of Thomas's efforts to connect with others.

"Oh, it was lovely. Thank you for asking, Thomas. Spent some time with the grandkids and caught a movie. How about you?"

"Quiet. Mostly stayed home, did some work. Finally fixed the roof."

"Nothing wrong with a quiet weekend. Sometimes we all need that."

He took another sip of the smoothie, letting the flavors anchor him to the moment.

"Anyway," Maggie continued, her eyes twinkling, "I tried that new Italian restaurant in the village. The food was exquisite, and the ambiance was perfect for a night out." She paused, glancing at Thomas's desk. "Oh, speaking of which, I almost forgot to mention—a package arrived for you on Saturday. It's right here."

She handed him a brown cardboard box with no markings or labels. Thomas took the package, his fingers tracing the edges of the box.

"No return address?"

"Afraid not. Do you want me to send it to the lab? They can check for things like anthrax."

"I doubt it is terrorism, Maggie. But if it's anthrax, I'll be caught in a mosh."

She looked at him cockeyed, and he cleared his throat, realizing his joke had fallen flat.

"It's a band," he said. "Anthrax."

She placed a hand on her chest and forced herself to laugh. "Oh, that's funny, Thomas."

She didn't listen to heavy metal music. He ran a hand through the mop of hair on his head.

"Anyway, I'll take the box back to my office. Excuse me. I need to greet the other deputies before starting my day." Thomas tucked the package under his arm. As he turned to leave, he noticed the concerned look on Maggie's face. He offered her a reassuring smile, hoping to put her at ease. "Don't worry, I'll let you know if it's anything interesting."

Walking down the hallway, Thomas made a point of acknowledging each deputy he encountered. He nodded at

Lambert, who greeted him with a knowing smirk. Undoubtedly, he had another prank in the works.

"Morning, Lambert. Busy day ahead?"

"Always, boss man," Lambert replied, his grin never faltering. "You know how it is around here."

As Thomas continued down the hallway, his thoughts drifted back to the package. Despite his attempts to concentrate on the day's duties, he needed to know what was inside and who had sent it.

Reaching his office, Thomas allowed himself a moment of solitude before diving into the day's work. The package beckoned to him from the corner of his desk, its contents shrouded in mystery. First he needed to attend to the more mundane aspects of his job.

As he settled into his chair and checked his emails, he stole one last look at the enigmatic box. Fingers tapping against the edge of his desk in a rhythm only his subconscious understood, he replied to a message from the mayor of Wolf Lake. The silence in his office was broken only by the distant hum of fluorescent lights and the muffled footsteps of deputies passing by in the hallway.

"Okay," he muttered to himself, "let's see what this is all about."

He reached for the pair of scissors that lay beside his computer monitor and cut through the tape sealing the box. As he worked, he glanced around the room, noting each familiar object—the framed diploma on the wall, the scattering of case files on his desk, the worn leather chair that had supported him through countless hours of paperwork.

The last of the tape gave way beneath the blades, and he lifted the flaps of the box to reveal its contents. A frown creased his brow as he stared down at the item nestled within the protective layers of bubble wrap. The contents seemed innocent enough, but it wasn't what he expected.

"Strange."

Thomas reached into the box to retrieve the item. He turned it over in his hands, examining it from every angle, searching for any clue as to its origin or purpose.

"Hey, Thomas," Aguilar's voice called from the doorway, causing him to start. "You all right in here? You've been awfully quiet since I made you that smoothie. You aren't sick, are you?"

"I'm trying to figure out this package I received."

He set a tiny white carving of a bird on his desk.

"A gift?" she asked, stepping into the room and peering over his shoulder. "Who's it from?"

"That's just it," he said, frustration creeping into his voice. "There's no return address, no note, nothing. And yet, someone went to the trouble of sending it to me."

"It's beautiful. Is that ivory?"

"I think so."

"Maybe it's a secret admirer," she suggested with a teasing grin, though her eyes betrayed concern.

"Chelsey wouldn't be happy about a secret admirer," he said. "I hope I don't have a stalker."

"Thomas, you need to relax," she said, placing a reassuring hand on his shoulder. "Sometimes a gift is just a gift."

"But why would anyone send me a gift?"

"Gee, I don't know. How many lives have you saved since you became sheriff? The universe is thanking you. Accept the gift."

"I suppose you're right. It is striking, isn't it?" He set the bird in a prominent location beside his monitor so he would see it all day. "I just wish they'd left a note so I could thank them."

"If you ask me, they're *thanking you*, Thomas."

5

An hour passed as Thomas sat at his desk, organizing case files. In the hallway, a phone rang.

Deputy Aguilar returned to his office. "I received a call about a domestic dispute outside of Coral Lake."

"Meet you at the cruiser."

He hurried to the vehicle, but she was already waiting for him. As they arrived at the house near Coral Lake, the sight of a woman, beaten and bloodied, shattered the stillness of the scene. She sat on the front steps. Her eyes were swollen shut, her lip split, and her body covered in bruises and cuts.

"Dear God," Aguilar whispered.

Thomas approached the woman. "Ma'am, we're here to help you," he said. "My name is Sheriff Thomas Shepherd, and this is Deputy Aguilar. We need to find your husband. Is he in the house?"

The woman struggled to speak through her injuries. "He's in the kitchen. Please, don't let him hurt me anymore."

"Did your husband do this to you?"

The wife hesitated, looking away from him. "Yes," she admitted, her voice cracking under the weight of her confession.

"Has this happened before?"

"Too many times," she whispered, shame and defeat etched into her expression.

"Are there any weapons in the house?"

"No, sir."

"Deputy Aguilar will stay with you. I promise he won't hurt you again."

Aguilar kneeled beside the woman, one hand resting on her shoulder as she murmured comforting words. Thomas could see the compassion in Aguilar's eyes, and he felt grateful to have such a supportive deputy by his side.

"Thomas," she called out as he moved towards the house. "Maybe I should come with you."

"I'll be careful."

As he entered the house, he remembered the countless victims of domestic abuse he'd encountered. Someone had drawn the curtains. It took a moment for his eyes to adjust to the dark.

"Sheriff's department."

Thomas's eyes scanned the living room and hallway, his senses heightened as he searched for the abusive husband. From the corner of his eye, he caught movement near the back door. A tall figure bolted into the sunlight.

"Halt!" Thomas yelled, but the man didn't heed his command. Instead, he quickened his pace.

Thomas sprinted after the fleeing man. His legs pumped like pistons, adrenaline coursing through his veins as he closed the gap between them. The husband stumbled through the snow, giving Thomas enough time to lunge forward and tackle him.

"Get off me," the man said, struggling beneath Thomas's grip. "You don't know what you're doing."

As they grappled on the ground, Thomas noticed the

wounds on the husband's knuckles. They looked like a boxer's hands. He sucked his teeth in disdain.

"Listen," the husband said, still attempting to squirm free. "She attacked me first. It was self-defense."

"Self-defense?" Thomas echoed skeptically, his eyes never leaving the man's face. "I saw your wife outside. She's hurt bad. That doesn't look like self-defense to me."

"Please, you have to believe me."

"Those bruises tell a different story than self-defense."

Thomas led the handcuffed husband to the cruiser. The snow and ice slowed them down.

"Get in," Thomas said, opening the back door of the vehicle.

The man paused for a moment before obeying, his face a mixture of fear and anger as he slid onto the seat. Thomas shut the door, the sound echoing through the neighborhood.

"Good job, Thomas," Aguilar said, joining him beside the cruiser. "You handled that well. You seem to be over your PTSD."

"I'm doing my best."

"Your growth is clear. Told ya you'd be fine if you took Dr. Mandal's advice."

"I should have listened to you from the beginning."

Thomas dropped his eyes to the ground, his thoughts briefly wandering to the horrors of the past. He could still see Bacchus chasing them into the cabin with an ax, a memory that would never fade.

Another cruiser pulled beside the curb. Now there were two more deputies to look after the woman and take her statement.

"Let's book him and get this paperwork done," Thomas said.

"Sounds like a plan," Aguilar agreed. "I hope the judge throws the book at this degenerate."

Together they climbed into the front of the cruiser. As they drove back to the station, Thomas allowed himself an inner smile. He had come so far in his journey as sheriff, overcoming personal demons and learning to trust in himself and his abilities. But it was his team that gave him the courage to grow.

At the department, Aguilar escorted the wife beater to a holding cell. Thomas set his hat on his desk and jumped into the paperwork. Lambert looked up from his desk, eyebrows furrowing.

"Hey, Thomas," Lambert said, crossing the room to examine the bird carving more closely. "What's this on your desk?"

Thomas followed Lambert's eyes. He had almost forgotten about the bird amid the day's chaos. "Oh, that. I received it in the mail. No return address or anything."

"Looks like a crow," Lambert said, picking up the carving and examining it with a mixture of suspicion and curiosity. "Kinda creepy, isn't it?"

Thomas shrugged, trepidation creeping down his spine. He couldn't quite put his finger on why the bird bothered him so much, but there was something unsettling about the carving, despite its beauty.

"I suppose so. Do you really think it's a crow? I can't tell."

"Maybe it's a message," Lambert said, half-jokingly. "You know, like a bad omen or something."

"You and Scout Mourning watch too many ghost shows."

"I don't know, Thomas. You need to respect the supernatural."

"Right. Or it's just someone's idea of a joke."

Now that he thought about it, the carving might be a prank. Had Lambert given him the package? If so, he couldn't determine what the joke was.

"Or fan mail," Lambert said with a chuckle. "Either way, it's definitely, uh, unique." He placed the carving back on Thomas's desk, giving it one last look before returning to his own workspace.

As Thomas settled into his chair, he stole a few more glances at the bird. Yes, it looked like a crow. Who had sent it, and why? The questions nagged like a splinter beneath the skin. His fingers traced the smooth edges of the crow. Lambert's words echoed in his thoughts, feeding his curiosity and unease.

"Hey, Thomas," Aguilar called out from her desk. "You got those reports on the domestic case ready?"

"Almost," he said, forcing himself to refocus on the task at hand. He'd already wasted five minutes staring at the mysterious carving.

"Just wanted to make sure you don't need my help."

"Thanks, Aguilar."

Thomas flashed her a wink before burying himself in the paperwork. But despite his best efforts, his attention kept drifting back to the crow.

Lambert leaned against the doorframe, watching him. "You really can't shake that thing off, can you?" he asked, an amused grin playing on his lips.

Thomas looked up. "All right, Lambert. Come clean. This is one of your jokes, isn't it?"

The deputy raised his hands in exaggerated innocence. "Who, me?"

"Just tell me the punchline. I don't get it."

"Seriously, boss man, this isn't my doing. Maybe LeVar is trying to pull one over on you."

LeVar. That was possible.

"Maybe you're right," Thomas conceded, pushing the carving aside with a sigh. "I guess I'm just overthinking things."

"Wouldn't be the first time," Lambert said, earning a wry grin from Thomas. "Anyway, I'll leave you to your reports. Just remember, it's only a bird."

Lambert's voice faded away as he sang, *"The bird bird bird, the bird is the word."*

6

The bell over the door to Wolf Lake Consulting jangled, and LeVar shivered as he entered the hallway. He shook off the chill of winter and took in the familiar scent of toner ink and fresh coffee. The converted two-bedroom house had become a second home for him since his sister Raven started working there with Chelsey Byrd.

"Hey, LeVar," Chelsey greeted him from her desk as she looked up from her computer screen. "What brings you here today?"

"Thought I'd get a head start on my college term paper. But before I go home, I wanted to see if y'all need help with anything."

"Always happy to have an extra pair of hands." She looked over at Raven, who was busy typing away on her laptop. "How about it, Raven? Could your brother be of any help?"

Raven paused her work, her dark braids swaying as she turned to face her brother. "I'm sure we can find something for him to do."

"Of course," he said, the corners of his eyes crinkling with amusement.

"All right then," Chelsey said, scanning her surroundings for a task that would suit their unpaid intern. "Let's see. How about organizing those case files on the shelf? Some of them are out of order, and I haven't sorted through them yet."

"Sure thing." LeVar rolled up the sleeves of his sweatshirt and approached the cluttered bookshelf. As he sorted through folders filled with pages of notes and photographs, he couldn't believe he was a part-time sheriff's deputy and an intern at a private investigation firm. His life no longer resembled the one he'd led growing up in Harmon.

"Thanks for helping," Raven said. "We're behind the eight ball."

"No problem. I enjoy contributing, even if it's just organizing stuff. You almost make me feel useful."

"I always appreciated your help, LeVar," Chelsey echoed from her desk, her eyes never leaving her computer screen. "You're a valuable part of this team."

As he slotted the last file into place, he brushed off his hands.

"I'm all done here," he said, stepping back to admire his handiwork. "Anything else you need help with before I head out?"

"Actually, there is one thing."

He watched as Chelsey and Raven shuffled through the stacks of case files crowding their desks, each one a testament to the mounting backlog that had become a constant concern for the small investigation firm. Among these cases was the search for a missing dog named Ned, who belonged to a loyal friend and client of Wolf Lake Consulting.

"Would you be willing to help us with this missing dog case?" Raven asked.

"No question. What can I do?"

"Here," she said, handing him a stack of missing posters

featuring a detailed description of the lost canine, along with contact information. "We need to post these on the lake road. Can you place these on your way home?"

As she spoke, Chelsey pinned a poster to the office wall.

"I got you."

"Thanks, LeVar. We really appreciate your help."

"Hey, we're family. And family helps each other out."

"Am I family?" Chelsey asked.

"You're my sis from another miss."

"Ha-ha, I like that."

"Hey LeVar," Raven called out, mischief sparkling in her eyes. "I hear you've been teaching Scout how to drive on ice and snow. That's brave of you."

"Brave?" LeVar smirked, turning to face his sister. "More like a public service. She needs to learn from the best, not someone who still can't parallel park properly."

Raven scoffed and tossed a crumpled-up sticky note at him. "I'll have you know I'm an excellent driver. Besides, I'm pretty sure that time you drove into a snowbank was entirely your fault."

"Low blow. At least I learn from my mistakes. How many times have you backed into the ditch at the state park?"

Raven coughed into her hand. "Darren exaggerates."

"Yeah, I'm sure."

Chelsey looked up from her work. "LeVar, did you play a prank on Thomas?" she asked, her tone serious. "He called earlier and told me he received a bird carving in the mail. It's not your style, but I thought I should check."

LeVar looked at her as if she had suddenly sprouted wings. "What? No, I didn't send him anything," he said, bewildered. "If anyone's behind it, it's Lambert. You know how he loves his pranks."

"True that."

"The saying is *true dat*. You grew up in the suburbs."

"Hundred percent."

He raised an eyebrow. "That's better."

"Anyhow, I just wanted to make sure."

"When I play pranks on Thomas, they're a helluva lot better than sending him some trinket. Do you have a picture or anything?"

Chelsey held up her phone, displaying a photograph of the bird carving in question. The intricate detail etched into the smooth material beckoned him to examine it further.

"This is what Thomas received," she said. "It showed up in the mail with no return address or note."

"Is that . . . ivory?" LeVar asked, his eyes widening as he took in the craftsmanship. He shook his head, chuckling. "I couldn't afford something like that just for a prank, Chelsey."

"Neither could Lambert. Weird, isn't it?"

"Well, when you get to the bottom of this mystery, fill me in."

His gaze wandered to Raven, who rose to retrieve another cup of coffee from the kitchen. Sensing an opportunity for a private conversation, he excused himself from Chelsey and followed his sister down the hallway.

"Hey, sis. I need to talk to you about something."

He leaned against the kitchen counter. Raven set her mug on the table.

"What's up?"

"Remember how you rode me about giving Scout driving lessons?"

"Yeah."

"She said Liz has a crush on me," he said, rubbing the back of his neck. "I don't know what to do about it."

She crossed her arms. "Be careful, LeVar. She's only sixteen."

"Don't you think I know that? I've been trying to avoid her, but she's infatuated or something."

"Maybe you should have a talk with her. Set some boundaries and make sure she understands the situation."

"That's not a conversation I look forward to. Just being in the same room with her gives me the creeps."

"What will people say if they think you're dating a teenager?"

"But I'm not."

"People gossip."

"I mean, she's fine and all. If she was twenty, I might be interested."

"Don't even go there," Raven said.

"I'm just saying." He blew out a breath. "Okay, I get your point."

"That's because I'm older and wiser."

"Well, you're older. Not sure about the wisdom part."

She shoved his shoulder. "Don't you have a job to do?"

LeVar looked down at the posters in his hand. "*Aight*. I'm on it."

He just hoped Liz wasn't at Scout's house when he returned home.

7

The bitter aroma of green tea and lemon wafted through Thomas's office as he took a sip from his chipped mug. His eyes lingered on the ivory bird carving he kept fidgeting with. Through the window, he caught sight of medical examiner Claire Brookins bundled against the cold and hurrying toward the entrance. Maggie greeted the woman and sent her through.

When Claire strode into the office, the scent of lilacs and rain followed in her wake.

"Thomas," she said.

"Claire, I wasn't expecting you this morning. What can I do for you?" His fingers curled around the bird carving, tracing its delicate wings.

"I was hoping we could discuss the Peterson case." She settled into the chair across from his desk, rust-colored curls spilling over her shoulders. "The toxicology report came back."

"And?" Thomas asked.

She looked out the window. "Nothing conclusive. No drugs or poisons in his system."

Thomas stared into his tea. Another brick wall standing

between them and the answers in a suspected teen overdose investigation.

"I'll keep looking," she said. "We'll figure this out."

For the first time since she'd entered, he met her eyes. In their mossy depths, he glimpsed the same determination that had led her to become the county's first female ME.

"You always find the answer," he said.

Claire sat forward, observing him. "How are you feeling today?" she asked, a hint of concern in her voice.

"I'm okay. Why do you ask?"

"You seem a little preoccupied."

"Just a lot of things on my mind. Seems like there's never a minute to sit back and relax."

"Did you finish the repairs on the lake house?"

"Finally, yes."

Their conversation shifted to mundane topics—the persistent cold, the latest case updates, and even Claire's frustration with drivers constantly running over her mailbox. As they spoke, she kept peeking at his hands, where the bird carving rolled between his fingers.

"Any plans for the weekend?" Claire asked, breaking into his thoughts.

"Nothing special. It's been a while since I stopped by Shepherd Systems, and Mother is pushing me to pay a visit. What about you?"

"Hoping for a nice, quiet weekend," she said, her eyes following the movement of his fingers on the bird. "Interesting piece you have there," she remarked, her russet hair framing her face as she leaned closer to inspect the carving.

Thomas looked up from his reverie, realizing the object had caught her attention. "Oh, this?" he asked, holding it up for her to see. "It's a bird, carved from ivory."

"Are you sure that's ivory? Where did you get it?"

"Someone sent it to me in the mail. No return address or note, just the carving."

"Strange. I wonder who would send something like that with no explanation."

"Your guess is as good as mine."

The ivory bird gleamed in the sun pouring through the window. Its eyes seemed to light with hidden knowledge. Why was Claire so interested in the bird's origin?

"Thomas, would it be all right if I borrowed this carving for a few days? I have a personal interest in it."

"Personal interest?" Thomas echoed, his blue-green eyes narrowing. He couldn't pinpoint why, but Claire's sudden fascination with the object made him uneasy. She was usually so pragmatic and focused on her work.

"Yes," Claire said, crinkling her forehead in thought. "I have connections that might know more about this kind of craftsmanship. It could help us find out who sent it to you."

Thomas considered her request, weighing the options in his mind. On one hand, he wanted to learn the truth behind the mysterious artifact. But on the other, she wasn't telling him the reason behind her interest.

"I suppose that's okay. But be careful with it. I've grown fond of the gift."

"Of course," Claire said. She reached out and picked up the carving, cradling it in her hands as though it were a fragile, living creature. She then tucked it into her coat pocket, securing it within the folds of the fabric.

"Thank you, Thomas. I'll return it as soon as I know more."

"Sure thing," he said, watching as Claire stood up and headed for the door. Apprehension gripped him as she left his office, taking the mysterious gift with her.

As soon as Claire disappeared, Aguilar strode in and took her place.

"Hey, what was all that about?" she asked, her dark eyes narrowing with curiosity as she shut the door behind her.

"Ah, Claire," he said, rubbing his neck as he tried to organize his thoughts. "She wanted to discuss the findings in the Peterson case. For whatever reason, she seemed interested in my gift."

Aguilar raised an eyebrow. "The ivory bird? Did she tell you why?"

"No, but she wants to borrow it for a few days. Said she had a personal interest in it."

"Personal interest?" Aguilar leaned against the doorframe. "That seems a bit odd."

"She didn't say much, just that she'd return it soon."

Aguilar frowned. "Whatever she comes up with, let me know. Now she has me curious."

Thomas watched as his deputy made her way back to her own desk. He removed the file on the Peterson investigation and reviewed what they knew. But he couldn't concentrate. His eyes kept drifting to the empty spot beside the monitor where the bird had sat. Picking up the mug, he took a sip of his lukewarm green tea.

Lambert poked his head into the office. "You okay in there, boss man?"

"Just thinking," he said, evading Lambert's inquisitiveness by staring into the pale green liquid in his mug. His fingers brushed against the cool metal surface of his Ford F-150 keychain.

"Heard the medical examiner stole your toy."

"It's not a . . . never mind. Hey, Lambert. You told me the truth, right? You didn't send me that gift for some elaborate joke, did you?"

"Have I ever lied to you?"

"Nope."

The deputy's eyes gleamed with mischief. "Are you sure?"

Thomas chuckled. "Now you're making me paranoid."

"I didn't send you the carving. If I had, I'd tell you. Want me to get on the horn and find out why the medical examiner took it?"

Thomas shook his head, his sandy hair falling into his eyes. "No, and I don't want to pry. But it's strange, isn't it?"

"A little. But you know how she is—always interested in the unknown. I'm sure it's just her curiosity getting the better of her."

"True."

As Lambert returned to his desk, Thomas wished he'd saved the package the gift arrived in. Had he thrown away evidence?

8

Thomas steered his silver Ford F-150 down the icy road, windshield wipers working furiously against the falling snow. He was heading to the house of Melinda Eland, the woman he'd tended to after arresting the husband for beating her. The man was now sitting in a jail cell, and Thomas wanted to check on the wife and offer what support he could.

As he spotted the modest house, its muted yellow exterior stood out against the stark white of the snow-covered landscape. It was a small Cape Cod-style dwelling with weathered shingles. The flower garden lay dormant under a thick blanket of snow, its life hidden away for another season. A rickety wooden porch, adorned with a single rocking chair, stretched across the front of the house.

He parked his truck at the curb and trudged through the snow to the front door, the cold biting at his cheeks. He knocked, hoping Melinda would hear him over the howl of the wind. After a few moments, the door creaked open, revealing a bruised and battered woman who seemed to hold herself together by sheer willpower.

"Good afternoon, Sheriff," she said, attempting a weak smile that didn't reach her eyes. "Come in, please."

"Thank you for the offer, Mrs. Eland, but I won't be staying long. I wanted to check on you and provide some information about local shelters and counseling centers."

At the mention of shelters, her eyes widened. She shook her head. "I appreciate your concern, Sheriff, but I want no part of a shelter. This is my home, and this is where I'll stay."

Her grip tightened on the doorframe, as if anchoring her to the house.

"I understand how you feel, Mrs. Eland. But sometimes seeking help is the best way to regain control over our lives."

Melinda's eyes dropped to the snowy ground, her thoughts miles away. She seemed to consider his words, weighing the risks and rewards of seeking help. After a moment, she sighed and looked up.

"Maybe I could talk to a counselor. But I won't go to a shelter. I need to stay here."

"Talking to a counselor is a great first step, Mrs. Eland. It's important to have someone who can help guide you through this difficult time."

Melinda wrapped her arms around herself as if trying to hold her world together. He remembered his experiences with counseling, and how it had helped him navigate the complexities of the Victor Bacchus murders.

"Thank you for thinking of me."

"We're here to help. Here." He removed a business card from his pocket. It was crisp and white, bearing the name Dr. Ryka Mandal in bold black letters. "This is the counselor I recommend. She's helped many people in similar situations."

He held out the card. She hesitated before reaching out with trembling fingers to take it. She stared at the name on the card for a moment.

"I don't need a psychiatrist."

"Mrs. Eland," he said, his eyes never leaving hers. "There's no shame in seeking help. In fact, I've seen Dr. Mandal myself. It's important to talk with a professional. Don't think of Dr. Mandal as a psychiatrist. Think of her as a counselor, but more qualified."

Melinda looked down at the card again, her grip tightening on its edges. Her thoughts seemed to be a whirlwind of doubt and fear.

"I wouldn't recommend her if I didn't believe in her ability to help," he said.

Her posture relaxed.

"I'll call her tomorrow morning."

"Please do so, Mrs. Eland. Remember, you don't have to go through this alone."

As he climbed into the driver's seat, he pictured the woman, standing alone in her house, clutching that small white card. He hoped she would find the strength to seek help, just as he had done, and start her journey toward healing.

Climbing into the cab and closing the door, he ran the wipers to clear a fresh layer of flurries. As he pulled away from Eland's house, the tires rolled over snow and ice, a sound that brought an unexpected memory to the forefront of his thoughts. He was scheduled to give Scout a driving lesson tomorrow, following in LeVar's footsteps. She would have to get used to these icy roads if she wanted to drive in Upstate New York.

His breath fogged the windshield momentarily before the defrost system kicked in. A thin layer of ice clung to the corners of the glass, but his vision remained clear.

The ring of his phone interrupted his musings about Scout's driving lessons. Claire's name flashed on the screen. He tapped the speaker button on the steering wheel to answer.

"Hey, Claire, what's up? Did you figure out who sent me that gift?"

"Thomas, I just finished examining the bird carving," she said, her voice strained with urgency. "We need to talk. Can you come by my office?"

"I'm on the road and need to get back to the sheriff's department. Whatever is, you can tell me on the phone."

"I don't think that's wise."

"Please tell me. If you don't, I'll obsess over the news. I don't have a secret admirer, do I? I'm about to become a married man."

The line went silent. He worried the call had dropped until her voice came through the speaker like thunder.

"The carving isn't ivory. It's human bone."

Her words removed the oxygen from the truck, echoing in Thomas's ears as he struggled to process the information. His grip tightened on the steering wheel. A million thoughts raced through his brain. She had to be wrong. There must have been a mistake.

"Are you sure?" he choked out.

"Completely." More silence. "I ran multiple tests to be sure. This is . . . well, it's beyond disturbing, Thomas."

For several beats, only the sounds of their respective breathing filled the silence between them. Thomas grappled with the implications of her discovery.

Human bone?

"Thank you, Claire. I'll come by later to discuss our next steps. First I should talk with my deputies."

"Be careful out there, Thomas."

She didn't have to warn him. Where did one acquire a human bone, and why would anyone make a carving and send it to him?

He ended the call. The blood drained from his face, and a

sudden wave of nausea washed over him. He had to pull over, or he'd risk losing control of the vehicle. With shaking hands, he steered the pickup to the side of the road and parked, taking deep breaths to steady himself.

"It's not real," he muttered, staring at his pallid reflection in the mirror. The thought of someone mutilating human remains for their own sick purposes revolted him.

At least he assumed the bone came from human remains. The alternative was unthinkable: it had come from a living person.

A logical explanation existed. Perhaps he had touched the life of someone who'd lost a limb, and that person fashioned a beautiful gift out of the bone.

Even to his own ears, the assumption didn't sound plausible.

9

Flurries floated past the window as Scout leaned against the counter, her straight brunette hair cascading over her shoulders. Naomi, her mother, stood by the stove, stirring a pot of tomato sauce.

"Mom," Scout said, "I've been thinking about taking my driver's test this summer. I'm sixteen, and I think it's time."

Naomi paused her stirring, setting the spoon down on the counter. "I know you're eager to drive, but sixteen is still very young. I'm not sure if you're ready for the responsibility just yet."

"But I've been practicing with LeVar, and he says I'm a natural behind the wheel. Plus, I've handled winter driving, which we both know can be really challenging."

Her mother sighed and pushed her hair back. "I know you're capable, but driving is a serious matter. Every teenager rushes the process, but waiting an extra year or two makes a tremendous difference. Do you know the accident statistics on sixteen-year-old drivers?"

"I regained my ability to walk, and I've been doing everything possible to regain my strength. I can handle it."

"Sweetheart, it's not that I don't believe in you. It's just that I want to make sure you're prepared before taking on something as important as driving."

"LeVar trusts me, and I trust myself. Please, just give me a chance to prove myself."

"I'll think about it. But remember, driving is a privilege, not a right. I need to be sure you're ready for it."

After dinner, Scout picked up a plate from the table and rinsed it under the faucet, her thoughts stuck on getting her license. Driving afforded freedom. Who wanted to beg for rides everywhere? Plus, LeVar would consider her more mature if she got her license.

Mom leaned against the kitchen counter, watching Scout as she scrubbed the porcelain. The rhythm of water hitting the stainless-steel sink filled the room.

"Scout," Mom said after a moment, "I want you to know that I'm proud of your determination and how far you've come after the accident. You've shown immense maturity and strength."

"Thank you."

Mom stepped forward, taking a clean plate from Scout's hands and placing it in the drying rack. "But I need you to understand that driving isn't just about skill. It's about responsibility and making good choices. This world is unpredictable, and sometimes even the best drivers can find themselves in scary situations."

"I understand." Scout attacked a stubborn stain on a fork. "And I promise, if you let me take my driver's test, I'll be responsible. No reckless speeding, no distractions, nothing like that."

"I wouldn't expect you to fall into those traps. It's important to stay on the straight and narrow, both on and off the road. That demonstrates trustworthiness."

As Scout handed her mother another clean plate, she mulled over the words. She knew all too well the impact a single moment could have on a person's life—the accident had changed hers forever. But she refused to let fear hold her back.

"When I get behind the wheel, I'll be the safest driver you've ever seen."

"I believe you, but let's not get ahead of ourselves. We'll take it one step at a time and see how you progress. Driving is an ongoing learning experience."

"Deal," Scout said, a small smile playing on her lips as she turned back to the sink.

They worked in companionable silence, the bond between mother and daughter stronger than any challenge life could throw their way. Scout's hand was still damp from the dishwater when her phone buzzed on the kitchen counter. The screen displayed Liz's name, and she looked over at her mother, who had just finished drying a plate.

"Mind if I take this?" she asked, nodding toward the phone.

"Go ahead. Just remember to come back and finish in the kitchen."

Scout grabbed her phone and retreated to the sanctuary of her bedroom, closing the door. The room, decorated with posters of her favorite bands and movie characters, felt like a refuge from the world outside.

Pressing the phone to her ear, she said, "Hey, Liz."

"Scout, how's it going?" Liz's voice always sounded animated.

"Not bad. I was just talking to my mom about the whole driver's test thing. She's still not on board."

"Really? That's too bad. Parents can be such a bummer sometimes."

"I'm doing okay. Just trying to convince my mom that I'm ready."

"Of course you're ready. You've been practicing with LeVar all winter, right?"

"Right. He taught me so much, and I feel comfortable behind the wheel."

"Then you'll be fine," Liz said. "You just need to get your mom to see that."

The last light of day faded outside the window. "Easier said than done."

"Hey, you know what always helps when I'm feeling stuck? A good old-fashioned vent session. Just let it all out, girl. I'm here for you. Speaking of feeling stuck, have I ever told you how absolutely frustrating the dating scene is? Boys at school are so immature."

Scout leaned back against her pillows, absently twirling a strand of her brunette hair as she listened. She could picture Liz rolling her eyes, and it brought a grin to her face. "Oh, trust me, I know," she agreed. "It's like they'll never grow up."

"Exactly. Just the other day, I overheard a couple of guys making crude jokes about bras in the hallway. It was so embarrassing."

Grimacing, Scout recalled the encounters she'd had with immature boys in school. The memory of whispered comments and snickering laughter made her feel uncomfortable.

"Remember last month when I tried dating Jason? He couldn't hold a conversation without turning everything into a competition or a joke. I can't believe I thought I liked him."

"Ugh, don't remind me," Liz groaned. "I still can't believe he tried to impress you by throwing a water balloon at Mr. Thompson."

"Right?" Scout laughed, remembering the spectacle. "He missed and soaked Mrs. Jenkins instead. Honestly, what was he thinking?"

"Who knows? Boys are childish lunatics. But seriously, we deserve better."

She nodded, even though Liz couldn't see her. And while she

was grateful for her friendship with LeVar, there was something special about bonding with a girl who understood her experiences.

"Maybe we just need to give them time to grow up. Or maybe we'll meet more mature guys when we're older."

"Let's hope so," Liz said, a wistful note in her voice. "Speaking of guys, how's LeVar doing? Is he still dating that girl you mentioned?"

Scout hesitated, her fingers tightening on the phone as an unexpected pang of jealousy hit her.

"Uh, I don't know." Scout battled to sound neutral. "I haven't asked him about his love life. Why are you interested?"

"It's just that he's so cute, and I'm sure it's only a matter of time before he's available."

Scout forced herself to smile.

"LeVar's great. But I think he's been pretty focused on work and school lately. I can ask him if you want, though."

"Would you?" Liz sounded excited, and Scout swallowed the bile that was rising in her throat. "That'd be awesome. Thanks, girlfriend."

Mom called from the kitchen, and Scout was more than happy to end the conversation. As she hung up the phone, she leaned against the wall and closed her eyes. LeVar was just a friend. Nothing more, nothing less.

She placed the device on her bed. The conversation lingered in the air. Her stomach roiled at the thought of LeVar with an immature girl, but she couldn't let herself dwell on those feelings. With a groan, she opened her eyes and returned to the task at hand. The dishes needed to be put away, and her mother was waiting in the kitchen.

Scout returned to the kitchen, where her mother was working. As they resumed putting the dishes away, she allowed herself to be enveloped by the comforting routine of the task. It helped distract her from the turmoil brewing inside.

"Everything okay?" Mom asked.

Scout hesitated for a moment. She couldn't mention her jealousy over Liz chasing LeVar. That was childish, and she was mature, right?

"Yeah, Mom. Just girl stuff."

While they cleaned the kitchen, Scout's thoughts drifted. She couldn't brush aside her emotions. At least she needed to be honest with herself.

But as Scout placed the last plate on the shelf, her mind returned to LeVar. His smile, his laugh, the way he always seemed to know exactly what she was thinking. She knew that even considering him as more than a friend was wrong. And immature.

10

Thomas sat in his F-150, gripping the steering wheel as if it were the only thing anchoring him to reality. Discovering that the bird carving was made from human bone had stolen the earth from under his feet. His memories returned to his days as a detective in Los Angeles, when he'd dealt with gang violence and gruesome crime scenes. But this. This was different. And personal.

Asperger's syndrome had never stopped Thomas from excelling in his field, but sometimes it amplified his reactions to stress. Yet this had nothing to do with his condition. Claire's news would have crippled any officer, no matter how grizzled. He needed to inform his team about this chilling revelation and hear their thoughts on the matter.

Reaching for his phone, he typed a text message to Raven and LeVar Hopkins, specifying the time and location of their meeting at the Slidin' Steer Steakhouse, where he was scheduled to join Chelsey for dinner. His fingers were still shaky, but he hit send. When he returned to the station, he would inform Lambert and Aguilar. He needed all hands on deck.

Raven and LeVar would sense the gravity hidden in the

message. They were more than just colleagues; they were family. As he waited for their replies, he stared out at the swirling snowflakes, hoping against hope that they could find some kind of explanation for the macabre artifact that didn't involve a deranged killer hacking off limbs in Nightshade County.

After he found the resolve to drive, he brought his deputies up to speed. Aguilar would work with Claire to determine the bone's origin. If that was possible. They'd faced nothing like this before.

The Slidin' Steer Steakhouse stood as a beacon in the growing darkness of Nightshade County and winter's early sunsets. Its flickering neon sign spilled a red and green glow over the parking lot, accentuating the rustic exterior of weathered wood and corrugated metal. Thomas pulled up in his truck and parked near the entrance.

Inside, the steakhouse was alive with the hum of conversation and clinking glassware. Cattle skulls and black-and-white photographs of ranchers hung from the walls, while the reserved lighting lent an air of intimacy. He scanned the tables, searching for Chelsey and Raven.

"Thomas." Chelsey's voice cut through the noise, her dark hair shimmering under the soft light. Thank goodness. He needed her company now more than ever. "Over here."

He spotted Chelsey at a secluded table in the back, next to Raven, who was shifting in her seat, her long dark braids brushing against her muscular shoulders. He made his way over, feeling the curious eyes of fellow patrons; the sheriff always attracted attention in the lakeside village.

"Hey," he said as he approached the table. "Thanks for coming on short notice."

"Anytime," Raven replied, her eyes holding concern. "You seemed pretty shaken in your text. What's going on?"

"Let's wait for LeVar," he said, avoiding eye contact as he

settled into a chair. "I'd rather not repeat it more than necessary."

The women shared an uncomfortable glance.

"As you wish." Chelsey rested a comforting hand on his arm. "We're here for you."

The cacophony of laughter and conversation swirled around them as they waited in silence, creating an uneasy contrast to the tension squeezing his spine. He drummed his fingers on the table, counting the seconds until LeVar's arrival allowed him to unburden himself of the gruesome news.

"Thomas," Raven said, her brows furrowed with worry. "You're tapping your fingers. You only do that when you're really stressed. Is everything okay?"

Forcing a tight-lipped smile, he stilled his hand and focused on remaining present for his friends. "I'll be all right," he assured her, though he knew it was far from the truth. "Where's LeVar?"

"Running late. He got caught up in some video game and lost track of time. Should be here any minute now."

Thomas surveyed the restaurant, his eyes lingering on the decor and the candles adorning each table. The Slidin' Steer was a popular spot in Nightshade County, but tonight it felt suffocating.

"Good evening, folks," a server said, approaching their table with a tray balanced in one hand. She set down a basket of warm crusty bread along with three glasses filled with ice water. "I'm Carrie, and I'll be taking care of you tonight. Can I get you started with anything else to drink?"

"Uh, just a Coke for me, please," Raven said, her eyes darting between Thomas and Chelsey as if trying to gauge the severity of the situation. He spied the gears turning in her head as her innate curiosity nudged her closer to the edge of her seat.

"Water's fine for me," Chelsey said, patting Thomas on the arm. He appreciated her attempt at normalcy, but his heart thundered in his chest like a caged animal desperate for escape.

"Water as well," Thomas echoed, doing his best to maintain eye contact with Carrie. She gave him a polite smile before disappearing into the kitchen, leaving them alone with their thoughts.

"Thanks for waiting," he said. "I need to tell everyone at once."

"Is it that serious?"

"You may want to hear me out before you order a rare steak."

The door swung open, and LeVar stepped inside. The sound of ice pellets hitting the pavement created a rhythmic backdrop for his entrance. He shook off his umbrella, causing granules to scatter across the floor like a painter's brush flicking excess paint from its bristles. LeVar appeared disheveled—his black dreadlocks dampened by the snow and ice, his eyes flying around as if trying to catch up with reality.

"Sorry I'm late," he said, pulling out a chair next to Raven and slumping into it. "Lost track of time playing that damn game."

"You made it. That's all that counts. I've got some news. It's about the bird carving."

"Shoot."

Thomas gathered his thoughts, feeling as if his chest might collapse under the weight of the words he was about to say. "The carving. It's made of human bone."

"Human?" Chelsey gasped, her eyes wide with horror.

"Bone?" LeVar echoed, his expression a mixture of shock and disbelief. His eyes searched Thomas's face for any hint that this was a joke, but finding none, they dropped to the table as he processed the information. "Are you sure?"

"Positive," Thomas said. "Claire Brookins tested the carving at the lab. The implications of this discovery are . . . significant." He paused, allowing the gravity of the situation to sink in. "Now I understand why she was so interested in the gift."

The three of them sat in stunned silence, trying to wrap their heads around the unspeakable horror. LeVar's fingers tapped on the table.

"Listen," Raven said, "I know this sounds terrible, but maybe there's another explanation. The lab could have made a mistake, right?"

Thomas hesitated. He wanted to believe that no one would commit such a monstrous act, but he knew better than to let hope cloud his judgment.

"It's possible," he admitted, "but it's unlikely. You know how thorough Claire is."

"Or maybe it's some kind of prank?" Chelsey said, playing with a strand of hair. "Some sick person trying to scare us?"

"I want all of you on high alert. If this is personal, he might go after my friends and family."

The evening was supposed to be a casual night out, a break from the relentless pressure of their investigations. Chelsey had been looking forward to an evening of laughter and lighthearted conversation. But now, with the disturbing revelation about the bone carving, the atmosphere had taken on a somber tone.

"Guess it's not really a night for karaoke, is it?" Raven said, staring into her drink, the colorful lights of the jukebox seeming garish and out of place.

"Probably not," LeVar said, his eyes fixed on the tablecloth as he traced its pattern with a fingertip.

Thomas felt a twinge of regret. People enjoyed their meals and conversations, oblivious to the darkness that had settled over their table. Chelsey longed for the simplicity of a normal night out, and he had robbed her of the opportunity.

Somewhere in Nightshade County, a demented killer carved figurines from human limbs. Was another gift in Thomas's future?

11

Thomas stood in his office, staring out the window at the night sky. Though the support of his deputies and friends grounded him, he couldn't escape the truth behind the carving. The fact that he had rolled the figurine around in his hand, entranced by its beauty, sickened him.

The phone buzzed on his desk. "Sheriff Shepherd speaking."

No one replied before the line went dead.

"Hello?" Thomas frowned at the silence, then hung up. An unknown number. Was it him? The person who'd sent the carving?

"Thomas," Aguilar said from the doorway. "You look like you saw a ghost."

"Unknown number." Pockets of anxiety bloomed in his chest.

"Could be a wrong number," she said, though her tone lacked conviction. "I'm going through the medical examiner's report. Holler if you need me."

He paced the room, his thoughts circling around the DNA test Claire was running on the bone used for the carving. It was human, and there was no denying the sinister nature of the gift.

But he hadn't heard from her yet, and the waiting drove him mad.

"Shouldn't Claire have called by now?" Thomas asked Lambert, who was lounging against the wall, sipping coffee from a chipped mug.

"Patience, my friend," the ex-soldier said. Lambert and Aguilar were working after hours like Thomas. "It's not like she can rush these things."

Lambert was right, but the frustration gnawed at Thomas. Was it possible to identify a victim from a bone? He knew tests existed to determine gender from bones. There was no guarantee the victim's DNA was in a dataset. What else could Claire accomplish?

Thomas needed air. Despite the chill, he exited the sheriff's office, his thoughts reeling. A gust of wind tugged at his hair and bit his exposed skin. He shivered, not just from the chill but from an unsettling feeling that had taken root deep inside him.

Night cast the parking lot in shadows, with only a few lampposts shedding their glow over the deserted space. Thomas approached his pickup, his breath visible in the frigid air.

As he neared his truck, he noticed a figure lurking in the shadows near the vehicle. He reached for his gun, removing it with trained precision.

"Show yourself," he said.

The figure stepped forward. It was Claire. He breathed again.

"Don't shoot, Thomas."

"Good lord, Claire," he said. "You could've given me a heart attack."

"Sorry about that." The wind whipped her hair around her face. "I wasn't trying to scare you. I just didn't want to wait any longer."

"What did you find?"

"Like I said before, it's human bone." She hesitated. "I need more evidence to prove a murder took place. The fact that it's human doesn't prove foul play. We need something more concrete."

"Who did the bone come from?"

"My tests prove it came from a man in his younger years. Between twenty-five and forty if I had to guess."

Thomas rubbed his temples, the gravity of the situation pressing down upon him. "So where does that leave us?"

"I can run more tests, but I suggest you search for missing males."

The wind howled, whipping up a frenzy of snow and ice that stung their eyes. The smell of exhaust fumes lingered in the air as Thomas considered Claire's words.

"That implies murder."

"I hope I'm wrong. Listen, I'll share my findings with the Wolf Lake Consulting team. Chelsey tells me they're helping with the investigation."

"Please share everything."

"I'll work with you on this, Thomas," she said. "We have to find out who sent that carving and why."

"But how did they get their hands on a human bone? Is it even possible for someone to just... buy one?"

"Oh, yes. There are companies that sell human bones, usually for medical research or educational purposes."

Thomas shook his head, disturbed by the thought. He tried to imagine the face of the person who had crafted the bird, but all he saw were shadows lurking in the corners of his mind.

"Focus on finding the sender," she suggested, pulling him out of his dark thoughts. "Maybe you can trace the package or find some connection between the victim and the person who sent it."

"I can't."

"Why not?"

"I disposed of the package."

Claire pulled her lips tight. She didn't need to point out his mistake. It would forever haunt him. He leaned against his truck and rubbed his arms against the cold.

"Sometimes I wonder if it's all just a game to whoever's doing this," he said, more to himself than to Claire. "A game where I'm the pawn. It feels personal."

"Like someone from your past?"

"I've made my share of enemies."

"And placed most of them behind bars. They can't hurt you from a prison cell."

"Then it's someone else. Maybe someone who sympathizes with a criminal."

She bounced on her toes to stay warm. "Why don't we continue this conversation inside?"

The door to the sheriff's department creaked open, the wind howling in protest as Thomas and Claire stepped inside.

"Keep analyzing the bone," Thomas said. "We need more information about its origin."

"Agreed. I'll look into companies that sell human bones and see if I can find any links to this specific piece. That would rule out mischief."

"Good idea. Aguilar is looking over your report. I'd like you to work directly with her."

"More than happy to."

In the silence that followed, the hum of the fluorescent lights seemed to grow louder, a constant reminder of the urgency of their task. With each passing moment, the unknown menace behind the bird carvings felt closer, more tangible.

His past had come back to haunt him.

12

Scout lay in bed, her phone pressed against her ear, the soft glow of the screen lighting her face from below as Liz discussed LeVar.

The sound of clattering dishes drifted through the downstairs, a reminder that her mother was still awake, tidying up. It made it difficult for Scout to concentrate on the conversation.

"Isn't he a little old for you?" Scout asked.

"Maybe. But remember what we said about high school boys and immaturity? I could see myself dating a college guy."

Her stomach tightened.

"A college guy? Are you sure?"

"Anyway, we need to discuss another ghost hunt."

"Oh, Liz. I don't know. I don't want to get into trouble again. Mom will never trust me if I screw up like I did on Halloween."

"This hunt will be totally above board. We'll get permission and everything."

"I'll think it over."

"I should go before my parents freak. Let me know if you think LeVar will talk to me. Goodnight, Scout."

"Goodnight, Liz."

Scout set her phone on her nightstand. She stared up at the ceiling, unable to shake the knot forming in her stomach. She tried to rationalize it, telling herself that she and LeVar were just friends. Which was true. But LeVar deserved a mature, trustworthy woman, not Liz. As much as Scout loved Liz, the girl made questionable decisions.

With a sigh, she reached for her phone again, her fingers hovering over the screen. No, she wouldn't message LeVar about Liz. He'd already said he was avoiding the dating scene while he concentrated on work and school.

The familiar hum of the living room television provided a backdrop to her thoughts as she lay in the darkened bedroom. She rolled onto her side, staring at the moonlight streaming through the window. Jealousy wasn't part of her vocabulary, but there it was, pulsing through her veins like an unwelcome intruder.

"Stupid," she muttered under her breath, hoping the word would somehow dissipate the frustration and longing that had taken up residence within her. It was ridiculous to be jealous of Liz dating a guy she had no romantic interest in. Where were these feelings coming from?

As she continued to look out the window, she imagined LeVar with his arm around some girl, laughing together at some private joke. What if Scout and LeVar were the same age? The fantasy took root in her mind, growing with each passing second.

She chastised herself, wincing at how pathetic she sounded in her mind. There was no denying the age difference between them, or that he was already in college while she was still navigating the treacherous waters of high school.

"Besides," she continued, attempting to sound logical and detached, "even if he was interested, it wouldn't be right."

The living room noises faded into the background as she

allowed herself to sink further into her fantasy, picturing what life might be like with a trustworthy college boyfriend by her side. They could study together in the library or share stories about their days over cups of coffee at their favorite café. And then, perhaps, they could steal a few quiet moments alone, wrapped in each other's arms. How much longer would she be a teenager? Twenty seemed decades away.

Maybe LeVar could introduce her to a friend from college, someone who was only two or three years older than her. Pinching the bridge of her nose, she closed her eyes and banished all thoughts of unattainable romance from her mind.

Scout sat on the edge of her bed, fiddling with her phone as she contemplated the message she was about to send. She took a breath and typed out the words, trying not to overthink matters.

Hey, LeVar. Are you sure you aren't seeing anyone right now?

Scout hesitated for a moment before pressing send. She couldn't help but wonder if her curiosity would come across as too intrusive. He would know she was asking for Liz.

Her phone buzzed, and she jumped at the sudden sound. She looked down at the screen and saw that LeVar had responded.

Hey Scout. Nah, I'm single, like I told you. Not really looking to date anyone right now. College and work keep me hella busy.

A streetlight shone outside her window. She stared at the words, allowing them to sink in. Good. His reply settled everything.

I totally get it. College and work must be tough to balance.

As she hit send, she experienced a visceral mix of emotions. Why would LeVar take an interest in Liz anyway? They weren't even friends.

The relief of knowing he was single washed over her like a gentle wave, but the undertow of disappointment at his disinterest in dating soon followed. Not that it mattered. Why should it?

When LeVar stopped responding, she worried she'd scared him off. When her phone hummed again, it was Liz checking in. Apparently, she wouldn't give up easily.

Scout hesitated before typing out a response.

LeVar is single, but he's not interested in dating right now.

Then maybe he'll change his mind. You never know what could happen.

Her eyes drifted to the calendar on the wall, and she thought about the day when she'd finally graduate high school and attend college. Hopefully Kane Grove University. Then she'd be old enough to attract a college guy.

Give him room, Liz. He has a lot on his plate right now.

Yeah, but he's so perfect.

I should get some sleep, Scout wrote. *We'll talk about it at school tomorrow.*

Sleep well, and remember, anything can happen. You taught me that.

Goodnight, BFF.

Scout set the phone aside and pulled the blanket up to her chin. The time for planning had come and gone. Tomorrow she would meet with her guidance counselor and explore options for graduating early. But what would Mom say?

Headlights and shadows danced across her walls as a truck drove past, but now they seemed to take on new shapes, hints of what the future might hold. As she drifted off to sleep, the unseen face of a true boyfriend intertwined with her hopes and dreams—a vision of what could be, if only time and circumstance allowed.

13

The night sky cast a somber pall over the quiet suburban street as Thomas parked his truck outside Deputy Aguilar's burgundy ranch house. He listened to the engine tick and turned his head toward her home. The door loomed large in his mind, a gateway to unburdening himself of the uncertainty eating at him. Rubbing his eyes, he turned off the engine and stepped out of the truck.

He approached the door, tugging nervously on the cuff of one sleeve. Was it right to bother her after work? After all, she had left the office an hour ago. But he needed someone to talk to about his concerns, and Aguilar was the only deputy with whom he could open up.

"Thomas?" Aguilar's surprised voice cut through the chill as she opened the door, revealing her stocky frame and short dark hair. "What brings you here?"

"Hi, Aguilar. I hope I'm not disturbing you. I . . . I just needed to get something off my chest."

She gave him a concerned look. "Of course. Come on in," she said.

He studied her living room. An eclectic mix of art hung from the walls, and a soft light emanated from a lamp by the couch. He noted the details: the worn couch, the stack of crime novels on the coffee table, the framed photograph of Aguilar's family on the mantelpiece. It was a life that seemed so much more grounded than his own, and yet she was willing to set it aside to offer him support.

"Can I offer you some tea?" she asked as she studied him.

"Uh, no, thank you." He tried to appear more at ease than he felt. "Caffeine this late will keep me up all night."

"Herbal tea?"

"I won't be staying long. It's bad enough that I'm bothering you after a twelve-hour day."

She took a seat on the couch and gestured for him to join her.

"Not a problem at all. I was just wasting time in front of the TV. So what's bothering you, Thomas?"

The uncertainty pressed down on him, making it difficult to put his thoughts into words. He appreciated her patience; she waited silently for him to gather his thoughts.

"We're looking at a potential murder investigation. I'm uncertain about my ability to lead. I don't know if I'm ready."

She nodded, understanding the unspoken complexities of his situation—the lingering trauma from the Victor Bacchus murders, the weeks of therapy sessions.

He stared at the worn pattern on Aguilar's rug, his mind racing. He needed to confide in her, but it wasn't easy for him to admit to vulnerability. She waited for him to continue.

"Maybe you should take the lead on this one," he said. "I just don't know if I'm ready."

She leaned forward, her eyes filled with empathy. She didn't show any sign of irritation or impatience, only genuine concern.

"Thomas, listen to me," she said. "You're an incredible sheriff and more than capable of handling this case."

"But what if I relapse? What if I make a mistake, or miss something crucial? People could get hurt because my head isn't in the game."

"Do you remember what Dr. Mandal told you during your assessment?"

His brow creased as he recalled the conversation with his psychiatrist. "She said I was ready to handle high-stress situations."

"Dr. Mandal knows what she's talking about, and she believes in your abilities. We all do—Lambert, LeVar, me, everyone at the station. So trust us, trust yourself, and trust Dr. Mandal's opinion."

That was just it. Dr. Mandal had voiced her opinion. No one could foresee the future.

"Now, let's talk about the case," she continued. "We'll tackle it together, step by step, and I promise you, we'll get through this."

As they delved into the details of the investigation, Thomas allowed Aguilar's confidence to buoy him, even as his own doubts lingered beneath the surface. He looked down at his hands. The demented eyes of Victor's Bacchus flashed in his mind like an old horror movie.

"Thomas," she said. "I know you're uncertain, but trust me when I say that I have full confidence in your ability. You've come so far over the last two months."

He looked up, noting the sincerity on her face. Still, the doubt persisted, and he couldn't help but voice his concern.

"I can't stop thinking about what happened. Laurel Mountain nearly broke me."

"Hey, we've all got scars. You remember what I went through?"

How could he ever forget those dark days when serial killer Justice Thorin abducted Aguilar and a young boy and locked them in underground cells? It had taken months of therapy before Aguilar regained balance in her life.

"Yes."

"But you're not the same person you were in December. You've grown."

Her words, though well-intentioned, did little to assuage his fears. "What if my condition gets in the way?"

"It's not your condition that defines you as a sheriff. It's your dedication, your intelligence, and your unwavering commitment to justice. I've seen it firsthand, and so has everyone who's worked with you."

He allowed her reassurance to wash over him and sought solace.

"I don't want to let anyone down. If you thought I wasn't ready, you'd tell me, right?"

"Would I lie to my friend?"

He rubbed his hands together. "I won't keep you up any longer. I appreciate the advice, Aguilar."

"Anytime, Thomas. You know where to find me if you still need to talk."

They shared an awkward hug, and he walked to the door, opened it, and stepped into the chilly night.

As he made his way to the truck, Thomas felt a mixture of relief and uncertainty. He couldn't erase the doubt that lingered in the shadows of his mind. The weight of responsibility hung on him like an iron yoke.

He climbed into the driver's seat of his F-150 and started the engine; the steady hum of the motor filled the silent night. As he drove through the village streets, he vowed to cling to his friends' support and their belief in him.

Maybe he could even convince himself that he was ready for the nightmares ahead.

14

Thomas tangled himself in the blankets. The image of Victor Bacchus haunted his dreams like an unshakable specter. Visions of Laurel Mountain swirled around him, a place of darkness and death.

"Thomas," Aguilar's voice echoed through the hazy fog of his dream, but it was distorted and unfamiliar. He reached out to her, but the shadows swirled, obscuring his view.

"Can't... see you," Thomas muttered.

"Over here," Lambert called from the distance, his voice strained. Thomas attempted to follow the sound, stumbling through the strange, unnatural landscape that warped with every step.

Goosebumps rose on his skin as he navigated the gnarled trees and jagged rocks. Victor Bacchus was never far behind, always lurking in the darkness.

Where was Chelsey? He had to find her.

Faceless figures emerged from the shadows, their silhouettes indistinguishable against the murky backdrop. They whispered unintelligible words in low, menacing voices. He shivered as the terror clawed at the edges of his mind.

The Carver

The shadows swirled and slithered across the icy landscape. The trees bent in crippled, grotesque shapes.

"Who's there?" Thomas called out. He strained to hear any response, but only the howling wind and the creaking tree limbs answered him.

The darkness closed in, suffocating. Panic clawed at his chest, but he fought the urge to run, knowing that doing so would only make things worse.

"I'm not afraid."

"Of course you're not," a disembodied voice taunted. It echoed through the trees. Maniacal laughter followed.

Thomas faltered.

"Victor Bacchus," he said, recognizing the voice of the man who had haunted both his dreams and his waking moments for months now.

"Do you really think you can escape me?"

Before Thomas responded, a gunshot rang through the air. He spun around, searching for the source of the shot, but the echoes came from all around him.

"Show yourself."

"Here I am," the voice whispered next to his ear, making him jump. Thomas whirled around, and there stood Victor Bacchus, his face contorted into a cruel grin. In one hand, he wielded a blood-crusted ax. Brown clumps of hair dangled off the blade. Chelsey's hair. "Time to die."

As the ax began its descent, Thomas braced himself for the blow, knowing there was no escape this time.

"Help me," he choked.

"Thomas," Aguilar's voice broke through the cacophony once more. "Thomas, wake up!"

His eyes snapped open, and he stared at the familiar ceiling of his bedroom. Sweat dripped down his forehead. It had been weeks since he'd experienced a nightmare like that, and the sudden resurgence left him shaken. Had Dr. Mandal been wrong about clearing him to investigate murders?

Morning sunlight streamed through the window, drawing familiar patterns on the hardwood floor. He blinked, trying to dispel the remnants of the nightmare. The bed sheets tangled around his legs served as evidence of his restless night. Faint sounds came from the kitchen: the clink of dishes, the sizzle of something cooking. Chelsey must be up already.

Dragging himself out of bed, he shuffled down the stairs to the kitchen, where he found her preparing breakfast.

"Morning," he said, his voice hoarse from the remnants of his nightmare.

"Are you okay?" she asked, concern on her face. "You look exhausted."

"I'm fine," he lied, unwilling to burden her with his fears. "Just a rough night. Maybe I need some time off."

"Dr. Mandal said you're ready to lead this investigation, right? You should trust her opinion."

"That's what Aguilar said."

"Listen to your lead deputy. What can I do to help?"

He kissed her on the forehead. "Just stay by my side."

"You're the law, so I have to obey." She returned his kiss. "Could you feed Jack and Tigger? I've got breakfast covered."

"Sure," he said, grabbing two bowls from the cupboard and filling one with cat food for Tigger and another with dog food for Jack. The animals appeared as if they'd been waiting for this moment all morning, their tails wagging and whiskers twitching in anticipation.

As he watched them eat, he considered the case that lay ahead. The bird carving made of human bone chilled him. He thought about the faceless figures in his nightmare and wondered if they were the killer's victims reaching out.

"Trust yourself," she said, touching his arm and sensing his discomfort. "You're the best sheriff this county has ever seen. If anyone can solve this case, it's you."

He observed her scrambling the eggs and felt a mix of emotions—gratitude for her presence and support, but also his own fears and doubts about the case.

After Thomas emptied the kitty litter and took Jack outside, Chelsey plated their breakfast. She gestured for him to sit at the table, which was set for two.

"You still think this is someone from your past?" she asked.

He hesitated, his fork paused in mid-air. "It's just a hunch. The carving. It felt personal."

"We can rule out Jeremy Hyde," she said with a smirk. "You made sure he would never hurt anyone again."

"All my enemies are dead or behind bars. I'm probably overthinking this."

He studied her face, her eyes filled with unwavering belief in him. He couldn't let her see his lingering doubts. His fingers tightened around the fork, a subtle reminder that he needed to regain control of his emotions.

Breathe, Thomas.

The weight of his nightmare began to lift, and the fear and uncertainty that had plagued him vanished in the face of his resolve.

"Whoever sent that carving," he mused aloud, "he can't hide forever. I'll find him."

"Of course you will." Her tone was reassuring and matter-of-fact. "You have the best team of deputies in the state."

He winked at her. "And I can lean on Wolf Lake Consulting."

Thomas appreciated her team as much as his deputies.

"We'll help you catch him. So Claire will report the test results to Aguilar?"

"That's correct. She'll work on the science side of the investigation. Lambert and I will do the grunt work in the field."

As they stood up to clear the table, Jack trotted over and accepted a pat on the head. The dog was fearless. Thomas could learn something from the wolf-like canine.

Somewhere in Nightshade County, a demented monster from his past taunted him.

Thomas would face his fears.

15

The bell above the door chimed as Scout and Liz entered The Broken Yolk, their laughter mingling with the aroma of freshly ground coffee beans. The afternoon sun shed its golden glow on the assortment of mismatched chairs and tables scattered throughout the cozy shop.

"Two caramel lattes, please," Liz ordered, her eyes twinkling. "Extra whipped cream for me and a double shot of espresso for Scout."

"Thanks, Liz," Scout said, pulling her glasses up the bridge of her nose as she looked around the coffee shop. They grabbed their drinks from the counter and weaved through the crowd. LeVar worked a few hours per week, but he wasn't here today.

"Over there." Liz pointed to a round table by the window with a clear view of the street.

"Perfect."

Scout slid into the chair facing the window. She took a slow sip of her latte, savoring how the bitterness of the espresso cut through the sweetness of the caramel.

"Anything new on the amateur sleuthing forum?" Liz stirred

the whipped cream into her drink. She knew how much Scout enjoyed profiling killers and catching criminals.

"Nothing major, just a few interesting discussions." She adjusted her glasses again. "But that's not what I wanted to talk about."

Liz studied her friend, observing the way Scout's fingers drummed an irregular rhythm on the tabletop. "What's on your mind?"

"Promise you won't freak out?"

"You can tell me anything," Liz said, reaching across the table to give her friend's hand a gentle squeeze. "What's got you so wound up?"

Scout hesitated, her eyes drawn to the sun-speckled windowpane, then back to her friend. "I've been thinking about this for a while. I want to graduate early and attend college."

"Wow, that's, uh, ambitious. But why?"

"It's like we talked about. There is so much immaturity at school, and I want to move on. I've already mapped out a plan."

"Tell me about it," Liz encouraged, leaning forward in her seat.

"First, I need to take extra classes online and during summer school." Scout's words tumbled out faster as she gained confidence. "Then I can finish my required courses by the end of junior year. My guidance counselor says it's doable if I stay focused and work hard."

"Sounds like you've thought this through. Are you sure you're ready for all that extra work? College isn't a walk in the park."

"I know. But this is what I need to do."

"Look, I just want you to be sure that this is what you really want, not just because the boys at school are so weird. It's going to be tough."

"I promise I won't take this lightly. I'll think it through before making any final decisions."

"Good. That's all I ask."

As they sipped their coffee, Scout's thoughts churned. She cradled the warm mug in her hands before setting it on the table.

"Another thing I'm worried about is winning my mom's approval. She has certain expectations, and . . . well, I don't know if she'll understand why I want to graduate early."

"Your happiness matters most. Just be honest with your mom. Tell her why this is important to you."

"I hope she understands."

Liz paused, her expression shifting from concern to melancholy. "Can I be honest with you, Scout? The thought of you leaving makes me sad. We've been through so much together, and I can't help but feel like I'm losing my best friend. And who am I supposed to conduct paranormal investigations with?"

Scout recognized the genuine pain in her friend's eyes. She realized the full impact of her decision.

"Hey, you're not losing me, okay? No matter what happens, we'll always be friends. Distance doesn't change that. Besides, Kane Grove is less than an hour away."

A hint of distress popped up on Liz's face. "Kane Grove. That's where LeVar goes." The girl crossed her legs. "Maybe you should think things over. Are you sure this early graduation plan will work?"

Weird. Why the sudden change in her stance? Was Liz jealous that she would attend college with LeVar? Scout stared down at her cup, watching the coffee swirl with each absent-minded stir of her spoon.

"Yeah, it's totally doable."

"Promise me you'll consider what's best for you, not just the quickest path to your career."

Scout hesitated, her emotions warring within her. Liz was right. She had to weigh her desires against the potential setbacks of her plan. "I promise I'll think about it before making my decision."

They fell into a comfortable silence, sipping their coffee and watching the world go by outside the window.

Internally, her thoughts raced. Her decision would have far-reaching consequences, not only for herself but for those she loved. In the end, she had to make the choice that was right for her, no matter how much it hurt. Liz's friendship would endure.

A couple strolled by the window, hand in hand, laughing at some private joke. Scout envied their carefree demeanor and the simplicity of their lives. They made their own rules, set their schedules, and had each other to lean on. Like Chelsey had Thomas and Raven had Darren.

Liz sighed. "If you leave early, things won't be the same without you here."

"Hey, we'll still see each other, even if I graduate early. And, besides, it's not like I'm leaving tomorrow. We've got time."

"Of course," Liz said, but her smile seemed strained. "It's just that, well, I guess I'm afraid that once you get to college and experience all those new things, you'll forget about me."

"Never. You've been my best friend since I returned to school after my surgery. That's not going to change."

Liz nodded, but her eyes looked distant, as if lost in thought.

After some consideration, Scout said, "Just think, Liz. You can visit and stay over in my dorm room. No more slumber parties on the floor."

The girl's eyes lit with hope. "Parties. And you could introduce me to college guys."

Scout bent her neck back and laughed. "Slow down, girlfriend. But yeah, sure. I'll introduce you to all the hot guys."

They finished their coffee in silence, each absorbed in their own thoughts.

"I'm not jealous of your plans. I just want you to be happy. You've always been the smart one between us, and you'll do great things in college. But just make sure it's what you really want."

Relief flooded through Scout as she wrapped her arm around Liz's shoulder. "I will," she whispered, grateful for her friend's honesty and support. "I promise I'll think everything through before talking to Mom."

16

Thomas strode toward his office. He nodded to Aguilar, who was hunched over a stack of paperwork at her desk, and then to Lambert, who leaned against the wall, sipping coffee from a chipped mug.

"Morning, Aguilar. Morning, Lambert," he said.

They returned his greeting in unison. As Thomas settled into his chair, he glanced around the room at the familiar faces of his colleagues.

In the quiet of his office, he attempted to focus on the case files scattered across his desk. But the memories of the Victor Bacchus trauma on Laurel Mountain refused to stay silent. The haunting image of the killer's grin flashed before his eyes. He shook his head, trying to clear away the cobwebs of fear and doubt.

"Hey, Thomas," said Lambert. "You got a minute?"

"Sure, Lambert." Thomas turned his attention to the tall ex-army deputy. He tried to keep his mind on the present, on the task at hand, but the specter of his past loomed large in the back of his consciousness.

"Any updates on the bone carving?" Lambert crossed the

room to stand beside Thomas's desk. "I've been going through the missing person's reports, but nothing seems to fit."

"Not yet, but we'll find a lead soon. We'll catch this guy."

"Damn right we will," agreed Aguilar.

"It's personal. That's my feeling. He could have sent the carving to anyone, but he chose me."

"Is your home security system working?" asked Lambert.

"Working fine. Plus, I have LeVar living in the guesthouse."

"Well, if the killer shows his face, he and LeVar can share a pizza. Damn, that deputy can eat."

As they delved into the investigation, Thomas forced himself to push aside the memories of Laurel Mountain and the Victor Bacchus trauma. He had a job to do, people to protect, and he would not allow fear or doubt to stand in his way.

He scanned the screen as he awakened his computer, searching the state database for investigations involving killers who carved their victims' bones. With each click and scroll, disappointment set in. He found no leads, no cases that matched the sickening details of what they were up against. Not a surprise. Had an active serial killer in New York State sent bones to public officials, he would have heard about it by now.

"Nothing," he muttered under his breath, the word tasting like ash in his mouth. Aguilar and Lambert were both focused on their own tasks.

His gaze drifted across his desk, settling where the bird had sat. He'd once believed it to be ivory. The knowledge that it was human bone pushed a wave of revulsion through him. Claire Brookins had the carving now.

"Find any cases matching this one?" Aguilar's voice.

"Nothing. I can't find any investigations that match what we're dealing with."

As his fingers danced across the keyboard, unease clawed at

his insides. The carving, the message it conveyed—this killer knew how to get under his skin.

"Hey, Thomas," Lambert called from across the room, pulling his attention away from the screen. "If you want, I can help you look. We can cover more ground that way."

"Thanks. I could use the extra pair of eyes."

He wondered what clues Claire might uncover, what secrets the bones might reveal about the killer and his victim.

Picking up the phone, he dialed Claire's extension. The line rang once, twice, before her voice answered.

"Brookins," she said.

"Hey, Claire. It's Thomas. I was wondering if you've run more tests on the bone carving."

"Actually, I have."

"What can you tell me?"

Claire hesitated for a moment, as if weighing her words carefully. "This carving is not just any human bone," she said. "It's a femur bone, and it was recently removed."

"Victim's gender and age?"

"Tough to ascertain from a piece of bone."

"Do we have any idea how this person died?"

"Unfortunately, no. I can't even say with certainty that the victim is dead. I'll run more tests."

Thomas pictured a man with a missing leg bleeding out on a dusty floor as a madman leered down at him.

"And we'll cross-reference your results with our missing persons database. We might get lucky and find a match. Thanks, Claire. Keep me updated on your findings, will you?"

"Of course."

The line went dead. He hung up the phone. The killer had chosen a victim and removed his leg. It was a calculated, twisted act that spoke volumes about the person they were dealing with. He loved torture and power.

The Carver

Thomas stood up from his desk. Aguilar and Lambert were deep in conversation down the hall.

"Hey, Aguilar," he said, beckoning for her to come over. "Lambert, you too."

The two deputies exchanged a look before approaching Thomas's desk, their expressions a mixture of curiosity and concern.

"Listen," Thomas said, his fingers drumming a staccato rhythm on the wood, "Claire thinks the carving came from a femur bone."

"I just received the medical examiner's results," Aguilar said. "She believes it came from a male in his mid-twenties to early forties?"

"Correct. I need you to compile a list of everyone in the area who went missing in the last two weeks. Focus on males in the assumed age range. Use a radius of fifty miles. If you strike out, expand the age range and go out a hundred miles."

Aguilar's eyes narrowed as she processed the request. "No matter how long it takes, we'll find who the bone came from."

"Our killer might choose another victim," Lambert said.

"Exactly," Thomas said, nodding. "We have to nail this guy before he strikes again."

The list of missing persons might hold the key to unmasking the killer, or it could lead them to a dead end. With every passing moment, the stakes grew higher. Could the victim still be alive?

He watched as Aguilar and Lambert dove into the investigation, their fingers tapping away at their keyboards, searching through databases and police reports.

After a moment, Lambert said, "I found someone who went missing last week. A truck driver named Martin Jenkins. Sending the police report to both of you now."

"Could be something," Aguilar said, her dark eyes locked on

her screen. "I've got a young woman, Sarah Daniels, reported missing two days ago by her roommate. Wrong gender, right age."

"Keep looking," Thomas said. "There might be more."

Each name seemed to hold a fragment of the truth, a potential glimpse into the demented mind of a murderer. How did the psycho choose his targets?

He busied himself by expanding his search to the East Coast, then the entire nation. No serial killers with a penchant for carving items from body parts. He emailed the FBI, hoping Neil Gardy or Scarlett Bell might lend their opinions.

An hour later, he studied the list of names that Aguilar and Lambert had compiled. The sickening gift held the key to unlocking the identity of the killer. The message it conveyed was clear: a taunt, an invitation to delve into his own past.

Lambert leaned back in his chair. "So, we're not just looking for a connection to these missing people. We're looking for a connection to you."

"I'm afraid so."

Ghosts and demons filled Thomas's past, the memories of which still haunted his dreams.

"That might narrow the list," Aguilar said, clapping her hands together. "Let's dig deeper. We'll cross-reference the missing persons list with anyone who might have a connection to you, Thomas. That means old cases, colleagues, even friends."

"Good idea," Lambert said. He cracked his knuckles and returned to the search.

The killer had thrown down the gauntlet, daring Thomas to confront the sins of his past. But in the end, it would be the killer who faced the consequences of his actions.

Thomas would see to it personally.

17

The guesthouse was a modest yet cozy abode, tucked away behind Thomas Shepherd's A-frame home. The icy tendrils of winter seeped through the cracks, weaving a chilly embrace around the interior. Despite the cold, LeVar appreciated the breathtaking view of Wolf Lake that unfolded before him like an enchanting painting, its icy surface reflecting the pale sunlight.

He stepped out of the shower and wrapped a towel around his waist before admiring his reflection in the fogged-up mirror. Satisfied with the body he'd built at the gym, he ran a hand over his sculpted chest and toned arms, pausing briefly over the scars that marred his otherwise flawless skin—the remnants of his past life with the Harmon Kings.

At each scar, memories of violence and brotherhood flashed through his mind, serving as a constant reminder to never go astray again. A jagged line snaking down his forearm made him recall the night a rival gang member's blade had sliced into his flesh. LeVar shook off the memory, focusing instead on the man he had become: a dedicated deputy, an intern for Wolf Lake

Consulting, and a steadfast friend to his fellow officers, Aguilar and Lambert. And especially Thomas, the father he'd never had.

As he patted himself dry, he felt grateful for his second chance. A chance to build a life beyond the shadows of the Kings. But even with his newfound purpose, some days the ghosts of his past threatened to claw their way into his present, taunting him with doubts.

He pushed those thoughts aside, determined not to let them take root. He couldn't change the past, but he could forge a better future for himself and those he cared about.

LeVar draped the towel on the shower door when a knock startled him. He spotted a youthful figure with long hair standing at his doorstep. It was Liz, Scout's friend from school. What on earth was she doing here?

Maybe if he pretended he wasn't home, she would—

"Hey, LeVar," Liz called out, peering between the curtains. "Can I talk to you for a minute?"

So much for fooling her into going away. He hesitated, unsure of how to handle the situation. Allowing a teenager into the guesthouse was a terrible look. Sure, Scout hung out all the time, but she was his friend. He valued his moral compass and didn't want to get in a compromising position.

"Uh, hey, Liz," LeVar said, opening the door just a crack. "What do you need? It's kind of cold out here."

Despite the frigid air, Liz wore a snug, low-cut sweater that accentuated her curves and left little to the imagination. Her miniskirt seemed impractical for the weather, but practicality wasn't her primary concern. A pair of knee-high boots completed the ensemble, making her appear both youthful and alluring.

"Could I just talk to you for a bit?" she asked, attempting to peer inside the house. "It won't take long, I promise."

LeVar's reluctance intensified as he tried to keep Liz from

entering. He knew people might talk if they saw her inside his home, and he didn't want to give anyone the wrong impression.

"Actually, it's not a good time right now. Is there something you wanted to ask me? We can chat out here."

Liz pouted, her eyes darting around the chilly exterior. "Well," she began, "I was hoping you could help me with a problem. But it's kind of hard to explain out here."

His curiosity piqued despite his determination to maintain boundaries. "*Aight*, what do you need help with?"

"Umm, it's just . . ." Liz stammered, shifting her weight from one foot to the other. "I wanted to ask if you could teach me how to drive in the snow and ice. You see, I have my license, but I'm kinda bad at winter driving. Well, horrible. Scout says you're teaching her."

"Isn't your dad around to help you? I thought he taught you how to drive."

"Uh, yeah. But he's been so busy lately, and I don't want to bother him. Plus, I think you'd be a better teacher. You're calm and cool."

LeVar frowned. There was something more to Liz's request than she was letting on.

"Maybe your dad can call me and tell me what he wants you to work on. You know, so I can help you with your weaknesses."

"Come on, LeVar," she said, rubbing the goosebumps on her legs. "I just need a little help. Don't you want to be my knight in shining armor?" She inched closer to him, her eyes locked on his as if trying to reel him in.

He was acutely aware of how close she stood. "Liz, I'm flattered, but I can't do this right now. It wouldn't be right."

"Fine," she huffed, clearly disappointed by his resistance. "But you're missing out on all the fun we could have had. I don't see what the difference is between teaching Scout and teaching me."

"I've known Scout longer." LeVar stepped back to create distance between them. "You're young, and I'm sure you'll find someone else who can help you with your . . . driving lessons."

He crossed his arms and leaned against the doorframe, noticing how her eyes darted over his shoulder and into the guesthouse, as if searching for a way inside.

"Please, LeVar. I promise I'll be a model student."

If Liz had ulterior motives, she needed acting lessons to hide them. For now, he played along.

"I can give you some tips, but we're not doing this alone. I'll ask Scout and her mother to join us. Would that be all right?"

"Uh, sure." Her voice wavered with disappointment. "That would be fine."

"Here's what we'll do. We'll set something up with Scout and Ms. Mourning. That way, you get your lessons, and Scout can pick up tips too. Deal?"

Liz hesitated for a moment before nodding. "Deal."

"Great. Now, if you don't mind, I have some things I need to take care of."

As Liz stepped into the cold, he watched her, noting the way she wrapped her arms around herself for warmth, her provocative clothing out of place against the harsh winter landscape. He felt sympathy for her. She was just a kid, and obviously she wasn't as sure of herself as she pretended to be. But getting close to a girl four years younger than him meant trouble.

Closing the door behind him, LeVar leaned against it for a moment as he processed the encounter. He sank into the worn couch near the window, his eyes skating across the icy expanse of Wolf Lake. He rubbed his temples to shake off the tension from his encounter with Liz.

"Too young," he muttered under his breath. "And too damn confusing."

Liz was undeniably beautiful, and there was something

about her that tugged at his heartstrings. What if there was more to her story than met the eye? And why the sudden interest in him?

He replayed their conversation in his mind, searching for any clues he might have missed. She'd seemed so desperate for his help, so insistent on learning how to drive in winter conditions. It didn't quite add up, especially given her established driving skills.

The sun began its westward descent. He turned on a corner lamp to keep the shadows at bay. Whatever was up with Liz, he needed to know.

LeVar messaged Scout.

18

Parry Bonner stood among the neatly arranged aisles of Kane Grove Builders, his tall frame slightly slouched and a hint of stubble on his square jaw. His eyes were red from allergens as he surveyed the shelf he'd arranged, taking in the tools and materials. At twenty-seven years old, he was a three-year veteran of Kane Grove Builders, familiar with every nook and cranny of the home improvement store and on the fast track to a managerial position.

"Excuse me."

Bonner turned to see a man standing beside him. The stranger had broad shoulders and watery eyes that seemed to stare right through him. His lips were thin, and cuts ran up and down his arms. He looked as if he'd lost a fight with a woodchipper.

"Can I help you?"

"I'm looking for a very sharp saw. Something durable. Something that can cut through anything."

"Sure," Bonner said as he led the man to aisle seven. "Over here, we have a selection of hand and power saws."

"Which one would you recommend?" the man asked, his

eyes never leaving Bonner's face. There was something unnerving about the intensity of his stare, as if he were a witch sizing up Hansel and Gretel.

"Um, well, this one is quite popular." Bonner picked up a heavy-duty hand saw. "It has a strong blade and comfortable grip. It should work well for most materials."

"Most materials? What about ... harder substances?"

"Like what?"

"Never mind," the man said, a tight smile playing across his lips. "I'll take this one."

He took the saw, his fingers brushing against Bonner's for a fleeting moment.

"Happy sawing. Let me know if you need anything else."

"Thank you."

The man's eyes lingered on Bonner before he walked away, the saw cradled in his arms like a precious treasure.

"Wait. I have one more question."

"Sure, what is it?"

"Can this saw cut through bone?"

The question caught Bonner off guard, and he felt a rush of cold air sweep through him despite being indoors. He swallowed, trying to ignore the pounding in his chest.

"I suppose so. It's a strong blade," he said hesitantly. The man's eyes gleamed, and Bonner felt unease creep into his bones. "You into taxidermy or something?"

"That's all I needed to know."

With that, he walked towards the checkout counter, leaving Bonner standing between the rows of tools, confusion and fear churning within him.

"Hey, Parry." It was Pete, Bonner's coworker in the tools department. "You look like you're about to lose your lunch."

"Man, you wouldn't believe this guy who just came in."

Bonner forced a laugh. "He asked me if our saws could cut through bone."

"Bone?" Pete raised an eyebrow, chuckling. "Sounds like a real weirdo."

"Tell me about it," Bonner agreed, shaking his head. "Wackos come in here sometimes."

"Was his name Hannibal?"

"That was just a movie. This guy was real."

"Ah, well," Pete said, clapping Bonner on the shoulder. "At least he's gone now."

"Right. Anyhow, it's time to exit stage right."

"Lucky you. I still have four hours left. Anything you need done?"

"Some kid spilled a soft drink in front of the screwdrivers. I mopped it up, but the floor is still sticky."

"I'll pull out the industrial cleaner. Have a good one. See you tomorrow."

The day had turned into night, and orange lights flooded the Kane Grove Builders parking lot. Bonner pulled up the collar of his coat as he stepped into the February chill. Kane Grove Builders required all employees to park at the back of the lot. Not a problem during July, but midwinter temperatures made the walk feel like a death march. His nose hairs froze every time he inhaled. The wind whipped at his face, causing him to squint as he hurried towards his truck.

He climbed in and started the engine, feeling heat seep through the vents. That was the best part about his pickup. The heater warmed up in less than a minute. He rubbed his hands together, trying to regain some feeling in his fingertips. As he shifted into drive, a jolt sent him forward against the steering wheel. In an instant, adrenaline surged through his veins, and he realized someone had smashed him from behind. Idiot drivers. He'd made the last payment on this truck a month ago.

"Damn it," he muttered, throwing the truck into park and stepping out to survey the damage. The frigid air cut through him like a knife, making him shiver.

The other car, a nondescript sedan with its headlights switched off, had a crumpled hood and a shattered headlight. Bonner's truck seemed to have fared better, but there were visible dents where the force of the impact had left its mark.

"Yo! What the hell?" Bonner stepped toward the other driver, who was just getting out of his car.

"Sorry," a familiar voice said. "My foot slipped on the pedal."

"Slipped? Look at this mess!"

As the other driver stepped closer, illuminated by the lights, a creepy realization hit Bonner. It was the same man who had asked about the saw. His mouth went dry.

"Small world, huh?" the man said with a grin, his eyes locked onto Bonner's.

"Look, we should probably exchange insurance information and get this sorted out."

"Of course," the man replied. "But first, I have something I need to show you."

Bonner hesitated, instinctively taking a step back. The wind howled through the empty parking lot, making him feel isolated. He looked around, hoping to see someone else nearby.

A sharp crackling sound filled the air, followed by an intense surge of pain through his body. The stun gun pressed against his chest. His muscles spasmed and he collapsed onto the ground, twitching and gasping for breath.

"Sorry about that," the man said, his voice void of any genuine remorse. "But I needed you to be cooperative."

Struggling to regain control of his body, Bonner tried to make sense of the situation.

The man popped the latch on his trunk and swung it open. He grabbed Bonner by the collar of his jacket, yanking him to his feet. Bonner tried to resist, but his muscles remained useless from the stun gun's effects.

The psycho gave him a push. He tipped forward, catching himself on the edge of the trunk. As he rasped a silent cry for help, the man tossed his legs over the side, forcing him further into the confined space.

Then the trunk slammed shut. Darkness enveloped Bonner, trapping him in a suffocating world of fear and pain.

Outside, the winter wind howled through the parking lot, the biting cold creeping into the trunk and through the thin layers of clothing, numbing his skin.

Inside, he crumpled against an ice scraper. His breath came in shallow gasps, the frigid air stinging his lungs at each inhalation. The car's engine rumbled beneath him.

He struggled to catch his breath. The smell of rubber and oil assaulted his nostrils, making it difficult to breathe. The effects of the stun gun lingered, but he could move his limbs now.

"Hey!" he yelled, kicking against the trunk. "Let me out of here."

Silence met his cries for help, followed only by the dull thud of his own kicks against the cold metal. For a moment, he allowed himself to hope that someone might hear and save him from this nightmare.

"Who are you?"

As the car sped away from the parking lot, Bonner strained against the confines of the trunk. The world outside seemed impossibly distant, separated by layers of metal and darkness, leaving him alone with his fear and the chilling knowledge that he wouldn't survive the night.

19

The man pulled into the driveway of his secluded house outside Wolf Lake. The trees swayed with each gust of wind, spinning shadows across the snow. He sensed the weight of his prey in the trunk, and a sense of satisfaction washed over him. Parry Bonner was in his grasp. Another gift for the loyal servants of Nightshade County.

"You will make a beautiful specimen," he said, stepping out of the car and slamming the door. He walked to the back, fingers tingling with anticipation. The moment had come.

After checking the road, he unlocked the trunk, revealing Bonner, who lay unconscious, a bruise forming on his temple from the way the car had jostled him around. A smile curved the killer's lips as he admired his handiwork, knowing that the man would soon serve a greater purpose.

"You're going to help me send a message," he whispered, reaching down to grab Bonner by the collar.

With effort, the killer dragged him out of the trunk. Bonner's body thudded against the ice before sliding towards the house. As they crossed the threshold, he felt power surging through him. This was his domain, and this victim would become another chapter in his story.

Inside, he wasted no time in securing the store worker to a sturdy wooden chair, tying up his hands and feet with rope. Grunting with exertion, he ensured each knot was tight, relishing the thought of Bonner's futile struggle once he regained consciousness.

"Can't have you escaping now, can we?" he said, chuckling.

As he stepped back to admire his work, he remembered Sheriff Thomas Shepherd and his deputies, Aguilar and Lambert. They were relentless in their pursuit of him, but he wanted them to come. As soon as he sent his next present, they would understand the depth of his power. He imagined the sheriff's expression when confronted with the gruesome reminder of his failure to protect his citizens.

The glow of the television screen kept him company as an old horror movie played in the background. He stood at his workbench, running a sharpening stone along the edge of his knife. The rhythmic sound of metal against stone punctuated the air, accompanied by the distant screams and ominous music from the TV.

His eyes shifted to the array of tools laid out before him, each with a specific purpose.

"You know, I've always had a flair for the artistic."

He picked up another knife, honing its blade with the same surgical precision. With every swipe, his excitement mounted at the prospect of what was to come. After a stroke of the sharpening stone, he set the knife down and flexed his fingers. And as the screams from the television echoed through the room, he knew those chilling sounds would be all too real. He thought of Sheriff Thomas Shepherd and his infuriating persistence. A self-righteous dictator.

The memory of a funeral came to him unbidden—two

somber faces, the lost hope, the icy rain. The man who lay in the casket hadn't deserved what happened to him. A misunderstood soul, tarnished by the actions of one man.

"They act like they're working for justice, but what about that poor man? Where was his justice?"

His grip tightened on the knife handle, knuckles turning white as his resentment grew. He resumed the rhythmic sharpening, each stroke fueled by thoughts of revenge.

The blade's edge glinted in the dim light. The sharp, bitter scent of oil mixed with the faint smell of mildew from old wallpaper that peeled at the edges. He could hear Bonner's muffled moans coming from the next room, yet he didn't let the sound distract him.

"Patience. A dull knife is a dangerous tool."

He turned his attention to the new saw lying on the table, its teeth like a row of hungry sharks ready to feast. As he lifted it, feeling the weight and balance, a thrill coursed through his veins.

"Sharp enough to cut through bone," he said as he inspected the teeth. He pressed the tip of his thumb against a tooth and drew a single drop of blood. Satisfied, he wiped it clean and placed it alongside the knives in an array of gleaming menace.

The door creaked open, revealing the room where Bonner sat, bound and helpless. A single light bulb served as a spotlight over his victim.

At first, Bonner didn't see him. His head hung over his chest in groggy submission. Then the man blinked and saw what was coming for him.

The screaming began.

20

The images of ghost hunters on a TV screen illuminated the basement. Scout and Liz huddled together under a blanket, their eyes glued to the show as they munched on popcorn and candy.

"My aunt told me she saw a shadow figure at the Radford mansion once," Liz said. "She said it was the scariest thing she'd ever seen."

"I can't imagine what I would do if a ghost floated by."

"Me too, but I'd feel safe if LeVar was with us."

Scout tried to focus on the TV, but the mention of LeVar's name stirred conflicting emotions. She recalled the message he had sent her about Liz stopping by his house and asking for driving lessons.

"Did you know he is teaching me to drive in winter weather?" Liz asked. "He said he wants you and your mother to come with us, but that's up to you guys. You don't have to."

"Really?" Scout asked, trying to keep her voice steady despite the growing discomfort in her chest. She shifted her weight on the couch and reached for a piece of candy.

"Uh-huh. He really is the greatest."

Scout popped the candy into her mouth, biting down hard to keep from saying something she might regret later. She knew about Liz's long-standing crush on LeVar, but lately it seemed like her friend's interest had become more intense, almost like she was determined to win him over as a boyfriend. The thought upset her, making her stomach churn with unease.

"I guess we could come," Scout said, forcing a smile onto her face. She kept her eyes on the screen, watching the ghost hunters explore a creepy old building, but their antics did little to hold her attention. Instead, her mind raced with questions. Why now? What had changed between Liz and LeVar?

"Hey, do you think LeVar would be interested in joining us for one of these slumber parties?" Liz asked. "We could watch the ghost hunting shows together. He'd love that."

"Doubt he'd be interested. I don't think he believes in all this paranormal stuff. But, you know, slumber parties are kind of our thing. Just the two of us."

"True." Liz's smile faded. "I just thought it'd be fun to have him around."

Scout stared at the screen, now showing a ghostly apparition, but all she could see was the image of LeVar and Liz together, laughing and enjoying each other's company while she was left behind.

"Hey, are you okay?" Liz asked. "Did I say something that upset you?"

"Just got a little spooked by the show, that's all."

"Me too. But that's what makes it so much fun, right?"

"Right."

Liz's excited chatter finally subsided as they watched the latest episode.

"Did you see that?" Liz whispered, gripping Scout's arm as an apparition formed on the screen. "That was so creepy."

Every time something spooky happened on the show, the

two girls screamed and jumped, clutching each other until the tension passed.

"Can you imagine if we ever ran into a ghost?" Liz asked.

"I don't know if I'd be brave enough to face it."

"Sure you would. And we'd be rich and famous after our video went viral. Think of it: Scout and Liz, paranormal experts. Hey, let's make a pact. This year, we'll record a ghost and face it head-on. Sound like a plan?"

"Deal," Scout said, the simple agreement giving her a small measure of comfort. If only she could make a similar deal with Liz to give LeVar space.

"I bet ghosts are more scared of us than we are of them. Like hornets."

"Hornet stings hurt."

The girls tensed, waiting for the next twist in the show. After a commercial, an announcement appeared on the screen.

"Breaking news," the man said. "New York Ghost Patrol is coming to Wolf Lake to investigate the notorious Radford mansion, believed by many to be the most haunted location in Upstate New York."

Liz and Scout shared an incredulous look.

"What if we went there ourselves?" Liz's eyes lit with excitement. "We could beat New York Ghost Patrol to the punch and check out the mansion before they arrive."

Scout hesitated, torn between her desire to spend more time with Liz and her fear of trespassing into unknown territory. She saw the eagerness in Liz's expression.

"Are you sure? The last time we tried something like this, we ended up grounded for a month."

"Come on, Scout," Liz said, her eyes sparkling with mischief. "It'll be an adventure. Besides, we made that pact, remember? We'll stick together and face whatever we find."

"Let me think about it."

As they resumed watching the program, Scout shuddered over venturing into dangerous territory, given both the looming investigation of the haunted mansion and the unspoken tension between them caused by LeVar.

"You can't say no."

"Why not?"

"This is our last hurrah. You know, before you graduate early and go to college."

"That plan isn't set in stone. I still have to talk to my mom."

"Please, Scout. This is our big chance. Heck, it's our last chance."

"Look, Liz, it's not a smart idea. The Radford mansion is private property. We can't just waltz inside."

"We'll find a way. Besides, it's not like anyone lives there anymore."

Scout shifted on the couch, her hands fidgeting in her lap. Liz's stubbornness wouldn't give way easily.

"I'm worried about our safety, and if we get caught again Mom will lock me in my room until I'm thirty. Besides, Radford Mansion has actual ghosts."

"Exactly!" Liz grinned. "That's what makes it so thrilling."

As they continued to debate, Scout struggled to maintain eye contact with Liz. She wanted nothing more than to put an end to their conversation and let the matter rest, but doing so would mean ignoring the unease in her gut. Instead, she focused on the way Liz's vibrant blue nails played with a loose thread on the arm of the couch.

"We don't know what could happen in there. It's not just about ghosts or trespassing. What if someone dangerous is lurking around? Or what if the place is falling apart and we get hurt?"

"I know you're worried, but I promise we'll be careful. We've got each other's backs, right?"

"Right," Scout agreed, though she still held doubt. Liz wouldn't give up on the idea, and Scout wondered if her friend's persistence had something to do with LeVar. "I just think we should think about it some more. Maybe come up with a plan before we get ourselves into a mess."

Liz rolled her eyes and tossed a handful of popcorn into her mouth. "You worry too much. Besides, what's life without a little spontaneity?" She grinned, nudging Scout playfully with her elbow.

"Spontaneity is one thing. Recklessness is another."

At last, Liz surrendered the argument, though the girl seemed sullen as they settled in for the next episode in the marathon. When they reached the bottom of the bowl, they popped another batch in the kitchen and returned to the basement. Scout turned off the lights, adding to the creepy atmosphere. All the while, the image of Radford Mansion loomed in the back of her mind, casting a shadow over the evening's entertainment.

As the final credits rolled and the girls prepared for bed, Scout worried they were about to step into a story far darker and more dangerous than anything they had seen on the screen.

21

The room was a grotesque canvas of gore and terror, the walls spattered with crimson stains. Its damp air, thick with the coppery scent of blood, clung to Parry Bonner's skin. The metallic taste lingered on his tongue as he tried to focus on anything but the excruciating pain radiating from his leg.

"Christ," he muttered through gritted teeth, sweat beading on his forehead.

His leg—or what remained of it—throbbed with ferocity. The madman had severed it just below the thigh, leaving a raw stump that pulsated in time with his racing heartbeat. The pain was unbearable, driving his every thought and every action. He squinted at the ceiling, fighting back the urge to scream.

"Please, just let it stop."

The sound of his own voice seemed distant. In-between gasps for breath, Bonner caught snippets of sounds—the creak of floorboards, the soft rustle of fabric. The killer was still there, somewhere beyond the door. Each thud of footsteps heightened Bonner's anxiety.

How could he escape? If he didn't, he would die here in this blood-soaked room. He blinked through a haze of pain, his vision swimming in and out of focus. His leg throbbed with white-hot agony. The room seemed to spin around him, and the blood-stained walls provided a macabre backdrop to his torment.

He had lost consciousness several times, each an all-too-brief respite. Every time he awoke, the reality of his situation crashed down upon him once more, filling him with a sickening mix of powerlessness and desperation.

His stomach churned at the memory of the blowtorch, of the searing heat as it cauterized his wound; the smell of burned flesh still lingered in the air. It clung to him like a noxious cloud, intensifying his nausea.

As the footsteps retreated, Bonner marshaled what little strength remained in him. His thoughts were muddled, clouded by pain and fear.

He slumped in the chair with his hands bound. The sound of doors opening and closing echoed through the house, a reminder that he was never alone.

"Help!" he yelled.

But the only response was the distant creak of the house settling, punctuated by the intermittent thudding of the killer as he moved from one room to another. The noises heightened Bonner's anxiety, as if the walls themselves had come alive.

The drugs in his veins dulled his senses and left him weak, helpless. Every thought seemed to slip away like water through his fingers. He strained to listen, hoping to gain some sense of the killer's whereabouts. The muffled footsteps grew louder, then faded again as the unseen tormentor had moved away.

Time stretched out, each second an eternity, as he remained immobile. Again, he heard creaking of doors and now of footsteps growing closer. Panic swelled inside him as he realized the killer was returning. In a desperate bid, he feigned sleep to lure the madman into a false sense of security.

Bonner slowed his breathing, forcing himself to relax despite the searing pain. He closed his eyes and listened to the approaching footsteps.

"Pathetic," the killer said, his voice cold and emotionless, as he entered the room. Bonner fought to suppress a shiver, acutely aware of the man's presence looming over him.

"Look at you," the madman continued, his tone dripping with contempt. "You're not even worth the effort."

Bonner maintained his ruse, keeping his breaths slow and steady.

The madman circled him like a predator sizing up its prey. Was this man seeking revenge for some perceived slight? Did he crave power and control? Or was he simply a monster who delighted in inflicting pain?

As the footsteps receded and the door closed with a chilling finality, Bonner allowed himself to breathe again. His fear and confusion remained. A clock on the wall ticked away the seconds, each one precious as he considered his options. He had deceived the killer, but it would take more than cunning to survive the ordeal that lay ahead.

Even if he freed his arms, how would he escape on one leg? Agony threatened to drive him into unconsciousness. If he mustered the willpower to endure long enough and crawl out of this hellhole, there might be a glimmer of hope.

He gritted his teeth and struggled against the bonds. Five minutes later, the ropes held fast. Bonner wept with frustration; his hands and wrists burned and his back ached. He slumped in the chair, drained by the effort but steeled by the thought of escape. Closing his eyes, he lay his head against the backrest. His mind drifted in and out of sleep.

Despite the torment, he must have fallen asleep; the gray

glow of the coming dawn pushed against the window as the smell of his own flesh lingered in the air. His thoughts swam through a sea of confusion, leaving him unable to comprehend his situation.

Somewhere in the house, a door groaned open. The madman was coming for him.

22

In the Mournings' basement, Scout leaned against a cluttered workbench, her glasses sliding down her nose as she spoke to Liz. Restlessness had kept her up most of the night, and it wasn't because the television shows scared her.

"Okay, I've come to an ultimatum," she said. "I'll do the ghost hunt in Radford Mansion, but only if we get permission from our parents and Thomas."

Liz frowned, her expression doubtful. "Really? You think that's a good idea? You know how the sheriff can be. He might shut us down before we even get started."

"If we want any chance of beating New York Ghost Patrol, we need to go through the proper channels."

They climbed the stairs to the kitchen, where her mom worked at the stove, flipping pancakes. Sunlight streamed through the window. Scout looked at Liz, who still appeared uneasy about their plan.

"Mom, can we talk to you about something?"

"Sure, what's up?" Naomi asked, sliding a fresh batch of pancakes onto a plate.

"We were thinking about investigating Radford Mansion.

You know, like a real ghost hunt. But we want to do it legally and with Thomas's permission."

Naomi raised an eyebrow, her spatula hovering over the sizzling pan. "You two are serious about this?"

"We can prove ourselves responsible and maybe even help solve the mysteries connected to the mansion." She hesitated for a moment, then added, "And we'd like to speak to Thomas about it."

As they sat down at the table, a stack of golden flapjacks between them, Scout noticed Liz's tense posture. She knew her friend was worried about Thomas's reaction, but if they wanted to be taken seriously, they needed to follow the rules.

"I'll see if Thomas is available to talk. But I want you both to understand that if he says no, or if he thinks this is too dangerous, then that's the end."

"Understood."

They spoke little as they ate. After stuffing themselves, the girls cleared the table and did the dishes. Maybe this was a mistake. Scout had injured her relationship with Thomas because of the Halloween fiasco, but he'd forgiven her. Was she pushing things too quickly?

A knock on the sliding glass door announced that Thomas had arrived. His sandy hair tousled, he entered the kitchen and took a seat across from the girls with a steaming mug of coffee in hand.

"Your mother said you have something to ask me," he said, taking a sip.

She swept the hair off her shoulder and pushed the butterflies down in her chest.

"Thomas, we want to investigate Radford Mansion for ghosts. We've done our research, and we're sure there's something going on there. But we want to hunt legally, not trespass."

"Radford Mansion?" Thomas raised an eyebrow. "That place

has been abandoned for years. What makes you think it's haunted?"

Liz jumped in, her enthusiasm shining through despite her earlier despondence. "I gathered accounts from locals who experienced strange occurrences inside. Unexplained noises, objects moving on their own, even sightings of ghosts. And with the New York Ghost Patrol planning to investigate soon, we want to prove that we can do just as good of a job."

"Even more than that," Scout said, "we want to show that we can follow the rules and do things by the book. That's why we're asking for your permission."

Thomas studied them for a moment, his expression unreadable. "I appreciate that you're trying to go about this the right way, but it's not that simple. Radford Mansion is private property. Not to mention the potential dangers lurking in an old, decaying building. There could be unstable floors, exposed wires, even wild animals taking shelter inside."

Liz clasped her hands on the table. "We understand the risks, which is why we'd ensure the mansion is sound before we step foot inside, and we'll have our phones with us. The New York Ghost Patrol already has permission to investigate Radford Mansion. Don't you think our local team should have the same opportunity?"

Scout said, "We won't take any unnecessary risks. This is important to us, and we're willing to do whatever it takes to prove ourselves."

His blue-green eyes searched their faces. Finally, he sighed, setting down his mug. "I'll think about it, but I need to discuss this with your parents first, and there are no guarantees."

Scout turned to her mother. "Mom, we want to do this the right way. We don't want to sneak around or break any laws. Please, can you trust us on this?"

Naomi knuckled her chin. "It's not just a matter of trust. I remember what happened on Halloween night. You girls snuck out and put yourselves at risk."

"We've learned from our mistakes, and we're trying to do things differently. If we have your permission and support, we won't feel the need to take risks like that again."

The thick scent of bacon still lingered in the air, and the sun streamed through the kitchen window.

"Look," Thomas said, breaking the silence. "I understand that you both are passionate about this, and I admire that. But I also have a responsibility to ensure your safety. If something were to happen to either of you while you were investigating Radford Mansion, I'd never forgive myself."

Liz bit her lip. "What if we had someone with us? Someone who could look out for our safety and make sure we don't take any unnecessary risks?"

"Like a chaperone?" Mom asked skeptically.

"Exactly. Someone to ensure we're safe."

Thomas and Mom exchanged a look. It felt like an eternity before he spoke.

"If your parents agree, and you find a chaperone, I'll allow it. But you girls need to understand this is a privilege, not a right. If we agree to let you investigate Radford Mansion, you must follow our rules and guidelines to the letter."

Scout asked, "What if Chelsey and Raven came with us? They're experienced investigators, and they'll be able to keep us safe while we explore the mansion."

A knot of hope grew in Scout's stomach. Liz gave her an encouraging nod.

"They would definitely know how to handle any situations that might arise during the investigation."

"Then we can check out the mansion?" Liz exclaimed, unable to contain her excitement. She caught herself and lowered her voice. "I mean, if you agree, of course."

"Wait." He held up a hand. "I didn't say they could go with you. I said they would be helpful, but unfortunately they're both unavailable."

"Unavailable?" Scout asked. "Why?"

"Chelsey and Raven are working on a high-profile case with my department."

"Isn't there anyone else who can go with us? Someone who can make sure we stay safe and follow the rules?"

"LeVar could chaperone," Liz suggested, her eyes narrowing as a sly smile formed on her lips. "He's faced tougher enemies than ghosts."

Scout sensed the ulterior motive behind Liz's enthusiasm. "LeVar is a smart choice," she said, trying to focus on the task at hand rather than her friend's hidden intentions.

"He's responsible," Thomas admitted, his voice measured and thoughtful. "If we were to allow you two to investigate Radford Mansion, having him there would be the safest option."

"However," Mom interjected, "if we agree to this, there will be strict rules and guidelines. We're not giving you free rein to run around the mansion unsupervised."

"Of course, Mom," Scout said. "We promise to follow the rules and listen to LeVar."

"But LeVar has to agree to work with you. If you promise to be careful, and Liz's parents give their permission, we will allow you to investigate."

As the conversation shifted towards logistics and preparation, Scout experienced a mix of elation and anxiety. Investigating Radford Mansion was an exciting prospect, but it also meant potential danger.

And what had she gotten LeVar into?

"Can you believe this is actually happening?" Liz whispered as they cleaned up the basement after breakfast, waiting for LeVar to arrive.

Scout grinned. "Hardly. I never thought we'd get permission, let alone have LeVar helping us."

"Right? He's so perfect."

Scout couldn't help but chuckle at her friend's obvious infatuation. "Just remember, we're there to hunt ghosts, not to flirt with our chaperone."

"Of course," Liz said, suddenly serious. "But a girl can dream, right?"

23

One advantage to his throbbing agony: Parry Bonner sweated until his clothes clung to his body. And all that perspiration slicked his wrists and allowed him to move his hands. Just a little further, and he'd free them from the ropes.

He leaned over in the chair. Sweat dripped from his brow onto the wooden planks beneath him as he fought to remain conscious. The madman had just exited the room, leaving him with an unbearable pain where his leg had been. Why was this happening to him? He couldn't understand the reason behind his torment.

"Please," he whispered, hoping against hope that someone would hear. "Help me."

He listened for the killer's return, but the man was outside. The sound of a car door in front of the house distracted him from his agony. This was his chance. If he didn't make a move now, he would never get another opportunity. Now he had to free his damn wrists.

With a pull, he ripped his arms free of the ropes. One wrist dislocated, but that was the least of his problems. Only one leg stood under him, and it had fallen asleep, as useless as the missing limb. He toppled forward and caught himself before he smashed his face against the floor.

Gritting his teeth, he dragged himself through the room. There had to be another door nearby. The chill bleeding across the floor directed him to the rear exit.

Each movement sent searing pain shooting through his body as his stump scraped against the rough wood. Catching, tearing. Yet he refused to give in. He would survive.

The madman opened and closed the trunk to his car, but the noise seemed so far away. It wasn't. The killer would come for him at any second. And when he found no one in the chair, he'd know his victim hadn't gotten far.

Bonner's progress was slow, but he was getting somewhere. The back door came into view. Almost there.

As he continued his desperate crawl towards freedom, he could no longer hear the madman. The sound of his bloodied stump scratching against the floorboards echoed through the house, a constant reminder of the horror that had befallen him.

But he would not stop. He could not stop. Not when survival lay just beyond the reach of his outstretched fingers, and the possibility of revenge against his tormentor loomed in his future.

Gritting his teeth, he pushed through the narcotics-induced haze that clouded his vision. His fear of the killer's return was stronger than any pain or confusion.

Survival. That's all that mattered.

Dust assailed his eyes and nose. His trek left a bloody trail through the kitchen, like mucus from a dying snail. The killer would have no problem following him.

With every labored pull of his arms, he drew closer to the back door. Thoughts of revenge rushed through his mind, but it was a need for justice that burned in him—a desire to see the psycho pay for what he had done.

What would happen if he made it outside? Then what? He couldn't drag himself through the February morning and live to tell about it. A half foot of ice lay beyond the back door. Even if the snow didn't get him, the cold would.

He reached the exit, his fingers trembling with effort as he grasped the handle. Help would come. It had to.

The door creaked open. As he crawled across the threshold, he noticed the stump where his leg had been, its raw, jagged edges a gruesome reminder of his ordeal. How had he ended up in this hell? He thought about the people who had come and gone in his life, their faces blending together in his drug-addled mind. Some brought smiles; others carried the weight of regret. They all served as a reminder of the life he still had left to live. If he could escape this nightmare.

He dragged his battered body into the yard, his senses heightened by adrenaline and fear. Birds chirped in the nearby trees, their songs a stark contrast to the terror that lingered in front of the house. The madman wasn't aware he was escaping.

He gritted his teeth and, with great effort, pushed himself to a kneeling position. His eyes darted around the yard, searching for something, anything, that could help him escape. A crutch or a walking stick. His eyes settled on a spade lying against the back wall of the house. He stared at it for a moment. Perfect.

With a grunt, Bonner lunged for the spade, gripping it as he hoisted himself up. The pain was unbearable, but he had no choice; he needed to move if he wanted to escape.

He leaned on the makeshift crutch, his steps a symphony of agony, but he refused to let it slow him down. He limped away from the house, each uneven step further from the nightmare within.

Almost there. Once he reached the back of the yard, he could vanish into the forest. As long as he kept moving.

He had barely made it ten feet when the sound of footsteps reached his ears. Panic gripped him. The killer was returning to the house.

Urgency drove him forward while his body screamed in protest. A bellow came from inside the house. He didn't dare look back. If he did, he was as good as dead.

Limping faster, he hurried toward the trees. Snow fell, but not fast enough to cover the blood dripping from his cauterized wound. More angry shouts from the house. How soon before the psycho saw the trail of blood leading out the back door?

The spade sank into the snow. He toppled. Caught himself. Then continued.

Faster now. Sounding like a gunshot, the back door banged open.

A crazed laugh escaped Bonner's lips. He was free.

24

With his head lowered against the frigid breeze off the lake, Thomas walked towards the guesthouse, flurries biting at his cheeks. He could see LeVar's silhouette through the window. It felt ridiculous asking his junior deputy to babysit two teenagers on a paranormal investigation, especially with the department hunting a murderer, but he wanted to ensure the girls' safety. Who better than LeVar to watch their backs?

"Yo, LeVar." Thomas knocked on the door. "Is it okay if I come in?"

"Shep Dawg," LeVar said, opening the door. His dreadlocks were pulled back into a loose ponytail, and he looked as if he'd been up for a few hours working on his term paper.

Thomas stepped inside, rubbing his hands together for warmth. The cozy interior of the guesthouse provided some respite from winter.

"I have to say, you've really made this guesthouse feel like home," Thomas remarked as he ran his fingers along the spines of the books that lined the shelves. They were mostly books from LeVar's college courses, but he'd added a few classic literature pieces.

"Thanks, man," LeVar replied, a proud smile playing on his lips. "It's been a lot of work, but it's worth it. You know, once we replace these windows during the spring, this place will be perfect. They're still a bit drafty, but they held up during the December blizzard."

Thomas raised an eyebrow, recalling what the storm had done to the A-frame's roof. That the guesthouse had weathered the onslaught was impressive.

"I've been putting the window replacement off for too long," Thomas said, glancing at the large pane behind LeVar. It looked a little worse for wear, but it was still holding up. "I remember what the temperatures were like. I can only imagine how cold it must've gotten in here."

"Man, you have no idea." LeVar chuckled, rubbing his hands together as if to ward off the memory of the biting chill. "But hey, we made it through and learned a thing or two about insulating this place."

"Seems like it's quite resilient."

"Resilience is key, especially when dealing with a structure like this. And it's not just the guesthouse either. We've all had to adapt and grow stronger in our own ways."

Thomas knew LeVar was referring to more than just the building. Both of them had faced their share of challenges, but they had come out the other side better for it. It was a quiet reminder that resilience wasn't just an attribute of physical structures, but also of the human spirit.

"Well said, my friend," Thomas said, his thoughts briefly drifting to the girls and the dangers that might lie ahead in the abandoned mansion. "Let's hope that same resilience can keep us steady as we face whatever comes next. Have you heard about the girls' plan to explore that abandoned mansion?"

He couldn't help but think of all the dangers lurking within Radford Mansion—vermin, collapsing ceilings, and who knew what else. Without question, he would send a building inspector to the mansion before he allowed anyone inside.

"Yeah, I've heard," LeVar said, avoiding eye contact. "Scout just sent me a text. They're pretty excited about some investigation they're planning."

"A paranormal investigation."

"Ghost hunting?" LeVar raised an eyebrow, disbelief on his face. "You mean like with EMF detectors and all that weird stuff?"

"I know it sounds strange, but they're determined to go through with it. And as much as I don't believe in ghosts, I do believe in the potential dangers of that old mansion."

"Man, I don't know." LeVar scratched the back of his head, uncomfortable with the situation. "I've never been one for spooky stuff, and I've got enough demons of my own without looking for fake ones."

"I'm uncomfortable with the idea too, but I think we can both agree that it's better for someone to be there with them, just in case anything goes wrong. We can't always keep them away from danger, but we can at least try to minimize the risks. Just so you know, I'm having an expert look the building over. It's been abandoned for years, and no one knows what kind of structural damage it sustained. I don't want them getting hurt."

"I know it's risky, but Scout seems determined. Want me to talk them out of it?"

"No. I understand their curiosity," Thomas said, running a hand through his hair. "But I need to make sure they're safe. I want you to accompany them on this adventure."

"Me?" LeVar's eyes widened in disbelief. "I don't know, Thomas. I mean, I'm not exactly an expert on ghost hunting or abandoned houses."

"Neither are they. That's why I need you there, to keep an eye on them and make sure they don't get into trouble. I can't have another incident like Halloween night."

"When will you know if the mansion is safe?"

"The village inspector owes me a favor, so I'll have an answer within twenty-four hours. My guess is the place is fine. Otherwise, New York Ghost Patrol wouldn't bring their cameras inside."

"New York who?"

Thomas waved a hand through the air. "Apparently they're a big deal in paranormal research."

"They aren't those goofs on television, are they?"

"I'm afraid so. Scout and Liz want to beat them to the punch and be the first to investigate."

LeVar hesitated for a moment, his eyes drifting over the room as if searching for an escape from the situation. Finally, he sighed and nodded. "All right, Shep. I've got your back. I don't want to let Scout down."

"You're a good sport, LeVar," Thomas said.

"A good sport? That saying went out of style decades ago."

"At least I didn't say 23 Skidoo. Listen, I know it won't be your idea of a fun time, but it's better than letting them go unsupervised."

"I'll take care of them. I don't like the idea of those girls wandering around alone."

"You're helping me a great deal. I know this isn't easy for you, but I appreciate the sacrifice."

"What's life without a little adventure?"

"True. Just make sure it's an adventure with a happy ending, okay?"

"But what about your investigation at the department? Don't you want my help to catch whoever sent the carving?"

Thomas's face paled. "Aguilar and Lambert are working with me, and you're not scheduled for a shift until next weekend."

"Just say the word. I'll work OT or off the clock. Whatever you need."

"I can't ask you to do that." He placed a hand on LeVar's shoulder. "But I promise you'll be the first person I call if we need help."

25

The hum of the vacuum cleaner filled the guesthouse as LeVar pushed it back and forth across the carpet. Thomas was on his way to work, and LeVar wanted nothing more than to join the investigation and protect his friend. But he was a part-time junior employee, the dude they called when someone needed a cat rescued from a tree. And now Thomas wanted him to babysit Scout and a sixteen-year-old girl who had eyes for him.

It was impossible not to think of Liz standing in the winter wind in a miniskirt, pretending she needed driving lessons. Her crush was undeniable. She was just a teenager, and he was a young adult, a former gang member trying to walk the straight and narrow.

As if summoned by his musings, Scout and Liz arrived at the guesthouse. Scout clutched her laptop while Liz practically vibrated with excitement. LeVar switched off the vacuum and plastered what he hoped was a casual smile on his face.

"What's good, ladies?" LeVar asked, attempting to hide his discomfort. "If you're searching for ghosts, ain't none here."

Liz nearly toppled over in laughter. "Nobody makes a joke like you, LeVar."

"Uh, okay. But I assume you're here to discuss Radford Mansion."

"Like, for sure!" The girl fixated on him like a moth drawn to a flame.

To her side, Scout rolled her eyes at the exchange but grinned all the same. "You won't believe the info we've gathered about Radford Mansion. There's definitely something paranormal going on there."

"Sounds intriguing," he said, though he knew he should focus on the serial killer investigation instead. "So when do y'all wanna start this ghost hunt? This spring?"

Liz shook her head. "Sooner than that. We have to beat New York Ghost Patrol and get our findings online. I'm dying to get started."

"Said the ghost."

She nudged Scout with her elbow. "See? He's hilarious."

LeVar hesitated. There was a delicate balance he needed to maintain—taking care of these girls during their silly excursion, dealing with the serial killer case, and keeping Liz at arm's length.

"Slow down," he said. "We've got a lot of ground to cover, and I don't want to rush into anything." He lifted his chin at Liz, who carried a bag. "Whatcha got there, Santa?"

"Yo, check this out," Liz said, holding up a small device that resembled a walkie-talkie. "This is an EMF detector. It picks up on electromagnetic fields. Ghosts are supposed to give off these energy fluctuations when they're present."

"Word?" LeVar asked, raising an eyebrow as he examined the device. He couldn't deny that it was fascinating, even if he didn't believe in what the device was meant for.

"Definitely," Scout said, opening her laptop and pulling up a video feed. "We have night vision cameras too so we can see movement and temperature changes. You're gonna love this stuff."

"This is a spirit box," said Liz.

He crinkled his forehead. "What the heck is a spirit box?"

"It's how ghosts communicate with us."

"So it's a CB radio to the underworld?"

"Something like that."

LeVar watched as the girls demonstrated the gadgets, their excitement contagious. He found himself drawn into their enthusiasm despite his skepticism, and it wasn't long before he felt a sense of responsibility for the success of the ghost hunt.

"*Aight*," he said, taking charge of the situation. "If we're gonna do this, we gotta have a plan. Thomas's buddy needs to inspect the Radford Mansion. Make sure it's safe and all that. I don't want anyone getting hurt. You feel me?"

"I feel you," Liz said. He wanted to vomit. "So when do we go? Tomorrow night?"

"Whoa, hold up." He needed more time to prepare. "I'm thinking more like in a couple of weeks. We have some other stuff to take care of first, you know?"

"Like what?" Scout asked, her curiosity piqued.

"Um, you know, like making an inventory of our gear, mapping out the mansion, getting some research done." He tried to sound as authoritative as possible. In truth, he was stalling for time, hoping to juggle his responsibilities and put off this ghost hunt until they lost interest.

"But we'll lose the investigation to New York Ghost Patrol," Liz said. "By then, they'll prove the mansion is haunted."

"I wanna make sure we do this right, and rushing in ain't gonna help nobody. We'll get there, I promise. I know you're excited about this ghost hunt and all, but I got other things on my mind, you feel me?"

"Like what?" Scout asked, tilting her head.

"Like catching a real-life killer, for one. That's my priority right now, not chasing after some pretend ghosts."

"Hey, ghosts are real," Liz said. "You'll see when we go to Radford Mansion."

He sighed, wondering how he had gotten himself into this mess.

"Radford Mansion isn't exactly in tip-top shape," he explained, shifting uncomfortably. There was something unsettling about the way she looked at him, like he was a prime steak on display. "We need to make sure it's safe to be in there, especially at night. Don't want you getting hurt."

Scout said, "We've done our research, and we gathered a ton of information on the mansion and its history. You should take a look."

"Appreciate the effort, but there's no time for that. First things first. Let's wait until Thomas gets back to us with the inspection results. Then we'll talk about catching Casper."

"Of course," Liz said, though her eyes lingered on him a moment too long, making his skin prickle with unease. "Safety first, right?"

"Right." Between Liz's crush and the serial killer investigation, he had more than enough to worry about.

"Glad we have a strong man to keep us safe."

"LeVar," Scout said, interrupting Liz's flirting, "we really appreciate you accompanying us. Our parents won't allow us to investigate without you, and neither will Thomas."

That was when LeVar realized he had to give his full attention to the ghost hunt, regardless of his belief that it was all hocus pocus. This investigation meant everything to Scout, and he would do anything for her. And if she loved Liz, then he would call the flirty teen a friend as well.

They finished displaying their wares. He had to admit their

enthusiasm was infectious. Even the YouTube video of some creepy professor discussing the history of Radford Mansion held his attention. Then the girls packed their belongings and headed back to Scout's house.

He stood at the window and watched them leave. The wind whispered through the trees, carrying with it more flurries and a hint of something darker, more sinister.

This ghost hunt was only the beginning.

26

The snow clung to Parry Bonner's remaining foot. He knew he couldn't outrun the killer, not with one leg missing and the bitter cold nipping at his exposed skin. But he had to try. The sound of the killer's footsteps echoed through the otherwise silent forest, and Bonner felt the man's deranged grin.

He couldn't go on much longer. Already, he'd pushed his body to its limits. Where were the sheriff and his deputies? How could they allow a maniac to abduct people from parking lots and cut off their limbs?

At the edge of the forest, he stumbled upon a sight that sent shivers down his spine: an old cemetery, long forgotten by the living. Gravestones dotted the snowy landscape, their inscriptions worn away by time and weather. Beside the graveyard loomed an abandoned chapel, its once-stately structure crumbling and covered with dead vines.

Maybe he could barricade himself inside. As he limped toward the chapel, he heard the madman's shoes pounding through the snow. Closer now. A desolate country road stretched out beside him like a pathway to the unknown. He urged a vehicle to drive past, but none came.

The blood from his cauterized wound soaked through a hastily applied bandage. Dots of red covered the ice.

Almost to the chapel. The footsteps of his pursuer grew closer, the chilling sound a constant reminder that there was no escape from the relentless killer.

His agony intensified as he leaned on the spade, his makeshift crutch; it sank into the snow with each step, slowing his progress. His breaths came out in jagged puffs, the frigid air stinging his lungs. He winced at the trail he was leaving behind. It was too easy for the killer to follow. He needed to reach the old chapel.

A branch snapped a hundred yards behind him. He turned, but it was just a deer pawing through the brush. A gravestone almost tripped him up, but he caught himself. His skin prickled. He wasn't alone.

Then a figure emerged from behind a decaying headstone. The madman. His eyes were wild, and his smile seemed impossibly wide, revealing a row of yellowed teeth.

"Thought you could get away?" the killer taunted, his voice holding an unnerving singsong quality.

"Stay back." Bonner brandished the spade. He couldn't outrun the maniac, but he could fight him off, give himself just enough time to escape into the chapel.

"Nice try."

The killer sneered and lunged, wrenching the spade from his grip. Now defenseless, he hobbled toward the chapel, desperation fueling his movements.

The cold truth settled in: He was alone. The killer's laughter echoed in the silent winter air.

Fight or flee? Given his state, he knew he couldn't win on

one leg. He was tired, injured, and with no means of defending himself.

The forest fell silent around them, as if even nature held its breath, anticipating the brutality about to unfold.

"Please," Bonner muttered, his voice barely audible through gritted teeth. "Don't do this."

The maniac's fingers curled around the handle. He stepped closer, and Bonner could see the veins bulging in his arms, the muscles straining beneath his skin.

"I don't even know you, man. Think . . . think about what you're doing."

The killer swung the spade down with a sickening crunch, striking Bonner across the chest. The force of the blow knocked him to the ground, and he writhed in pain, gasping for air.

"Stop. Please," he choked out, struggling to breathe as he twitched on the icy snow. The killer ignored his pleas, landing another brutal hit to his skull.

"Never should have run," the killer growled, his face a mask of rage. With each swing, he grunted.

Blood spattered across the pristine snow, painting it a grotesque crimson as the madman continued his relentless assault. Bonner's screams became gurgles, his body convulsing with each hit. The sound of metal meeting flesh echoed through the clearing, punctuating the chill of the winter air.

But as the darkness closed in around him, Bonner knew there was nothing more he could have done. He had fought as hard as he could, and now it was over.

∽

THE KILLER HOISTED Bonner's lifeless body over his shoulder, the icy air biting at his face. Too heavy. He let the corpse fall to the ground and grabbed it by the ankle. With a chuckle, he dragged the corpse through the forest.

Too bad. He'd wanted to play with his victim a little longer. The thought of sending another bone carving to Sheriff Shepherd sent a shiver of excitement down his spine. The game they played had been exhilarating so far, and the stakes were only getting higher.

But would another gift be enough to break Shepherd? He pondered this question as he trudged through the woods toward his house.

No. If he wanted to destroy Shepherd, to gain true revenge, he needed to strike the man where it hurt. He envisioned the look of anguish on Shepherd's face when he realized someone he cared for was in the hands of a madman. That a loved one's bone lay on his desk in a beautiful form. He reveled in the thought of Thomas suffering. Every nerve in his body sang with anticipation.

As he approached his house, dragging Bonner, the thrill of the hunt coursed through his veins. It was time to take things to the next level, to make Sheriff Shepherd truly understand what it meant to play with fire.

He crossed the threshold of his isolated home, with Bonner's body leaving a bloody trail. The house was quiet, save for the television droning in the background. He grunted as he lowered the corpse onto the floor, careful not to disturb the myriad of trophies that lined the walls. Each told a story; each was evidence of his power over life and death.

The madman strode to his workbench, where an array of tools chosen for their ability to inflict pain lay organized. His eyes scanned the assortment before settling on the saw Bonner had sold him.

"Time to make amends," he whispered, gripping the saw tightly with a sense of grim satisfaction. In his mind, he could already hear the teeth chewing through bone, the sound of Bonner's remains being shaped into a symbol of artistry.

It was time to begin anew, to set the stage for his final act of torment against Sheriff Shepherd.

"Let the games begin," he said, lowering the saw onto Bonner's flesh.

And with that, he began to carve.

27

LeVar's phone buzzed on the card table, its vibrations almost imperceptible over the hum of his computer. He read the message from Thomas. The inspection was over; Radford Mansion had been deemed safe to explore.

"Just my luck."

The ghost hunt was becoming more real by the second, and there was no backing out now. The fear of the unknown lurked at the edges of his mind, and it wasn't because he believed some angry poltergeist would attack him. No, he worried about escorting a sixteen-year-old girl who was in love with him, and he fretted over keeping Scout and Liz safe. Let them charge up their paranormal gadgets and have their fun. As long as they came out of the mansion in one piece. He drummed his fingers against the table, lost in thought about what lay ahead.

A knock on the door jolted him back to reality. He got up and opened it, finding the girls on the doorstep, their faces flushed with excitement.

"Hey, LeVar." Scout beamed. "We just heard from Thomas. The inspection's done and we can go in."

He shifted his jaw. They must have received the same news and couldn't wait to rush over. "Yeah, I got the text too."

"Isn't it exciting?" Liz asked, eyes sparkling with anticipation. "I can't believe we're actually doing this. We'll all be internet legends."

"Exciting isn't the word I'd use." He tried to keep the tremor out of his voice. Stepping aside, he allowed them to enter.

The three of them settled into the living room. The teens chattered away, discussing plans for the ghost hunt while he lounged in a chair, listening but not replying.

"LeVar, you all right?" Scout asked, noticing his silence. "You're not very chatty today."

"Yeah, I'm fine," he lied, forcing a smile onto his face.

Liz turned to him. "Are you worried about the investigation?"

"Maybe," he said, rubbing the back of his neck. "I mean, I'm not afraid of ghosts. Heck, no. But just because the inspector gave us the thumbs up doesn't mean it's safe inside."

"Hey, nobody will get hurt," Scout said, placing a hand on his shoulder. "We'll stick together and be careful."

"Let's see what we're up against." His fingers danced over the keyboard as he typed "Radford Mansion" into the search bar. Scout and Liz leaned in close, their eyes glued to the screen as he scrolled through the results.

"Look at this one," Liz said, pointing to a link. "It says there have been multiple sightings of ghostly figures in the mansion."

"Here's another," said Scout, tapping the screen. "A family went inside for a dare, and they claim they heard whispers and footsteps when no one else was around."

He threw up his hands. "Wait a minute. How do we know these stories are true? You can post anything on the internet."

"True, but some of these accounts are corroborated by multiple people. Besides, wouldn't it be more fun if there was something to find?"

LeVar hesitated before typing again. He wasn't sure why, but he wanted to uncover more about the mysterious Radford Mansion. His curiosity overrode his initial worries, propelling him to dig deeper.

"*Aight*, let's see what else is out there."

He clicked another link. As they delved into the stories, they grew darker and more disturbing: tales of shadowy figures lurking in the corners, cold spots that made the hair on the back of your neck stand, and disembodied voices echoing through the halls filled the screen.

"Guys, I don't know about this," he said. "The more I read, the more freaked out I'm getting. Not that I believe in ghosts."

"Yeah, right," the girls said in unison.

"But this place is obviously dangerous. Why don't you leave the investigation to the pros?"

Scout widened her eyes. "What, and let those New York Ghost Patrol prima donnas steal our thunder? Not a chance."

"Besides, we'll be well prepared when we go in," Liz said. "We'll have all the latest ghost-hunting equipment, and we'll be sticking together. And we'll have you to keep us safe."

He ignored that comment. From the corner of his eye, he caught the girl batting her lashes.

"Look at this one," he said, pointing to an article on the screen. "It says here that a farmer disappeared after visiting Radford Mansion just after midnight on a Saturday night in 1855. And this other story talks about strange lights flickering in the windows late at night, accompanied by moaning sounds coming from inside. An off-duty police officer told that one."

Liz flicked the hair off her shoulder. "Well, if a police officer told the story, it must hold some weight, right?"

The words on the screen seemed to take on a life of their own, and each new tale was more chilling than the last.

"Maybe we should call it a day. I don't know about you guys, but I'm getting hungry. Time to cook dinner."

Scout laughed. "You're always hungry."

His thoughts turned darker every time he pictured the mansion. He wondered if this was a case of his imagination running wild, or if there was some truth behind the tales they'd uncovered. What if they came face-to-face with the unexplained during their investigation? Well, that was impossible. And yet . . .

"One more story and then we're done for the night," Liz said, clicking on a link that caught her eye. As she read the first few lines, her eyebrows rose in surprise. "Okay, guys, you have to hear this one."

"Go ahead," Scout said.

"According to this account," Liz began, her voice taking on a dramatic tone, "a group of tourists had a close encounter with an old woman who appeared out of nowhere during their visit to Radford Mansion."

"Out of nowhere? Please," he said, maintaining a brave facade despite his inner turmoil.

"The woman materialized out of thin air, right in front of them. She warned them to leave 'or else,' and then vanished as suddenly as she'd come."

"Creepy," Scout said.

"Or else what?" He imagined the scene unfolding before him—a darkened room, the sudden appearance of a ghostly figure. How would he react? He attempted to inject some levity into the conversation. "Sounds like a classic haunted house tale."

Liz leaned back in her chair, a mischievous gleam in her eye. "That's exactly what makes this whole thing so thrilling. Think about it. If we uncover information that even New York Ghost Patrol hasn't found yet, we'll be stars."

LeVar sensed the cold fingers of fear reaching out for him, and he knew that their research was only adding fuel to the fire.

"Okay, I think we've found enough stories. Let's call it a day and get some rest. We'll need our energy for the hunt next week."

Liz's mouth fell open. "Next week? No way. We're doing this tomorrow night."

He lost the ability to speak. Tomorrow night? That was too soon. He needed more time to . . .

To what? Chicken out?

Scout gave her friend a high five. "Before the investigation, we'll dig even deeper and find a story that'll blow away anything those New York guys could ever hope to come up with."

As they said their goodbyes and headed back to Scout's house for another sleepover, he stared at the empty computer screen, its glow now extinguished. The room fell silent, and the only sound was the faint hum of the space heater.

The stories they'd discovered painted a chilling picture of what might lie ahead for them at Radford Mansion. As the sun dipped below the horizon, elongating the shadows across the frozen lake, he didn't expect he would sleep much tonight.

And, for once, he'd lost his appetite.

28

Pale morning light, interrupted by snow squalls, filtered through the windows of the Nightshade County Sheriff's Department. It was early—just past seven—and the air outside held the chill of a February dawn. The rattling of the office heater provided little comfort as it fought against the lingering frost.

But as Thomas entered the office, the first thing that struck him was the funereal silence. No one spoke. Not Maggie or Aguilar. Not even Lambert. They were all staring at him.

And on Maggie's desk sat another package addressed to Sheriff Thomas Shepherd.

"When did it arrive?"

"First thing this morning," Maggie said, wringing her hands.

Thomas approached and scrutinized the mysterious package that held no labels or sender identification. The serial killer case had everyone on edge, and this unmarked delivery did nothing to alleviate the anxiety.

"Any ideas?" Thomas asked, looking up at Lambert. The tall ex-army man stood nearby, arms crossed and eyes fixed on the package.

"It's feather light. I think I can guess what's inside."

"Great," Thomas muttered, rubbing the back of his neck. He often found it difficult to read people, but the tension in the room was palpable. He looked around the office, spying the worried faces of his colleagues, before turning his attention back to the package.

"Here we go," he said, taking a deep breath. "Let's see what we're dealing with."

Carefully, Thomas reached for the package, his hands steady despite the anxiousness thrumming through his veins. He couldn't afford to make any mistakes, especially after he'd tossed away the first delivery. Was this another gift from his deranged foe?

"Keep everyone back," Thomas instructed, his eyes never leaving the package. "I don't want anyone touching this until I know what we're dealing with." All around the office, deputies and staff members exchanged nervous looks, but they complied with the orders. "I'll dust for prints first. Everyone, back off and give me space."

Deputy Aguilar pulled out her phone. "I'll call the county forensic team."

"Thanks, Aguilar."

He reached into a nearby drawer and pulled out a pair of latex gloves, snapping them on with practiced precision. His mind raced with thoughts of the serial killer, wondering who would be brazen enough to send evidence to the sheriff's department.

"Thomas, if you're looking for prints, what about the delivery guy?" Lambert asked, concern etched on his face.

"Good point. Send a junior deputy to interview him and get his prints, just in case."

As he worked, the office seemed to hold its breath. With one gloved hand, he applied fingerprint powder to the surface of the package, revealing the faint outline of a single print. Using a piece of adhesive tape, he lifted the print and placed it on a small evidence card.

"I'll be damned," he said, holding up the card for the others to see. He allowed himself a moment before returning his attention to the task at hand. "Aguilar, run this through the database while we wait for forensics."

"Will do," she replied, taking the evidence card and heading toward the computer terminal. The other deputies and staff members watched in tense silence, each hoping the print would provide a lead in the investigation.

"Wait, Thomas." Lambert cut through the silence, his eyes intense. "Shouldn't we call the bomb unit first? Just to be sure?"

Thomas hesitated, considering Lambert's suggestion. Something horrific lay inside, but it wasn't a bomb. The killer wanted to toy with them, not blow them up.

"No. The killer wants us to see what's inside."

He ran a box cutter along the edges of the package, making sure not to damage the contents. As he peeled back the layers of cardboard, anxiety and anticipation warred inside him.

The contents of the package came into view: another bone carving, this time in the shape of a fox. His breath hitched as he took in the intricate details of the sculpture.

"Another carving?" Lambert asked.

"Seems that way."

Was the fox some kind of message? A clue to the killer's identity, perhaps?

As he continued to examine the sculpture, his eyes darted to the window. Someone was watching him.

"Lambert, I have a task for you."

"Anything you need."

"Take a casual stroll outside. Make it look like you're heading to the coffee shop. If you see anyone watching the sheriff's department—"

"Say no more, Thomas."

The lanky deputy set his hat on his head, bundled into his coat, and headed out the door.

"Stay sharp, everyone. We need to be ready for anything."

He set the macabre gift on a layer of tissue paper and warned everyone not to touch it. Without another word, he hurried to Aguilar, who sat at the computer terminal, her fingers hovering over the keyboard as she prepared to enter the print data into AFIS. She looked at Thomas before returning to the task at hand. This could be their first break in the case.

"Okay, let's see what we've got," Aguilar said, typing in the information and initiating the automated search process.

He held his breath.

"Nothing," she finally said, her voice laced with disappointment. "No match in the database."

Thomas wasn't surprised. They were dealing with a cunning and elusive killer. He lifted the fox carving with his gloved hand, careful not to smudge any remaining evidence. He walked to a nearby table with an LED panel. Holding the carving by its base, he examined it under the bright, unwavering light, scrutinizing every minute detail.

"Look at this thing," he muttered, his voice low and filled with a mixture of awe and revulsion. "Who would make such a thing?"

As he studied the object, his coworkers gathered around, taking in the carving's craftsmanship. The fox appeared almost alive, its tiny, vivid eyes seeming to hold keen intelligence. The artist had captured the animal's lithe form in mid-leap, its tail extended as if caught in a breeze. It appeared that with just a little more pressure on its haunches the fox might leap from

Thomas's palm and scamper into the shadows of some distant forest.

A whoosh of winter air announced Lambert had returned. Thomas looked up, but the deputy only shook his head.

"Did that . . . thing come from some poor soul's body?" Maggie asked, holding a hand over her mouth.

He couldn't give her a comforting answer. The individual hairs of the fox's fur were painstakingly rendered, each one distinct and lifelike. Even the pads on the underside of its paws bore delicate whorls and ridges, mimicking the unique patterns found on real foxes.

"So much effort just to send a message."

Was this relic from the same victim as before, or had the killer claimed another life? Aguilar and Lambert came over to stand by his side.

"Maybe it's time to let you two take over," he said, his voice strained. "I don't want my mental condition to hinder the investigation."

"Thomas, we've been through this before," she said. "You're more than capable of leading this case. You've never shied away from a challenge."

"Besides," Lambert chimed in, a touch of humor in his voice, "you've got us to back you up. We'll catch this psycho together."

Thomas looked from one deputy to the other, feeling a rush of gratitude for their unwavering support. "Thanks for having my back. I promise not to let you down."

"What's our next move?" she asked, her eyes fixed on the fox carving.

"Lambert, give Wolf Lake Consulting a heads up about this new gift. They need to know what we're dealing with. If there's another victim, I want to know who it is."

"Will do, boss man," Lambert said, grabbing his phone.

"Let's hope Chelsey's team can shed some light on this," he

murmured, more to himself than to his colleagues. Deep inside, he knew that the weight of solving this mystery rested on his shoulders.

"I'll assist the forensic team," she said. "They should arrive soon."

"Good, and I'll contact Claire."

He removed his phone and dialed her number. The phone rang twice before she picked up.

"Brookins here."

"Claire, it's Thomas. We've got another bone carving. Can you swing past the department?"

"Give me twenty minutes."

"Thanks, Claire."

As Aguilar had predicted, the Nightshade County forensic team entered the building as he ended the call. Their leader, a baldheaded man with an eagle tattoo on his arm, approached Thomas for instructions.

"Analyze the packaging for any trace evidence that could lead us to the sender."

"Understood," the leader said.

As he waited for Claire to arrive and work alongside the forensic unit, he returned to the window. He swore someone had been watching him, but the street lay empty.

"I'll find you, you son of a bitch."

29

The heavy wooden door of the village library creaked open. A musty scent hung in the air, mixing with the aroma of old leather and decaying paper. Rows of light shone above, drawing out the books that seemed to stretch on forever.

"Excuse me," Scout said, approaching the librarian seated behind a worn oak desk. The woman's silver hair was pulled back into a tight bun, and her round glasses magnified her pale blue eyes.

"Can I help you?"

"We're looking for information on Radford Mansion," Liz said.

"You mean you're looking for details about the hauntings?"

"Yes," the girls said in unison.

"Especially a legend people don't talk about these days," said Scout.

The librarian tapped a bony finger against her lips. "Then you'll want to read about Virginia Radford and the tragic tale of a future heiress. I've heard quite a few legends about the mansion over the years, but this is the most strange."

"Where can we learn more about Virginia Radford?"

"Head toward the back of the library," the woman instructed, pointing down a narrow aisle lined with towering bookshelves. "You'll find a section dedicated to our town's history, including digitized newspaper articles about supposed hauntings. That should keep your research focused."

"Thank you."

Scout led Liz deeper into the library. As they navigated the maze of shelves, she sensed eyes on her. All she saw were the disorganized stacks of books and the occasional cobweb clinging to a forgotten corner. It was as if the very air within the library held secrets.

"Can you believe this place?" Liz whispered, her eyes wide with fascination. "It's like stepping back in time."

"There's so much history here, just waiting to be discovered. And if we can find something that will help us understand what caused the hauntings at Radford Mansion, we'll be way ahead of those New York goofs."

They stood side by side, their fingers tracing the yellowed pages of old newspaper articles. The printed versions only encompassed the last ten years, so they shifted their attention to the computers in the corner. The digital versions they held went back to the turn of the twentieth century.

"Check this out," Liz muttered, pulling up an article from 1915.

Scout squinted at the words. The headline read: "Mysterious Death at Radford Mansion—Daughter of Wealthy Family Found Dead."

"Virginia Radford. This must be it."

Scout and Liz huddled around the article. The story told of the gruesome discovery of Virginia Radford's body, shattered after falling from the upper floor and striking the ground. The circumstances surrounding her death were shrouded in mystery, with some people believing it was a suicide or an accident, while others whispered of murder.

"Look at this." Liz pointed to a passage that described the state of Virginia's room. "It says her belongings were scattered all over the floor, as if there had been a struggle."

"Maybe she was trying to fend off an attacker?"

"Or maybe"—Liz paused for dramatic effect—"she discovered something she wasn't supposed to, and someone wanted to silence her."

"Either way, it's clear that there's more to this story than meets the eye. We need to find out what really happened to this girl."

"Definitely."

"Let's go through these other articles. There might be more information about the mansion or the Radford family that could give us some clues."

"Good plan," Liz said, pulling out her notebook and pen.

As they continued their search, the shadows in the library seemed to grow darker. The chilling tale of Virginia Radford's death had taken hold of their imaginations.

"Scout, what if we try to contact Virginia Radford during our ghost hunt?"

"Interesting idea. It's worth a shot."

"Right. I say we use the EMF detector to locate phantoms, then switch to the spirit box and hope they communicate with us. We'll ask to speak to Virginia."

"Especially near the window she fell out of. We should also bring candles and salt for protection, just in case."

"This is going to be amazing."

Their research left more questions than answers. The police had ruled the death as accidental, but Scout wasn't so sure.

They left the library as the sun was beginning its descent. Spring was only a month away, but it felt like years.

"I'm so relieved LeVar will be our chaperone," Liz said, a dreamy expression on her face. "We won't have anything to fear with him there."

"Uh-huh." Scout rolled her eyes behind her glasses.

"And he's really intelligent too. He always knows exactly what to do in difficult situations."

"Okay, Liz. Enough," Scout finally snapped, unable to hold back. "He's four years older than us. You need to stop pursuing him. It's not a good look."

"I don't see what the big deal is. When he's thirty, I'll be twenty-six. He's perfect and exactly what I'm looking for in a boyfriend."

"He's a great guy, but that doesn't mean you should chase after someone so much older than you."

"Age is just a number. Besides, we connect on so many levels."

As far as Scout could tell, LeVar tried to avoid Liz. If there was a connection, it went one way.

"Fine." Scout realized she wouldn't be able to change Liz's mind.

Her worries about her friend lingered. What was causing this sudden pursuit? They continued their walk back to Scout's house in tense silence, each lost in thought as the sun dipped below the lake.

"Look, I don't want to pry, but what's going on with you lately?" Scout asked with caution. "I mean, you've been talking about LeVar night and day. It's not like you to fixate on someone."

Liz hesitated, biting her lip. Something weighed on her mind.

"Okay, fine," Liz said, her words coming out in a rush. "I

guess there's just something about him that makes me feel . . . I don't know . . . safe. He's different from all the other guys. And he's dependable."

"But you hardly know him."

"I know him better today than I did yesterday. Seems our relationship is progressing."

Their relationship? It was obvious Scout wasn't getting through to her friend. Maybe this ghost hunt with LeVar was a mistake.

"Scout," Liz said, breaking the silence, "I promise I'll keep my focus on the investigations tomorrow. I won't let my feelings for LeVar distract me."

Scout knew her friend meant well, but she suspected something would go wrong. She'd never seen Liz act this way before. As they rounded the corner, the wind picked up, sweeping snow across their path. The sight of her house in the distance brought with it a small sense of relief. Tonight they would engage in another ghost show marathon. The action might distract Liz from talking about her crush.

Not that Scout was jealous. LeVar wasn't interested in Liz.

A black-winged bird landed on a fence post and squawked at them.

"Hey, look at that," Liz said, pointing at the crow. Its beady eyes seemed to follow their every move.

"Creepy."

Scout tried not to let the bird get to her.

"Scram, bird. Go back to Radford Mansion."

As they reached the front door of Scout's house, the last of the light disappeared behind the distant hills, plunging the village into twilight.

"I don't know about you, but I'm ready for popcorn," Scout suggested, her hand on the doorknob.

"With extra butter."

Liz took one last look at the crow before stepping inside with Scout.

As the door closed behind them, the bird took flight, its dark silhouette disappearing into the gathering night.

30

Evening shadows crept across the office space in Wolf Lake Consulting's converted house. The bustling room, filled with four desks and matching chairs, was where Thomas, Chelsey, and Raven met to collaborate. They bent over the photographs before them.

"Can you believe someone would actually do this?" Chelsey shuddered, her dark waves of hair brushing against her shoulders as she examined the intricate designs etched into the bones.

"Definitely the work of a demented mind," Raven said.

"The package containing the new carving arrived at the office this morning," Thomas said. "Like the last one, it came wrapped in plain brown paper and tied with a string."

Claire and the forensic team were currently poring over the package and carvings, trying to decipher any clues that might lead them to the person responsible. He shifted from one picture to the next.

"Have you heard anything from Claire about the origin of these bones?" asked Chelsey.

"Nothing yet. She's still examining them with her team. I can't help but feel like we're dealing with a serial killer here."

"Perhaps, but we can't jump to conclusions. We need to gather more information."

The bone carvings were a dark enigma, and as the evening wore on, it became clear that solving this case would push them to their limits. Chelsey picked up the latest edition of *The Bluewater Tribune*, which had arrived at Wolf Lake Consulting earlier that day. She unfolded the newspaper and showed it to Thomas.

"Look at this," she said.

The headline screamed in bold, black font: "The Carver Strikes Again. Serial Killer on the Loose in Nightshade County?" The words were plastered across the top of the front page, dominating the layout.

Thomas stared at the headline, his eyes narrowing in disapproval. "The Carver?" He shook his head. "That's what they're calling him? Sounds like something out of a bad horror movie."

"Regardless of the name, the media is all over this. They're speculating that we have a serial killer on our hands."

Raven scratched her arm. "I don't understand why there has been no communication from this . . . carver person. No letters, no phone calls, just the figurines. What is he after?"

"Perhaps he gets a thrill from watching us scramble to figure things out."

"Whatever his motives are, we need to get ahead of this," he said, his jaw tightening as he read the ominous headline. He felt a deep sense of responsibility for the safety of Nightshade County and its residents. These bone carvings were more than just a sick game. They were a threat to the community he had sworn to protect.

Raven nodded. "We can't afford to let this escalate any further. If we want to understand this killer's motive and behavior, we need to dig into his psychology. Maybe he came from a history of violence or has a personal connection to the victims."

"Good point," Chelsey chimed in. "We should go through more recent missing persons reports and see if there's a pattern. Perhaps the Carver has a type. Thomas, have you called the Behavioral Analysis Unit?"

"I did. Agents Bell and Gardy are out on assignments. The receptionist took down my information, promising a callback, but no one got back to me. I suggest we divide the work. Chelsey, you look into the missing persons reports. Raven, cross-reference criminal records with grave robberies. I want to believe this guy isn't taking live victims."

As the team members scrambled for information, Thomas felt a twinge of doubt. They were grasping at straws, hoping to find some tangible connection that would lead them to a killer. Time was running out, and the pressure to solve the case mounted every day.

Chelsey sifted through her database, Raven typed away on her laptop, and Thomas paced the room with the phone pressed to his ear. He fell into a messaging system at the BAU and hung up. How could he make sense of the killer's actions—the intricate bone carvings, the lack of communication?

"Anything useful?" he asked after a while, stopping by Raven's side to peer at her screen.

"Still checking," she said, frustration evident in her voice. "I'm not finding anything I can link to our killer."

"Same here," Chelsey chimed in, looking up from the missing persons reports. "I've gone through everything from the past month, and nothing stands out. These people come from different backgrounds, ages, and genders."

Thomas sighed. The room felt darker, the shadows creeping in as stars sparkled outside the window. They were no closer to catching the Carver than when they had started.

He fell into a chair across from them. "First of all, we have no evidence that a murder occurred. All we have are these carved bones, a crow, and a taunting fox left on my doorstep. I'm considering calling in the FBI, but without solid proof, I worry they'll refuse to take the case seriously."

"They might think we're overreacting and question our competence."

"Exactly." He rubbed his temples. "For all we know, this could be an elaborate prank using legally purchased bones. But we can't ignore the possibility that there's a serial killer out there, and we need all the help we can get."

The three of them mulled over their options, and Thomas remembered something Claire had mentioned to him the day before. "Claire told me people can actually order human bones off the internet," he said, a hint of disgust in his voice. "Can you believe that?"

"For science, I suppose."

"Yes. There are websites where you can buy human bones for research or educational purposes."

"Does that mean the Carver could have purchased the bones online instead of taking them from actual victims?" Raven asked.

"Potentially. But there's a message behind all of this, and we need to figure out what it is."

"What do you think the message is?"

"I don't know, but it's personal. He hasn't sent gifts to anyone but me."

"Hey, Thomas," Chelsey said, her attention fixed on the screen. "I found something. A man named Peter Morgan was reported missing six days ago. Not much info on him, but it says he was last seen at a bar in the northern part of the county."

"Good find. Any others?"

"The other disappearance are from a few weeks ago. I'll keep digging."

Raven printed Chelsey's results and stuck pins into a map, marking the missing people. "Maybe there's a pattern or message we're missing."

If a pattern existed, Thomas didn't see one. And it drove him mad.

31

LeVar sat on the couch, tapping his foot against the floor. He read the clock hanging above the sink, the hands ticking away like a metronome, each second fueling his anxiety. The ghost hunt loomed, and he worried about what Liz would do once they were alone in the dark.

What had he gotten himself into? He checked his phone, hoping to see a message from Scout or Liz canceling the whole thing. His dreadlocks swayed as he shook his head, trying to shake off the growing sense of unease.

His thoughts wandered back to his previous life with the Harmon Kings, when fear was a driving force. This time, it wasn't the threat of violence bothered him; he dreaded the responsibility he took upon himself for the girls' safety.

Someone pounded on the door. The girls couldn't have arrived already. Through the curtains, he saw Deputy Lambert blowing on his hands to stay warm.

"What are you doing here, dawg?"

"LeVar, you look like you've seen a ghost already."

"Ha, hilarious. I don't know, man. I got this bad feeling about tonight."

"Look, if those girls want to scare themselves silly, let them," Lambert said with a shrug. "Just make sure no one gets hurt, and you'll be fine."

LeVar nodded, taking in Lambert's words. In the back of his mind, he knew the senior deputy was right. He couldn't control everything, but he had to try.

"You just here to razz me?"

"And to tell you that Claire is working on the latest carving."

"I wish I was part of that investigation and not running after phantoms."

Lambert slapped him on the back. "You're back on shift soon. I'll be happy to have your help. Talk to you later."

The afternoon wore on, and LeVar's nervousness escalated. Each passing hour brought him closer to the hunt, and his hope for a last-minute cancellation grew more desperate. He paced around the guesthouse, glancing out the window every few minutes, as if expecting the girls to show up waving white flags, admitting defeat.

"Come on, just cancel already," he said, staring toward the Mournings' house. If something happened to Scout or Liz under his watch, he'd never forgive himself. The weight of responsibility bore down on him. The thought of canceling the hunt crossed his mind again, but he knew it wouldn't be easy with the girls so invested in the idea.

As if on cue, there was a knock at the door, followed by the excited voices of Scout and Liz. He steeled himself, putting on a confident smile as he swung the door open.

"Hey, ladies. Y'all ready for this?"

"Absolutely," Scout said.

"Listen, I've been thinkin'. Maybe we should reconsider this whole ghost-hunt thing. I ain't really, you know, into all that paranormal stuff."

"Come on, LeVar, don't chicken out now," Liz teased, nudging him. "We'll just explore the mansion and see if anything strange happens. It'll be fun."

Scout agreed. "Besides, we've done our research. We know what we're getting into. If anything, you'll be there to protect us, right?"

Their eagerness to begin the investigation was evident on their faces. With a resigned sigh, he threw up his hands, knowing he couldn't let them down.

"All right, fine. Let's do this."

"Great. We have all our equipment ready, so let's head out."

As they walked toward LeVar's car, he felt a mix of fear and determination swirling inside. While he hoped the investigation would prove uneventful, he worried about traipsing around in the dark. Despite the inspector giving Radford Mansion a thumbs up, the man hadn't walked through its corridors with two teenagers and the lights off.

"We'll follow the plan we discussed earlier. Head to the mansion, set up your equipment, and see if we catch any paranormal activity. Then we're outta there."

"And if we capture something really cool, maybe it'll be enough to trump the New York Ghost Patrol."

Liz laughed, a mischievous glint in her eye. "That would be amazing. We'll show them who the experts are."

The girls climbed into the backseat of LeVar's black Chrysler Limited. The sound of the car door slamming echoed in the quiet evening air, and as they buckled their seatbelts, he remained determined not to let his own apprehension dampen their spirits. With a turn of the key, he started the engine and pulled onto the road.

The first stars shone while they drove toward Radford Mansion. The darkening sky seemed to mirror his growing unease, and he gripped the steering wheel tighter the closer they came.

"Did you see that video from New York Ghost Patrol last week?" Liz asked. "They caught this creepy mist moving through a cemetery. It was scary but awesome."

Scout checked her phone. "Yeah, I saw that one. Imagine if we find something even better. This mansion has such a rich history; there is bound to be activity there."

LeVar scratched behind his neck, focusing on the road rather than the butterflies in his chest. He forced himself to think of his mother and sister, with whom he was scheduled to eat dinner next weekend. He had come so far since leaving the Harmon Kings and becoming a deputy, and he wouldn't let fear hold him back now.

Liz patted his shoulder from behind, her hand lingering a little too long. "We're almost there. I can feel it; we'll find something amazing tonight."

The imposing silhouette of Radford Mansion stood stark against a backdrop of night.

"Look, there it is," Scout said, her face pressed against the car window as she pointed.

"Wow. It's even more impressive up close."

Impressive was one word. Chilling was another.

He pulled the car up to the entrance and parked under a canopy of tangled branches. The sky was now a deep purple that reflected in the building's windows.

"Okay, let's do this," Liz said, rubbing her hands together in anticipation. She rummaged through their bags, pulling out a variety of ghost-hunting equipment.

"Here, LeVar." Scout handed him a flashlight. "You might need this."

"Thanks, but I got one. A deputy always comes prepared."

He watched as the girls fastened their gear belts, the zippers and metallic clasps providing a soundtrack to their eager preparations. They each donned a pair of headphones connected to their EVP recorders.

"Remember," Liz said, "we're here to document everything we can. The New York Goof Patrol won't know what hit them when we're done."

With the gear secured, the trio made their way toward the massive wooden doors that served as the entrance. The mansion's history pressed down on him like an icy wave, and he wondered if the girls felt it too. But their eagerness seemed undiminished as they approached the doors.

He led them into the dark, dusty halls of Radford Mansion. The sound of his footsteps echoed in the empty space, a constant reminder of the distance between them and the outside world.

"Did you hear that?" Scout whispered, pausing to listen.

He hadn't heard a thing.

"Probably just the old house settling," he said.

"Or it's our first encounter. Either way, we should keep going."

He stayed close to the girls as they explored.

"Listen," Liz said, holding up a hand for silence. They all stopped, straining to catch a faint moaning sound.

Scout leaned close to Liz. "Where's it coming from?"

"Sounds like it's coming from down there." Liz pointed to a room with the door ajar at the end of the hall. "Shouldn't we be recording this?"

Liz fumbled with her EVP recorder.

"Already on it." Scout pressed her record button as they neared the room.

The moaning sound beckoned them, urging them to uncover whatever lay hidden within the mansion. LeVar's pulse quickened as they reached the door. He tried to ignore the unsettling feeling that they were being watched. So what made that noise?

It was wind curling around the eaves. That had to be the answer.

Scout reached for the doorknob. "Ready?"

The moment the door creaked open, a frozen pocket of air struck them, as if the coldest January night lay hidden in this room. The air felt oppressive, and a metallic scent lingered in the air.

"Wow," Liz said, her voice wavering. "This place feels, uh, different."

Shadows played tricks on the walls, creating unsettling shapes that moved in tandem with their breathing. LeVar hesitated at the threshold, his instincts screaming at him to turn back. But with Liz and Scout already inside, he couldn't let fear dictate his actions.

Liz removed a night-vision video recorder and panned across the room. A large table stood amid the decay, dust-covered and surrounded by overturned chairs.

"Ain't nothing to worry about," he said. "This is where the previous owner tossed his stuff." He got the feeling that they were walking into a trap, that something or someone was manipulating them from behind the scenes. He wondered if Lambert had set up an elaborate prank to scare them. "Or someone wants to play a joke on us."

"Are you saying it's staged?" Liz asked, raising an eyebrow.

"Maybe. I don't know."

Scout raised a hand for silence while she listened. After she turned off the recorder, she motioned at them to follow. "Let's keep exploring. We came here to find proof of the paranormal, and we won't leave until we do."

He rolled his eyes. "Yippee."

Every instinct told him to get out while they still could, but if

Lambert was behind the unexplained moans, he couldn't let the prankster win. Should LeVar run off, Lambert would never let him hear the end of it.

He followed the girls as they moved down the corridor, their flashlights cutting through the darkness to reveal more unsettling details: scratches on the walls, broken mirrors, and a thick layer of dust that seemed to cling to everything. He sneezed.

Liz crouched beside a pile of debris near a cracked window, sifting through the remains of what looked like old newspapers and books. "These are from decades ago. Look at the dates."

"Careful," LeVar said, watching as she picked up a brittle page, the edges crumbling under her fingers. "You don't want to damage anything."

"This is incredible. It's like stepping back in time."

Scout crouched next to Liz and threw an alarmed look back at LeVar. "The newspaper—it's from 1915."

"That's impossible," he said. "No way a newspaper would survive over a century in these conditions."

"But it's here. How do you explain that?"

He couldn't.

32

The dashboard lights illuminated Thomas's face as he maneuvered his truck onto the winding road leading to the Nightshade County Coroner's Building. His fingers tapped the steering wheel, drumming out a rhythm only he could hear. He glanced at the clock in the corner—8:47 p.m.—and reached for his phone, dialing Chelsey's number.

"Hey, I'm heading over to see Claire Brookins right now. I'll be home late."

"Checking on her test results?"

"That's right. I want to check if she's found anything new. Can you send me the list of missing people we've compiled? I want to see if any of them pop out as a potential victim."

"I'll email it to you right away." Thomas pictured her sitting on the couch with Tigger, the orange tabby, curled up nearby. "Be careful, okay?"

"Always am," he said before hanging up.

The Nightshade County Coroner's Building loomed ahead. He parked his truck and hurried inside to escape the wind, the heavy door slamming shut behind him. The smell of antiseptic greeted him as he walked down the hallway, the silence broken only by the sound of his footsteps echoing off the walls.

He found Claire hunched over a microscope in her office, russet hair pulled back into a tight ponytail. The bone carving of a fox lay on a metal tray beside her.

"How's it coming along?"

She looked up, her eyes darting from the carving to him. "I didn't expect you, Thomas. Working late?"

"The new carving—I need to know if we're dealing with a human bone again."

Claire's expression turned serious, and she straightened her posture. "Give me a moment." She adjusted the microscope and peered through the eyepiece.

Thomas watched her work, his mind going over the information Chelsey was sending him. Whoever had made these carvings had taken great care, and the thought that the killer had used human bones for his murderous art made him shudder. He needed to find this person before they claimed another victim.

"Definitely bone," she said after a moment, pulling away from the microscope. "I'll need to run some tests to determine if it's human."

"I'll hang around if you don't mind."

"Feel free."

"Oh, and one more thing."

"What is it?"

"Keep this between us for now. I don't want news of the results getting out and compromising the investigation."

"Strict confidentiality is part of my job. You can count on me."

"I always do."

"Want to help?" she asked, holding up the DNA extraction kit.

"I'm game," he said, watching as she took the fox from its evidence bag with gloved hands.

She worked with meticulous precision, using a small swab to extract DNA from the strange fox carving. She then placed the sample into a vial and sealed it shut. As Thomas pulled gloves over his hands, she loaded the vial into the PCR machine. It hummed on the countertop.

"Does this take long?" he asked.

"Actually, it should only be a few minutes." She studied the PCR machine's digital display. "It's amazing how quickly we can get results these days."

As they waited, Thomas paced around the room. The killer had made this personal, but why? Who had he crossed that would want to terrorize him?

"Got it," Claire said, examining the results on the screen. "The DNA test confirms our fears. This carving is human bone."

"I figured, but I hoped I was wrong. How does this work, anyway? The PCR machine, I mean."

"It amplifies specific segments of the DNA so we can see if there are any matches. In this case, I matched the bone carving's DNA to human sequences," Claire explained, her voice taking on an excited tone as she shared her knowledge. "It's a powerful tool in forensic investigations."

"And I thought I was cool when I had one of those home electronic kits as a child," Thomas said. "You know, the ones with the wires."

"Ah, nostalgia. I had one of those."

Small talk didn't quiet Thomas's anxiety. He processed the implications of what they'd discovered. A torture victim in Nightshade County—it was a nightmare he'd hoped never to face.

"Here," she said, holding up a caliper. "I'll measure the

minute differences between the fox and the first carving. The crow."

Thomas observed as she placed the caliper against the carvings. The fine lines of the fox's fur seemed to come alive under her steady hand.

"See how the depth of each carved line is almost identical?" she asked, glancing at Thomas.

"Remarkable."

She measured various aspects of both figurines, jotting the results in a spiral-bound notebook.

"Now, let's run these measurements through statistical analysis software."

He spied the tension in her shoulders as they waited for the results. Even though she was an expert in her field, this case had shaken her.

"Here it is," she said, her voice strained. "The software confirms that the carvings came from different people. The chances of them being from the same individual are astronomically low."

"He's torturing his victims. Is there anything more we can do to identify the victim?"

"I'll continue running tests and comparing the DNA samples with any missing persons we have on file. Few people are in the database."

"Do everything you can to learn who our victims are. That's our best shot of learning the killer's identity." He pinched the bridge of his nose. "The media is already calling this guy the Carver, and with the investigation gaining attention, we don't need reporters throwing the county into hysterics."

"I'll do everything I can to help you catch this monster."

"I'm heading back to the station. If you learn anything new, call me day or night."

As Thomas prepared to leave the lab, he took one last look at the carvings. They were a grim reminder of the psychotic mind he was up against. The Carver. He'd faced demented murderers before, but this was a new level of insanity.

He exited the building, his eyes scanning the empty parking lot as he walked towards his pickup. The all-too-familiar sensation of someone following him made him spin around. Just like the feeling he got after opening the second package.

The wind tossed his hair. Endless night blanketed the land. He unlocked his truck and climbed in and searched for a hidden figure.

Nobody.

As he pulled out of the parking lot, he checked his mirrors before driving away. His phone buzzed with an incoming email from Chelsey. The list of missing people she'd promised to send him had arrived.

He needed to review it as soon as possible. Somewhere on the list was a torture victim.

33

LeVar, Scout, and Liz found themselves at the end of a long, narrow corridor, facing a door that led to the next room they were about to investigate. Over the last hour, there had been no unexplained occurrences, no moaning, and the paranormal-sensing equipment never activated. LeVar hoped the girls would soon grow bored and call it a night. He wanted to get out of there. Plus, his allergies were on fire from all the dust.

Scout reached for the doorknob. "Are you guys ready?"

"Hundred percent," LeVar replied, attempting to sound confident despite the unease growing in his chest.

Liz checked her equipment. "Ready when you are."

The door opened with a groan. Peeling wallpaper hung from the walls like ancient skin, and dusty furniture lay scattered about, untouched for what seemed like centuries.

"Okay, let's see if we can find anything here."

"Whatcha got there?" LeVar asked.

"This?" Liz asked, producing a small EMF meter and a spirit box. She handed one to Scout and held on to the other. "This is an electromagnetic field meter, or EMF. It measures changes in the electromagnetic field around us. Some people believe that ghosts cause these fluctuations, so we'll know if there's any paranormal activity around."

"Interesting. And what about the spirit box?"

"Ah, the spirit box." Liz grinned. "It scans through radio frequencies, creating white noise. The theory is that spirits use this white noise to communicate with us. If we hear anything unusual, it could be a sign."

"Sounds like a plan." LeVar was skeptical but didn't want to dampen the enthusiasm of his friends. "Make your magic happen."

As they scanned the room with their devices, the EMF meter started beeping and flashing, indicating a sudden spike in electromagnetic activity.

"Whoa, look at this. There's definitely something going on here."

"Or it could be faulty wiring," he said, not ready to accept a supernatural explanation. "Old houses have electrical issues."

"Maybe," Scout said, "but let's not dismiss the evidence just yet. Let's see if the spirit box picks up anything."

Scout handed him the spirit box, a small handheld radio with a speaker and a microphone. "Here, why don't you try talking to the so-called ghost? See if it responds."

He hesitated for a moment, staring at the device in his hands. Pressing the button on the side, he addressed the empty room, feeling like an idiot. "Yo, if there's anyone here with us, give us a sign." After a moment, he turned to them. "See? Nothing."

"Try again."

He blew out a breath. "*Aight*, spirits. Who's with us tonight?"

The white noise from the spirit box grew louder, and then a raspy voice echoed through the speaker. The air grew colder. "Leave. Now."

He tried to debunk the supernatural. "This has got to be a trick."

"That was a ghost," Scout said. "LeVar, you just contacted the spirit world."

"Must be my vibrant personality. But I'm telling you, there's a logical explanation for all of this."

He scanned the room, his eyes shooting from one corner to the next. The peeling wallpaper seemed to mock him as he searched for the source of the bone-chilling voice.

"Where did it come from?" he muttered under his breath. "There has to be a speaker somewhere."

"LeVar, are you okay?" Liz asked.

"Fine," he groaned, not wanting to admit how rattled he was. As he continued searching, a thought struck him. "This has to be Lambert pulling a prank on us."

"Deputy Lambert?" Scout raised an eyebrow. "You really think he'd go this far?"

"Wouldn't put it past him. Don't worry. He'll get what's coming to him."

"Let's not jump to conclusions," Liz said, her attention focused on the various paranormal tracking devices she had brought along. "We still have half the mansion to search through."

Just as he was about to respond, Scout's eyes widened, and she pointed toward a shadowy corner of the room. "Oh my God."

Following her gaze, they all saw it—an old rocking chair, hidden beneath layers of dust and cobwebs. It was an antique piece of furniture with a faded floral pattern and a wooden frame that spoke of its age and long-forgotten history. It moved. Just for second, but they'd all seen it.

"Did . . . did that just move on its own?" Liz asked.

"Must be the wind," LeVar said, his voice cracking. There was no breeze in the sealed-off room, no logical reason for the chair to rock.

"Or maybe we've just found our ghost. We can't ignore what's happening right in front of us."

"There has to be a scientific reason for everything."

"Like what?" Scout asked. "You saw how the EMF meter spiked."

Liz nodded, her eyes wide as she clutched the spirit box to her chest. "And that creepy voice? There's something here, LeVar, whether or not you want to believe it."

"Look, Lambert loves to kid around." He was determined to debunk what they had experienced, despite the mounting evidence. Deputy Lambert was behind the mystery, pulling his strings.

"LeVar, if you're so sure it's Lambert, then prove it," Scout said.

He set his hands on his hips and addressed the dark hallway. "Okay, buzz cut. I know you're behind this. Show yourself. I've had enough of the parlor tricks."

Silence followed, the only sounds the creaking of the old floorboards beneath their feet. The three of them waited for a response that would never come.

"Right," LeVar said after a long pause, an uneasy mix of triumph and apprehension coloring his tone. "Nothing. I bet he's hiding somewhere, laughing at us."

"Or maybe whatever is here doesn't want to make itself known."

Liz turned to him. "We can't ignore what we've experienced. The EMF meter, the voice through the spirit box, and the rocking chair. We have to keep investigating."

"Let's just finish this investigation and get out of here."

It had to be Lambert. He must have rigged the chair to rock

when they entered the room. That was the only explanation that restored order to his shaken world.

The three investigators proceeded down the next corridor. Scout, ever the curious sleuth, hung on to her EMF meter and spirit box, eager to uncover further signs of supernatural activity.

"LeVar, you're a brave man," Liz said, sidling up to him and casting a flirtatious glance in his direction. "Few people would have the guts to face a poltergeist."

"Uh, thanks." He found it increasingly difficult to concentrate because of Liz's advances.

"Maybe once we solve this mystery and become big stars, we could celebrate together."

"Let's just focus on the investigation for now, shall we?"

"Of course." Liz flashed a coy smile before turning her attention back to the paranormal equipment.

That girl would be the death of him.

Each creak of the floorboards, every rustle of decaying curtains heightened his nervousness. With two doors to either side of them in the corridor, he stopped, sensing they weren't alone.

"Give me that spirit-box thing again."

Scout handed it to him.

"This time for real. If there really is something here, let's see if I can make contact." He stared at the spirit box in his hand, its buttons and dials reflecting in the flashlight beams.

"Are you sure about this? You've never done this before tonight, and we don't know what we're dealing with."

Liz hooked elbows with him. "It's the only way to prove it's real, right?"

"Exactly," LeVar said, pulling his arm free. "Let's give it another shot."

He switched on the spirit box, adjusting the frequency while static buzzed through the speaker. "If there's anyone here, holler at me."

For a moment, nothing happened. Then, the static gave way to a faint whisper. His grip tightened on the device.

"Did you hear that?" Liz asked.

"Keep going," Scout said.

LeVar cleared his throat. "Who are you? If you have something to say, speak up. Ain't no time to act shy."

The whisper grew louder, more distinct, though the words remained indiscernible. This differed from before. As the sound intensified, he felt an electrical charge swimming around him.

"LeVar, I think we should stop."

He hesitated, torn between his desire to prove that Lambert was behind this and the creeping dread that settled in his chest. But before he could respond, the spirit box emitted a sudden, piercing screech. Then it fell silent.

"What the hell was that?" He caught them staring. "Pardon my French."

Was this all an elaborate hoax, or had he stumbled upon something unexplainable? A faint musty odor permeated the mansion, mingling with the anticipation that clung to each step.

As they approached the end of the corridor, a dull thud echoed behind a decrepit door. He exchanged looks with his companions before reaching for the handle. It might be an animal. Or a vagrant. This seemed like the perfect place to hole up. It sure beat a frigid night on the street.

"Nightshade County Sheriff's Department," he said outside the door. "This is Deputy LeVar Hopkins. I don't mean you any harm, but I'm coming in." He looked over his shoulder at the girls, who hugged each other. "Here goes nothing."

The room before him was a study in decay. Cobwebs draped from shelves sagging with dust-covered books. An ancient desk sat in one corner, its surface marred by the passage of time.

Despite the disarray, there was an unsettling stillness in the air, as if the walls were holding their breath.

"Something doesn't feel right," Scout said, her flashlight beam cutting through the gloom. "I don't like it."

"Isn't this what you wanted?"

His eyes scanned the room for any sign of Lambert's handiwork.

The EMF meter flashed its lights, accompanied by a beeping that grew more insistent.

"Has to be a ghost."

"The old wiring in this place is bound to give off interference."

A guttural voice boomed through the spirit box. "Get out."

"Is that you, Lambert? If this is your idea of a joke, I swear—"

"LeVar," Scout said, her voice trembling. "I don't think it's a joke anymore."

As they turned to leave the room, LeVar looked back one last time, unable to shake the nagging sensation that they were missing something crucial.

His determination to uncover the truth, whether it lay in the realm of the supernatural or in the games of a prankster, burned brighter than ever.

But Lambert wasn't in Radford Mansion. Something else was.

34

On the way back to the station, Thomas wondered again about the killer's motivation. Taunting wouldn't satisfy the psychopath. The Carver wanted more. Yet he hadn't called the station or included notes with his carvings.

A vibration alerted Thomas to a message appearing on his phone. Unknown sender. He stopped the truck along the shoulder and read.

Coral Lake gala tonight at 9 p.m.
Join the dance. I wish to see you unmasked.

Thomas's head swam. The killer had gotten his number and texted him. Before he pulled onto the road, he called his lead deputy, who was working the evening shift tonight.

"Hey Aguilar. The Carver contacted me."

"How?"

"Sent a message. At least I assume it's him. He must have found my phone number."

"What did he say?"

"There's a gala in Coral Lake tonight," he said. "He wants me to attend. Can you meet me there?"

"Is this wise, Thomas? It sounds like a trap."

"What choice do I have? Besides, he can't murder me in front of a few hundred guests."

"Everyone wears a mask at the Coral Lake gala."

Thomas paused. "I guess that's what he meant by seeing me unmasked."

"Excuse me?"

"Just meet me there. And bring backup. I don't want this guy escaping our net."

"I'll have my eyes on you the entire time."

"Thank you, my friend. See you there."

Aguilar arrived seconds after Thomas. A dome of illumination bubbled skyward from the luxurious event which took place at the country club. With the parking lot full, they had to trudge through the snow to reach the dance.

"We'll communicate through our earpieces," he said.

"Don't get too far ahead of me in there, Thomas. You need me to watch your back."

As they entered the grand ballroom, the opulence of the gala surrounded them. Glittering chandeliers hung from the high ceilings, and the rich scent of gourmet food wafted through the air. Everyone wore a mask. How the hell would he recognize the killer with everyone disguised? He realized his target held the advantage.

"All right, I'll head toward the bar area and mingle with the guests," Aguilar said into her microphone, her eyes scanning the crowd. "You focus on finding the person who sent the message. Keep me updated."

"Got it."

Except he wouldn't find the person who'd texted him. The Carver would find him.

Thomas adjusted his shirt collar. Goodness, it seemed hot inside. Everyone recognized his uniform and stared, as if he were the one wearing a bizarre mask. He walked toward the center of the dance floor as instructed, trying to remain inconspicuous while observing the various attendees.

"Excuse me," he said to a server passing by, "has anyone asked to speak with me?"

The server shook his head. "No, Sheriff, not that I've noticed. But there are so many people here tonight, it's hard to keep track of everyone."

As he continued to search for the mysterious sender, Aguilar's voice crackled in his ear.

"Thomas, I've been asking around, but no one seems to know anything about these bone carvings. Keep your eyes peeled. This person could be anyone."

"Understood."

If only he had more information to work with. As he studied the room, a wave of unease suffocated him. The gala attendees wore an array of masks, their faces hidden behind intricate designs and menacing expressions. His pulse quickened as he tried to focus on his task, but the sensory overload only heightened his anxiety.

"You all right, Thomas?"

Aguilar's voice.

"Yeah, fine. Should have eaten a bigger dinner."

Thomas inhaled and navigated through the sea of masked faces, each triggering a different emotion inside him. A few masks caught his attention: a grotesque, leering clown with hollow eyes, a crimson devil with horns, and a black raven with beady eyes and a sharp beak. Their presence chewed at his subconscious, feeding into his fear that one of them could be the killer.

"Good evening to you," the raven said in passing.

A black raven. The Carver's first gift had been a crow.

He spun to find the dancer, but the costumed man had disappeared into the mass of bodies.

Someone in a comical bird mask with an elongated beak bumped into him.

"My apologies, Sheriff," the bird said, rejoining the dance.

Thomas concentrated on his surroundings, trying to block out the unsettling masks and noisy chatter.

"Thomas, I'm near the stage." Aguilar's voice came through the earpiece again. "Nothing suspicious so far."

"Copy that. I'm beside the fountain. The target hasn't made contact yet."

At least he thought his quarry hadn't. How could he tell?

Deeper into the crowd, Thomas noticed a woman wearing an elegant silver mask adorned with delicate feathers. Its beauty stood in stark contrast to the grotesque masks he had seen earlier. She grinned and motioned him forward. He shook his head and moved on.

"Thomas, there's a man in a hooded cloak near the bar. I can't see his face. Can you head over and look?"

"Roger that."

He made his way through the throng of dancers. With every step, it felt as if the walls were closing in on him, the pressure building beneath his skin. The cacophony of laughter, music, and conversation assaulted his senses, making it difficult to focus.

As he approached the hooded figure, he couldn't help but notice the intricate detail of the mask the man wore under his hood—a disturbingly lifelike wolf with haunting yellow eyes. The sight sent a shiver down his spine, fueling his paranoia.

The lights flashed. Music pounded. And the wolf creature tossed his hood back and howled at the domed ceiling, drawing applause and laughter.

Thomas's head throbbed. He backed into a server carrying a

tray of drinks and almost caused a disaster. His legs buckled, and the room spun as he crumpled to the floor. Gasps and murmurs filled the air, drowning out the music.

"Someone help!" a woman cried, her voice shrill with alarm. "That poor man just collapsed."

More voices.

"It's the sheriff."

"No, it's someone dressed as the sheriff."

"William, you fool. That's Sheriff Shepherd."

"Call an ambulance. I think he had a stroke."

A cluster of masked faces leaned over Thomas, their expressions hidden but their eyes wide with concern. A man in a tuxedo and a grotesque snake mask kneeled by his side, checking for a pulse. Another, wearing a tree mask that seemed to writhe in the dim light, loosened Thomas's shirt collar. The scent of expensive perfume mingled with the odor of fear and sweat.

"Give him some space," said a woman, her face obscured by an elegant Venetian-style mask. The crowd parted, allowing fresh air to flow through.

"Thomas, can you hear me?" Aguilar's voice cut through the chaos like a lifeline. She was suddenly there, parting the sea of dancers, her brow furrowed with worry. "Stay with me, Thomas."

"What happened?" Thomas croaked, his mind foggy and disoriented.

"You collapsed. Take a deep breath and try to relax. I'm calling an ambulance."

"Don't. I'm not dying. I just had . . . an episode."

"And you need a medical professional to check you out." He tried to sit up, and she blocked him with her hand. "Rest for a few minutes."

The crowd backed away at Aguilar's command. Two junior

deputies pushed through the crowd to help. It took a minute for the room to stop spinning. He found his sea legs.

"All right, I think I can get up now."

She gave him a doubtful look before helping him to his feet. Thomas felt all those watching eyes. He coughed, fighting the urge to retreat into himself.

"How's your head?"

"Better," he whispered, steadying himself against her powerful frame. "I don't know what came over me."

"We need to get you somewhere quiet to recover." She motioned the deputies forward. "Fan out. Keep your eyes open and your radios on. I don't want our target slipping past us."

Thomas blinked, his thoughts still disjointed as they left the suffocating atmosphere of the gala. The dance resumed, and he sensed the Carver laughing somewhere. The psychopath had known the spectacle would overwhelm Thomas's senses.

Once outside, he breathed in the night air, feeling the tension in his muscles dissipate. At every inhalation, the stimuli from the gala faded further into the background. As Aguilar led him toward a quiet corner away from prying eyes, he regained his composure.

"Take a seat here," Aguilar said, pointing to an ornate stone bench nestled among some snow-covered shrubs. Thomas complied, resting his head in his hands as he tried to make sense of what had transpired.

"Here, drink some water," she said, handing him a bottle she'd grabbed on their way out.

"Thanks." He sipped the water until the cool liquid soothed his parched throat.

Something was wrong. His jacket felt heavier than before, and a sharp object jabbed into his ribcage.

He rummaged through his pockets, looking for his phone, and his fingers brushed against a solid object. Another bone carving, this one shaped like a raven, its wings outstretched mid-flight.

"Where did this come from? How did it get in my pocket?"

Though he'd already touched the figurine, he donned gloves before examining further.

"When did you get this?"

"I don't know. He must have slipped it into my pocket." He held her eyes. "I saw him, Aguilar. A raven. He spoke to me."

She lifted her radio. "All officers be advised—the target may be disguised as a raven."

The noise of the gala continued to drift out to them, a haunting reminder of the potential danger lurking behind every mask. The soft melodies of a string quartet intertwined with laughter and clinking glasses. Thomas could almost taste the rich flavors of gourmet hors d'oeuvres—smoked salmon canapés, seared scallops, and delicate pastries.

Somewhere in the ballroom, a man in a raven mask blended with the dancers.

Thomas stood.

"We know who we're looking for. Nobody leaves the gala without my permission."

35

Despite the drama caused by Thomas's spell, the Coral Lake gala remained in full swing, a dazzling spectacle of glitz and glamor. A soft golden glow emanated from hundreds of candles suspended from crystal chandeliers. Champagne flowed as the guests mingled, their laughter and excited murmurs creating a hum that blended with the sultry jazz.

Ice sculptures glistened on every table, while the fragrance of fresh lilies and roses filled the air. Women in shimmering gowns twirled around the dance floor, leaving trails of glitter as they moved to the rhythm of the music, their masked faces adding an air of mystery.

Thomas surveyed the scene. The serial killer lurked among the guests, hiding behind one of those masks.

"Backup is here." He spoke into his radio. "Lock down all entrances immediately."

Lambert, who had arrived moments ago, nodded and glided through the crowd, signaling to the other officers stationed around the room. Within moments, they secured the doors, leaving the attendees trapped inside like sparkling fish in a gilded aquarium.

"Showtime," Thomas muttered to himself. He studied the faces as they noticed the uniformed officers blocking their exits.

Whispers turned to gasps and exclamations as realization set in. The music faltered for a moment before resuming at a more subdued tempo, the band members exchanging nervous glances.

"Attention, everyone!" Thomas called out, his voice cutting through the din. "I'm Sheriff Thomas Shepherd with the Nightshade County Sheriff's Department, and I need your cooperation." He paused, letting the chatter subside. "We believe a dangerous individual is among you this evening. Please remain calm and do not leave the premises."

The room erupted into chaos as guests clamored for answers, their voices rising in a cacophony of confusion. Thomas winced at the overwhelming noise.

"Everyone stay where you are," he said, raising his hands to restore order. "We will check everyone's identity, one by one. I assure you, your safety is our top priority."

A murmur of trepidation rippled through the crowd as they took in Thomas's announcement. Some guests clutched their ornate masks to their faces, as if seeking protection from an invisible threat, while others stood in defiance, arms crossed and chins lifted.

"Is this some kind of joke?" a woman in a red gown sneered, her voice dripping with disdain.

"No, ma'am. I assure you, we are taking every precaution to ensure your safety."

A man in a tuxedo stepped forward, the muscles in his jaw tense. "You expect us to stand here while you interrogate us at a private function? This is outrageous!"

"Sir, I understand your frustration. But the sooner we verify everyone's identity, the sooner you can all return to enjoying the evening."

The man exchanged words with another guest before reluctantly nodding. In the background, a server's hand shook as he offered a tray of champagne-filled glasses to a group of uneasy revelers.

"Thank you for your cooperation," Thomas said, addressing the entire room. "We need everyone to stay together in this area. If we work efficiently, we can speed through the checks. Anyone who attempts to leave or disrupt the process will be treated as a suspect."

His words echoed in the air. Conversations ceased, replaced by hushed whispers and the rustle of silk and velvet as guests shifted uncomfortably.

"Deputy Aguilar, please assist me in organizing the guests into a line."

As she directed the attendees, a sense of urgency drove Thomas. Time seemed to slow as the line progressed, each guest stepping forward to be identified, their expressions a mixture of terror, indignation, and curiosity. The raven figurine felt like an anvil in his pocket, but there was no sign of the man in the raven mask. He tried to piece together the puzzle, the fragments of evidence and the killer's potential motive swirling in his head.

His eyes never strayed from the ever-shifting sea of faces. The clock was ticking, and every second counted.

"All right, everyone," Aguilar said. "Please remove your masks as you step forward."

Several people groaned. As they complied, each unadorned face revealed another piece of the puzzle that Thomas was desperate to solve.

"Deputy Aguilar, take down their names and any relevant information," he said.

Aguilar removed a notepad and pen. He observed as she

assessed the first guest, a tall man with silver hair who seemed uncomfortable with the situation.

"Name?" she asked.

"Robert Sinclair. I don't see how this is necessary."

"Thank you for your cooperation, Mr. Sinclair," Aguilar said, scribbling down the name. She asked him several questions before moving on to the next guest.

Each guest presented a new possibility, a potential suspect, and Thomas scrutinized every detail, from the lines around their eyes to the nervous tapping of their fingers.

"Excuse me, Sheriff." A voice cut through his thoughts, drawing his attention to a middle-aged woman with auburn curls cascading around her shoulders. Her eyes were wide with trepidation. "Is there anything I can do to help?"

"Stay calm and follow our instructions," Thomas said, forcing a reassuring smile. "We'll handle this."

"We're not under arrest, are we?"

"Of course not. We're here to ensure your safety."

"Thank you," she whispered before stepping forward to be identified.

As the last of the guests removed their masks, dread crept into Thomas's chest. The room was now filled with unmasked guests. He scanned the sea of faces as a chilling thought crossed his mind: What if the killer had already slipped away?

The gala attendees stood clustered together, their masks discarded like fall leaves on the polished marble floor. Some fidgeted with their gowns and tailored suits, while others whispered among themselves.

"Did you see anyone leave?" Thomas asked Lambert.

"No one has left since we locked the doors," Lambert assured him.

"Unless they snuck out before," Thomas muttered under his breath.

His fainting spell had provided the perfect opportunity for the killer to escape without drawing attention. This was his fault.

He studied the guests, noting the way a man in a pinstriped suit tugged at his cufflinks, and how a woman with dark curls played with a strand of pearls around her fingers. Each mannerism held potential significance, but determining which were genuine reactions to the situation and which signaled guilt proved challenging.

A woman in a silver gown caught his attention. Her hands trembled as she clutched a bejeweled purse. He remembered her. Moments after the man in the raven mask passed by, this woman had bumped into Thomas.

"Excuse me, madam," he said. "May I have a word with you?"

"Of course, Sheriff."

"Can you tell me where you were between 9:30 and 9:50?"

"Mostly by the dessert table," she said with a smile. "I do have a weakness for chocolate."

"You bumped into me earlier."

She placed a hand over her chest. "Did I? I must apologize. Too much champagne, you understand."

"Did you notice anything unusual or anyone acting suspiciously?"

"Nothing comes to mind," she said. "But then again, everyone was wearing masks."

"Do you recall a man in a raven's mask?"

"Why, yes. I do."

"Can you tell me who he is?" he asked.

"I would if I could, but the unmasking wasn't to occur until midnight."

Aguilar approached, handing over her notepad. "I have all their names. What's next?"

"We need to cross-check these names with professions and hobbies. Focus on males with a flare for the artistic."

"In this crowd? That could be half the attendees."

With the interviews complete, Thomas allowed the gala to recommence. Of all the people questioned, no one had worn a raven mask.

The killer had slipped through his fingers.

36

"Man, this place gives me the creeps," LeVar said, taking in the staircase that led to the second floor of Radford Mansion.

The inspector had deemed the steps sound, but he wasn't so sure. They bowed downward at the center, and the heads of rusty nails protruded upward like meerkats looking over the savannah.

"Isn't that the point?" Scout asked. She wiped her glasses on her shirt. "We're here to explore and uncover any signs of paranormal activity."

"Right," said Liz, shivering as a wintry draft swept through the mansion. "Lead the way up."

As they made their way through the dusty halls of the once-grand home, he sensed they weren't alone, that someone—or something—watched from the shadows.

Scout looked over her shoulder. "There's that moaning sound again."

LeVar shrugged. "Probably just the wind."

A thud sounded from upstairs, reverberating through the walls and jolting the trio into silence.

"Okay, that wasn't the wind," he admitted, now on alert. The sound was heavy, like a massive object crashing to the floor. It left an oppressive silence in its wake.

Scout's eyes sparkled with curiosity as she nudged him up the steps. He hesitated for a moment, weighing his options. The rational part of him wanted to dismiss the noise as a random occurrence, but another portion of his brain now believed anything was possible.

"I guess there's a broken window. That's why it's so cold."

Instead of agreeing with him, they stared. He led the way down another hallway, one hand on the flashlight, the other brushing against the wall for balance.

"If a window had broken, you'd hear the wind screaming through the opening," Scout said. Her fingers played with the strap of her camera bag.

"Everybody, stop," Liz said. She pointed at a protrusion on the wall, partially obscured by a moth-eaten tapestry. "It looks like a hidden door."

LeVar and Scout moved closer to inspect the anomaly. It was indeed a door, camouflaged within the intricate woodwork of the wall. An old-fashioned keyhole, caked with dust and rust, stared back at them from the center.

"Wow," Scout breathed, awestruck. "I never thought we'd actually find something like this."

"Neither did I," LeVar said, his skepticism momentarily forgotten.

He pushed the door open, revealing a narrow passageway.

Liz stepped into the corridor, followed by Scout and LeVar. "Here goes nothing."

The air inside was musty, thick with the scent of aged wood and decay. Another door blocked the way forward, this one more imposing than the hidden entrance. With a lump in his throat, he turned the handle, and the door creaked open to reveal a room frozen in time. A layer of dust blanketed every surface, from the ornate wooden furniture to the moth-eaten curtains that framed the windows. Cobwebs hung from a chandelier, their delicate threads swaying.

"Shouldn't be too difficult to find paranormal activity in this room," Scout said. "This is where the crash came from, but what fell?"

Scout and Liz took out their equipment, including an EMF detector and a digital recorder, and scanned the room. LeVar couldn't tear his eyes away from the portraits that lined the walls. Each depicted a member of the Radford family, their eyes seeming to follow him as he moved around the room.

"Anything?" he asked, his voice cracking.

Liz chewed her lip. "Nothing yet."

"Maybe there's no ghost after all."

"Or maybe it's just biding its time," Scout said. Her eyes never left the device in her hands.

LeVar rubbed his chin, his skepticism growing. "You sure it wasn't just the wind?"

"What wind? The windows are closed."

"Yo, this place is old," LeVar said. "It's falling apart."

"True," Liz said, "but that doesn't explain the secret passageway or the untouched room."

"Let me try that EMF detector."

"Go ahead."

He swept the room with the electromagnetic field detector. The LED lights indicated fluctuations. The device remained silent, however, and the lights didn't flash. Frustration bubbled; a part of him wanted to believe, but the lack of evidence made it difficult.

"See?" he said, waving the device. "Nothing."

"Maybe we should use the digital recorder to capture EVPs."

"Electronic voice phenomena?"

"That's the idea," Scout said. "Sometimes spirits communicate through frequencies we can't hear, but digital recorders pick them up."

Liz handed Scout the recorder, and she pressed the record button. "Is there anyone here with us?"

He stood aside as Scout and Liz took turns asking questions and leaving space for responses. The effort seemed futile, but he kept his thoughts to himself. After several minutes, Scout stopped the recording.

"Let's play it back," said Liz.

The room filled with the sound of their voices, echoing questions from earlier. LeVar shifted his weight from one foot to the other, waiting for something to happen. But as the recording played on, no unexplained voices came through the speaker.

"We're not asking the right questions," Scout said.

"Or maybe there's nothing here," he said. He should be working with Thomas to solve a murder investigation, not playing games in a dilapidated mansion.

They gathered their equipment. As they continued down the narrow hallway, he felt the hairs on his arms stand, but he attributed it to the drafty old house, not some lingering specter. They hadn't traveled a dozen steps before Scout grabbed his arm.

Ahead, a light drew moving shadows on the floor. "Still think it's the wind, LeVar?"

"We should turn around. I've seen enough for one night."

"Come on, tough guy," Liz chided. "This is what we came here for, right?"

"This is what *y'all* came for, not me."

Together they approached the door. Shadows danced across the walls, taunting them with sinister movements.

"That's candlelight," Scout said. "See how it flickers?"

Candlelight? Impossible. They were the only people in the mansion, and Lambert wouldn't leave a candle burning in a decrepit house.

"Someone needs to open the door," Liz said.

LeVar scowled. "I suppose that means me."

"Wait," Liz said, her hand on LeVar's arm. "Be careful. We don't know what's behind that door."

"On the count of three."

"One, two . . . three."

He grabbed the handle. The door shrieked open on seized hinges. Pitch black. No flickering candle.

"Flashlight," he said.

Liz clicked the button and aimed the beam around the room.

"Whoa," said Scout. "Look at this place."

A child's bed stood in the corner with a nightstand beside it. Grime coated every surface, betraying years of neglect.

"We should have brought some more equipment," Liz said. "Let's just search and get out of here,"

Scout fidgeted with a strand of hair. As they stepped into the room, the air grew heavier.

"Nothing seems out of the ordinary," he said, his voice quiet and tense. "Just a bunch of old junk."

"What if . . . what if whatever made those noises is still in here with us?"

Scout narrowed her brow. "Stop it, Liz. You're going to freak us out even more."

"If you've seen one bed," said LeVar, "you've seen them all. Time to hit the road."

"Not just any bed," Liz said, struggling to regain her composure.

Scout nodded. "We found Virginia Radford's bedroom. Start recording."

"Already on it."

Liz narrated as she panned the camera across the room. Somewhere in the mansion, a child screamed.

37

The moon hung over the Coral Lake country club as the last of the gala guests filed out, their whispers punctuated by the crunching of snow underfoot. Kane Grove police officers arrived and set up barricades around the perimeter while others secured the mansion. The festive air had dispersed, leaving behind emptiness and agitation.

"Thomas," Deputy Aguilar said.

Thomas, who was busy examining the raven figurine he had discovered in his pocket, looked up.

"Kane Grove's here," Aguilar said, nodding towards the approaching uniformed officers. "Time to fill them in."

Together, they approached the senior officer, a stout man with graying hair.

"Evening, Officer," Thomas said, extending a firm handshake. "I assume someone briefed you on the carvings."

"Lieutenant Barnes. What have you found so far?"

"Earlier tonight, someone in a raven mask bumped into me. It didn't seem significant at the time, but this ended up in my pocket." He held up the raven figurine for Barnes to see. "It's like the ones that were mailed to my department."

"Interesting," Barnes said, studying the small object. "Anything else?"

"Actually, yes," Aguilar said. "We've been looking into the guest list, and we believe the killer was at the gala tonight. On our instructions, everyone removed their masks, but no one was wearing the raven mask Thomas described."

"Sounds like he escaped before you locked the place down."

"That's what I'm afraid of," said Thomas.

"I understand you collapsed, Sheriff. Are you well?"

"Hanging in there." He glanced over his shoulder at the ballroom as if the crowd hadn't dispersed. "It got a little warm in there."

The moon bathed the building, its walls seeming to hold secrets only the shadows knew. He adjusted the collar of his coat and directed the officers.

"Okay, everyone. Comb every inch of the estate. Check the rooms, closets, and any hidden spaces you come across. We're looking for someone who hid to avoid the unmasking and for a discarded raven's mask. And if you see a figurine like this," Thomas said, holding up the carving, "don't touch it. Contact me or Lieutenant Barnes."

The officers nodded in agreement, splitting up and making their way into the country club. Thomas, Lambert, and Aguilar entered each room with caution, examining the contents.

As the search progressed, detectives made their way to the staff, questioning them about the evening's events. Thomas approached the head server, who appeared shaken but eager to help. He remembered the man in the raven mask.

Thomas's thoughts were a hurricane of theories and possibilities. The killer had invited him here and risked capture to further taunt him. To attend the gala, the man must be affluent. Aguilar had acquired a guest list, but there were over two hundred names to sift through.

With the search of the mansion underway and the questioning of the country club staff completed, he turned his attention to the security footage. He holed up in the security room with Lambert and Aguilar, surrounded by monitors displaying various angles of the property. The monitors painted the room in a cold, bluish glow.

"Let's start from the beginning," Thomas said, his eyes fixed on the screens.

Lambert nodded, rewinding the footage to the start of the evening. They watched as guests arrived, mingling and sipping champagne. Thomas leaned forward. His fingers drummed against the edge of the table.

"Stop right there," Thomas said, pointing at a screen. "Zoom in on that corner."

Lambert followed his instruction, bringing up a grainy image of a man standing alone, partially obscured by shadows. However, it was impossible to tell if he wore a raven mask or not.

"I thought that was him," Thomas murmured, rubbing his temples. "Keep going."

"Thomas," Aguilar said, "even if we find this guy on camera, it won't help us. It's not like he'll unmask and show his face."

"At least it will prove I'm not losing my mind."

The security footage told them nothing new. He stood at the edge of the grand ballroom, his eyes scanning every detail as the police officers searched the room. The chandeliers spun ethereal lights across the empty dance floor, making it seem like a haunted ball from a bygone era.

"Nothing here," one officer reported, stepping away from a stack of chairs in the corner.

"Same over here," another added after checking behind the stage where the band had played.

"Keep looking," Thomas urged. "Check the surrounding grounds and any nearby buildings."

"Will do, Sheriff," the officer replied, heading toward the exit with a few others in tow.

Lambert approached Thomas, his expression somber. "We've been at this for hours. Are you sure we're not chasing a ghost?"

"Every instinct tells me he left another clue behind," Thomas said, rubbing the raven figurine in his pocket. "I can't explain why, but he wants me to find it."

"We'll keep at it, then."

As the search continued through the mansion, the officers found nothing out of the ordinary. Their enthusiasm waned, but he refused to give up.

"Anything?" he asked Aguilar, who was overseeing the search of the mansion's extensive grounds.

"Nothing so far," she replied, her voice weary. "But if you say something is here, I believe you."

"Thank you."

Midnight had fallen over the estate by the time the search concluded. Officers trudged back to their vehicles looking defeated while he stood on the terrace, the raven figurine secured in an evidence bag.

"Thomas," Lambert said, joining him. "We searched the entire mansion and grounds. There's nothing here."

"Something's not right. I can't let it go."

"Maybe we should call it a night. Get some rest and regroup in the morning."

"You're welcome to head back, but I want to keep looking."

Lambert met Aguilar's eyes. She shrugged.

The night turned darker, the stars and moon obscured by thickening clouds. He was about to surrender hope when the bartender's voice caught his attention.

"Hey, Sharon. Did you leave these scissors beside the register? These blades could remove a finger."

Before Sharon replied, Thomas spun and rushed to the bar. "Don't touch them. Let me see."

Aguilar and Lambert joined him beside the register. Thomas shined the beam of the flashlight on the scissors.

"Those aren't ordinary shears," Aguilar said.

The blades gleamed with malice.

Lambert wiped his mouth. "Those are dissection scissors. The kind used to cut body tissue during an autopsy. Is this what the Carver uses on his victims?"

"I'd bet my life on it," said Thomas. "But they're more than that. These scissors are another clue. More taunting."

"How?"

Thomas had no answer for his deputies.

38

LeVar couldn't find his breath. He stood in Virginia Radford's bedroom, where she'd fallen to her death. Or where someone murdered her. The legend Scout and Liz had unearthed became real. He was here, in this hidden section of the mansion. Someone had tried to bury the past, but the past refused to be quiet.

A bed stood in the corner, its once-white mattress now yellowed with age. Vermin, bugs, and neglect had devoured the sheets and blankets. A cracked porcelain doll lay on a wooden chair, its glassy blue eyes staring back at them.

"Not trying to be a Debbie downer," he said, "but maybe it's time we got out of here. Take your videos and measurements. It's time to leave."

"Not until I set up the spirit box," Scout said, taking a seat on the edge of the bed.

He cringed, as if the bony, pallid hands of the dead would drag her under for disturbing its rest. Setting the device on a small table beside the bed, he looked back at the girls, questioning them with his eyes. They nodded. His fingers trembled as he switched on the device, which sent a low hum through the air.

"Virginia Radford, are you here?"

He looked at Liz, who wound her hand in the air, gesturing for him to continue. Silence filled the room.

"Virginia, can you hear us?" he tried again. "We're in your bedroom. Ain't tryin' to be disrespectful by sitting on your stuff." Scout got the picture and stood up from the bed.

Still, there was no response. He exhaled. "Maybe we've got enough evidence already. We should go."

"Wait. Just one more try."

"Last one. Virginia Radford, if you're here, give us a sign. We want to know your story. How you . . . died. Did someone hurt you, girl? Just say so. I'll take care of it."

The room remained quiet, the spirit box's hum the only sound. As LeVar's hope faded, a sudden gust of wind blew through the room, rustling the curtains despite the closed window.

"Did you feel that?" Liz asked, her eyes wide.

"Yeah," he said, trying to hide the unease in his voice. "Looks like these windows are draftier than they appear." He looked at Scout, who seemed lost in thought. "Come on, pack up so I can take you home."

Something was watching them, waiting for them to leave the sanctuary of Virginia Radford's bedroom. The shadows blackened, as if the spirits of Radford Mansion were closing in around them.

As he reached for the spirit box, the scent of perfume filled his nose, reminding him of honeysuckle. But it wasn't Virginia Radford's ghost creeping up on him. It was Liz. Her fingers traced the ridges of his tattooed forearm.

"Thank you for keeping us safe."

"Uh, sure. That's my job. Thomas insisted."

"LeVar, I always wondered what it feels like to be a deputy and hold so much power," she purred. "A man like you, so strong and capable, must have lots of admirers."

Scout rolled her eyes at Liz's blatant attempts at flirting. He tried to ignore her, focusing on packing up the equipment. "It's not really that interesting," he said, avoiding eye contact.

"Come on, don't be modest. You ran the Harmon Kings."

"No, Rev ran the Kings. I was just part of the crew."

"The best part. Then you escaped the streets—"

"Thanks to Thomas."

"—and became a deputy and a dean's list student. I bet you could do anything you set your mind to."

"Can we just focus on getting out of here?" Scout snapped.

"I'm just asking what it's like to be so awesome," Liz huffed, but her eyes undressed LeVar. "You can't blame a girl for being curious."

"Enough, Liz. He's clearly not interested, so just leave him alone."

"Or what?" Liz sneered, turning her attention to Scout. "Maybe you're just jealous because you want him all to yourself."

LeVar's cheeks flushed. He wished he could crawl into a hole and disappear. "Girls, really. This has gone too far."

The tension in the room increased, as if someone had tightened an invisible cord around his neck. He'd never seen Liz or Scout act like this, and he needed to defuse the situation quickly before the argument escalated.

"Look, let's just forget about all this and hit the road," he said. "We came here for a reason, and it's not to fight."

Liz glared at Scout one last time before shifting her gaze to the floor, her anger simmering beneath the surface. Scout returned the murderous glare. The quiet that followed was laden with unspoken words and bruised egos.

"Admit it, Scout," Liz said. "You're jealous because I'm after the guy you want."

"I'm not jealous. It's just that—"

"Help me."

LeVar snapped his head up, locking eyes with Liz. The voice had come through the speaker. "Ain't funny, Liz. This isn't the time for games."

"LeVar, I swear, it wasn't me," Liz insisted, shocked.

Scout's mouth hung open until she grabbed her EVP recorder. "I'm recording now. Everyone stay quiet. Virginia, was that you? Do you want our help?"

For thirty seconds, they stood in tense anticipation, straining their ears for any sign of the mysterious voice. When Scout stopped the recording and played it back, the girl's voice returned.

"He'll kill me."

A deep growl boomed through the recorder, causing them to jump. LeVar, caught off guard, dropped the spirit box on the floor.

"My bad," he said, bending to retrieve the device. His previous skepticism was replaced by a fear that they might have stumbled upon something far more dangerous than he'd expected.

"Okay, this is getting real," Scout said. "I don't know what we just tapped into, but it doesn't feel right."

"I yelled at you," Liz said, her earlier flirtatiousness entirely forgotten. "Oh my God, Scout. That wasn't me. I would never accuse you of being jealous."

A tear crawled out of Scout's eye. "I didn't mean what I said either. It was like I wasn't the one speaking."

"I know, right? It's the energy in this room."

"You argued right after the wind blew through," he said.

"He's right."

LeVar hesitated, torn between wanting to investigate further and knowing that they were potentially putting themselves at risk. He recalled his own troubled past with the Kings, and how he'd fought to leave that life behind him. Now, as a deputy, he vowed to protect others from harm. Getting Liz and Scout out of the mansion alive was his priority.

"We have evidence of something happening here, but we need to be smart about how we handle it."

Scout turned to Liz. "Please tell me you recorded those voices."

Liz slapped her forehead and twirled to search for her video recorder. "No, I never started it." Yet when she lifted the camera, a red light shone above the lens. "Wait, it's recording. I must have forgotten to turn it off after I ... after we ..."

Yet they all knew the truth. The recorder had started on its own.

A door slammed outside the room. LeVar leaped out of his skin before throwing protective arms around the girls. Liz gasped in terror, her eyes wide.

"Yo, what was that?" he asked.

"That wind we felt might have caused the door to close," Scout said, though the tremor in her voice betrayed her lack of conviction.

Liz threw the equipment bag over her shoulder. "We should get out of here."

He said, "Like I've been tellin' you for hours."

As they moved down the constricted corridor, cobwebs dropped past their eyes like descending spiders.

"Here's the door," Scout said, aiming her flashlight. Her hand gripped the doorknob, but it wouldn't turn. She tried again, harder this time, but the door remained unyielding.

"Let me try." His powerful hands grasped the knob, twisting

and pulling with all his might. The door stood firm, refusing to open.

"What's happening?"

"This ain't right." Beads of sweat formed on his brow. He looked back at Liz and Scout, who stared at him with a mix of desperation and dread. "Something doesn't want us to leave."

Liz covered her mouth. "You don't think it's her, do you? Virginia?"

"Whatever it is, we need to find another way out."

"The only other way out is a three-story drop."

Scout's breath quickened. "Like the way Virginia Radford died."

39

Claire Brookins hunched over a table in the lab, her hair pulled back into a messy bun. She studied the bone carvings that rested at the center of Sheriff Shepherd's murder case.

The Carver. Even the name set her on edge.

Her student intern, Kalifa, a tall and slender young woman with tight braids and an air of quiet intelligence, checked her watch and realized the shift was over.

"Kalifa, before you go, have you seen my dissecting scissors?" Claire asked, her brows knitting together in frustration as she rummaged through her instruments.

"Can't say I have, Dr. Brookins. But I can help you look before I head out."

"Thanks, but don't worry about it. I'll find them. You worked yourself ragged today. Go get some rest."

"What's on the agenda for tomorrow?"

Claire paused, considering their ongoing investigation. "I want to finish analyzing these carvings and send the results to the sheriff's department. Also, I should check on that toxicology report for that teenage drowning victim."

Kalifa nodded, slipping on her coat. "See you tomorrow, Dr. Brookins."

"Goodnight, Kalifa."

Now alone, she continued her examination of the figurines. She knew how important her findings would be for Thomas and the rest of the team working to catch the killer. Her job was to identify the victim, but his DNA wasn't in the national database. It was like feeling her way through a maze while wearing a blindfold.

The room seemed colder now that Kalifa had gone. The harsh lighting reflected across the counters and instruments. She shook off her discomfort and ran another test. The missing scissors nagged at her. When had she seen them last? Yesterday, if she wasn't mistaken.

A muffled thud came from somewhere in the facility.

"Hello?" she called out, hoping Kalifa had returned for a forgotten item. "What did you forget?"

There was no response, only the hum of the lights and the distant whirr of the ventilation system. Claire debated whether to investigate or stay put in the safety of the lab. She grabbed a flashlight and headed toward the sound.

As she approached the supply room, she noticed the door was ajar.

"Kalifa?"

Holding her breath, Claire pushed the door open, revealing the origin of the disturbance. A box had fallen off a shelf, scattering evidence markers and adhesive labels across the linoleum.

"What the hell?"

She studied the shelf for a moment, trying to determine if there was any obvious cause for the accident, but she found none. How had the box fallen? The cleaners worked overnight and wouldn't arrive for another three hours. She crouched to clean the mess.

The missing shears popped into her mind again. A thief? Why would anyone steal her dissection scissors? Gathering the last of the scattered items from the floor, she released a nervous laugh.

"Boxes fall. Life happens."

She placed the recovered supplies on the counter, intending to reorganize them later. For now, she needed to finish her work.

Returning to the lab, she resumed her examination of the horrific figurines. As she traced the patterns etched into the bone, she marveled that a twisted mind had created them. She wondered what drove someone to commit such acts.

Her thoughts drifted back to the disturbance in the supply room. Each strange noise made her jump. The nagging feeling of being watched gave her goosebumps, and she shot furtive glances over her shoulder. She shook her head to dispel the irrational fear. Allowing the case to worm into her mind didn't serve her.

As she returned to the lab, she barely registered the faint click that echoed through the now empty facility. Darkness enveloped her. It wasn't until she caught her breath that she realized what had happened: The lab lights had shut down. They used motion sensors and turned off if you stood frozen for too long. She was all for saving energy, but this was ridiculous.

A quick wave of the hand turned on the lights. Before she returned to the carving, a crash spun her head around. A metal tray had fallen to the floor, louder than someone striking a cymbal.

Then dead silence. Her ears rang, and her pulse scampered like a jackrabbit.

"Okay, you know what?" she said to no one in particular. "I'm done for the night."

She packed the carvings away, her hands trembling. It was irrational, she knew, but she hated working alone in this place after dark. Strange that she could cut open corpses and go about tasks with bodies tucked away in steel drawers behind her, but being by herself in the lab made her grind her teeth.

As she stepped into the darkened hallway, she forced herself to breathe, convinced that any second now, she'd hear footsteps behind her or feel an icy hand on her shoulder. The exit stood ten steps away.

Claire stepped into the frigid night, pulling her coat together with one hand as she locked the doors. Nothing moved in the parking lot, which included only one vehicle—hers. The distant hum of the highway traveled on the wind. She turned up her collar.

She made her way across the parking lot, her eyes scanning the darkness. Her car sat under a lone light. She fumbled for her keys.

Just as her fingers closed around the metal keyring, a rustling sound came from behind her. She froze.

Fighting the urge to run, she forced herself to walk toward her car. But as she reached for the door handle, a figure emerged from the shadows and snatched her from behind. She screamed, struggling against the vice-like grip.

A stun gun pressed against her side. With a high-pitched whine, it sent shockwaves of agony through her body. Her vision blurred. Her strength ebbed away as the stun gun continued to buzz, and her limbs grew unresponsive.

In a matter of seconds, she fell limp into the attacker's arms. He lifted her with surprising strength. Her eyelids fluttered. Insane eyes peered through a raven mask.

In her mind, she batted at his face and kicked her legs. But her limbs refused to move. He rounded the building, where she saw another car hidden from view. The raven-man popped open the trunk and tossed her inside.

The darkness was suffocating, closing around Claire as she lay crumpled. Panic clawed at her chest as she tried to make sense of what had just happened. She needed to find a way out of this. If this was the Carver, she knew her fate. Would he dismember her while she squealed?

The car roared to life and pulled away, tossing her like a rag doll.

She screamed, but no one heard.

40

Thomas lay awake in the bedroom of his A-frame, staring at the exposed wooden beams overhead. The room's decor was simple and rustic—a few landscape paintings and an antique dresser. The king-sized bed, positioned across from a window that overlooked Wolf Lake, felt empty despite the warmth of the quilted comforter.

He replayed the events of the Coral Lake gala in his head. The Carver had coaxed him into visiting the gala, then walked right past him. And somehow another bone carving had ended up in his pocket. He had failed not only himself, but the people of Nightshade County as well.

The ring of his phone made him jump. He squinted at the screen and saw Aguilar's name. Was she still at work? He hesitated for a second before answering.

"Thomas," she said, "we've got a situation. A deputy found Claire's car in the parking lot of the county coroner's building, but the lab lights are off, and no one seems to be inside."

"Maybe she broke down and found another way home."

But he didn't believe his own words. He processed the information as a sick feeling of dread crept through him. "Okay, I'll call you back in a second."

Hanging up, he tried to stay quiet. Chelsey lay beside him, her chest rising and falling with the slow rhythm of deep sleep. He scrolled through his contacts and located Claire's cell, praying she would answer.

"Hey, this is Claire," her recorded voice said. "Leave a message and I'll get back to you."

He tried four more times, each voicemail message like a punch to his gut. It wasn't like her not to answer the phone in the middle of the night. Being on call was part of a medical examiner's job.

Not wanting to wake Chelsey, he grabbed his clothes and slipped out of the bedroom. Jack lifted his head in curiosity, then went back to sleep. Downstairs, he dialed Aguilar.

"Any luck?" the deputy asked as soon as she picked up.

"Nothing. Just her voicemail. I'm worried."

"So am I. Are you at the county coroner's building?"

"On my way."

"Give me ten minutes to get there."

Thomas hung up the phone, grabbed his keys, and raced out the door. As he climbed into his truck, his chest tightened with anxiety. He started the engine and sped off, hoping against hope that there was a logical explanation for Claire's car sitting abandoned in the parking lot. It was a challenge not to fixate on the worst outcomes.

He arrived at the county coroner's building and spotted Aguilar standing outside, her face tight with worry. A junior deputy checked over the car. Thomas parked his truck and surveyed the pavement. In the beam of his flashlight, signs of a struggle became clear—scuff marks on the pavement and tire tracks leading away from the scene.

"Looks like there was a fight," Thomas said.

"I stopped by to speak with her yesterday, and these tire tracks weren't here. They're fresh."

His mind spun with memories of the Coral Lake gala, and suddenly it all clicked. The dissecting shears. The Carver had left them at the gala, a cruel hint that Claire was his next target. There was no doubt the shears had come from the medical examiner's lab.

He rubbed his forehead. "The clue at the gala. It was right there in front of me."

"What clue?"

"The dissecting shears," Thomas said. "They belong to the medical examiner's lab. The Carver . . . he was telling us he planned to take Claire next, and I missed it."

"You can't blame yourself."

She was right, but the thought of what could happen to Claire if they didn't find her in time haunted him.

"If anything happens to her," Thomas whispered, "I don't know if I can live with myself."

"We'll find her. You have to believe that, Thomas."

"I'm trying. She's a friend. I just...I can't lose her. I can't."

He tried again to call Claire and got the same voicemail message.

"Still not answering?"

"He took her."

He pocketed his phone and scanned the deserted parking lot, the glow of streetlights doing little to push back the darkness.

Armed with a key to the facility, Thomas unlocked the door so his deputy could check inside. The Carver had broken into the lab just to steal the shears. Brazen. He joined Aguilar and assessed the parking lot, searching for evidence as to the identity of the killer.

He should have figured out the clue. The weight of that failure settled on him. Claire's blood was on his hands.

Would the Carver simply kill Claire, or would he go further? Thomas's stomach churned at the thought of receiving pieces of her, bone by bone.

He pushed those thoughts aside and focused on the present. "Keep searching the area," he said. "I'll issue a BOLO."

Together, they walked around the parking lot. Aguilar spotted a shiny object near the back of the building and called Thomas over. It was a silver bracelet, one that Claire always wore.

"That's hers," Thomas said. "She must have lost it in the struggle. Bag it as evidence. If we're lucky, we'll find his print on the bracelet."

"He's sending us a message. He wants us to know that he has her."

Thomas agreed. The Carver didn't make mistakes and leave clues behind. He wanted them to find the bracelet. He should have done more to protect her, but he hadn't understood the message at the gala.

Was the killer holding Claire hostage nearby, or had he taken her out of town? The man was affluent and possessed artistic ability. Not a lot to go on.

The sound of sirens approached. A state trooper patrol car screeched to a halt in front of the coroner's building. Two more officers jumped out, one of them holding a K-9 unit. He recognized the man with the dog as Trooper Fitzgerald.

"Thomas, what's going on?" Fitzgerald asked.

"It's Claire. She's missing. We found her car here, and there are signs of a struggle."

"We'll get a search party together and comb the area. I'll get bloodhounds on the scent. We'll find her, Thomas. Don't worry."

The K-9 unit sniffed around Claire's car, then led the

troopers toward the tire tracks. Much as he appreciated the help, the bloodhounds couldn't follow someone who'd departed the scene in a vehicle.

He stared into the darkness and sensed the night laughing at him.

41

The county coroner's building loomed before Thomas, the facade glowing under the icy February moonlight. His breath plumed out as he paced.

Where was Claire? In the office, he'd located the contact information for her student intern. He dialed Kalifa's number, cursing to himself when it went to voicemail. On the second call, she picked up, her voice thick with sleep.

"This is Sheriff Shepherd. Claire Brookins disappeared this evening, and her vehicle is still at the facility."

There was a sharp inhale on the other end of the line. "What do you mean, you can't find her? Have you checked inside the building? Sometimes she works too hard and falls asleep in her office."

"No one's in the building." He scrubbed a hand over his face. "I understand you worked with Claire this evening. I need you to come to the facility right away."

The line went quiet for a beat. "I'm on my way," she said, and the call disconnected.

Thomas resumed his pacing. His stomach churned as he thought about what the Carver was doing to Claire.

Don't go there. Not yet.

There were other explanations. Had to be.

Ten minutes later, he heard the approaching motor: Kalifa, pushing her little sedan to the limit to get there as fast as she could. Like him, she wouldn't rest until they found Claire.

He braced himself. Waiting. Hoping the intern would provide something, anything, to point him in the right direction.

The sedan skidded to a stop, and the door flew open. Kalifa stumbled out, shrugging into her coat.

Thomas went to meet her. "Thank you for coming. I need the security footage."

"Sheriff, the building doesn't have security cameras. There's no footage to look at." Her eyes were wide behind her glasses, pupils dilated in the sodium glow of the streetlights. "Sheriff, you don't think—"

"No." He cut her off before she could say it, the thought he'd been battling to suppress. "We don't know that."

Thomas paced back and forth. He needed to find Claire, and he had to find her now.

"I'm so sorry, Sheriff," Kalifa said, wringing her hands. "There aren't any cameras in the parking lot. The county never had a reason to install them."

The admission sent a jolt of frustration through Thomas, his body tensing with anger. "What do you mean there is no need for cameras? This is a government facility. How can you not have security measures in place?"

"Sheriff, please—" Kalifa interjected, but he was beyond listening.

"The lack of security might have cost us Claire's life."

"Hey, Thomas, let's take it easy, all right?" Aguilar said, emerging from the shadows.

Aguilar pulled him aside. "Listen, I understand you're scared for Claire. We all are. But yelling at Kalifa won't help. You need to communicate more effectively, or we won't get anywhere."

He clenched his jaw, trying to process Aguilar's words. In times of stress, he struggled to interact with others.

"A friend's life is on the line. How am I supposed to react?"

"Keep your emotions in check. When you're angry, people may feel defensive and less likely to cooperate. Also, make sure you're listening to what they have to say. Consider their perspective."

He knew all these things, but there was no time for polite conversation.

"I'll try my best to stay composed."

"Kalifa understands. She's just as scared as you are. Maybe more so."

He turned back to the intern, softening his expression. "Kalifa, I'm sorry for my outburst earlier. It was uncalled for. I know you'll do everything you can to help find Claire."

Kalifa looked at him for a moment, her eyes searching his face. She seemed to recognize the sincerity in his apology, and her tense posture relaxed. "It's not a problem. Just find her, please."

They were all on edge, desperate to find their missing friend. His phone buzzed with a message. He dared not read the text, afraid the killer was sending him pictures of what he was doing to Claire. But the message had come from Deputy Lambert, who was on his way to aid in the search.

The K-9 unit couldn't help, and the county had shirked its responsibility by not providing the coroner's building with security cameras. Despite everyone's willingness to help, there was only one thing Thomas could do.

Wait for the killer to send him a carving from his friend's bones.

42

LeVar stirred awake, the cold air of the dark corridor nipping at his skin. Opening his eyes, he saw Scout and Liz huddled together and shivering on the floor. He noticed the fear etched on their faces, even in slumber. How could he have fallen asleep? The locked door at the end of the hallway still prevented them from escaping.

"Scout, Liz," he whispered, shaking them. "Wake up."

Both girls opened their eyes, startled, as if waking from a nightmare. They looked up at him in confusion.

"What happened?" Scout stammered.

"Somehow, we fell asleep. We need to get outta the hallway. This place ain't safe."

Above their heads, the ceiling sagged as if it might collapse and crush them at any second.

"Where do we go?" Liz asked.

There was only one choice.

"Back to Virginia Radford's room. We're out of options."

The trio picked themselves up, their bodies stiff from sleeping on the hard floor. They made their way back to the bedroom.

As they entered the room, he sensed eyes watching him from the darkness. He looked at Scout and Liz, noticing their body language shift into a more defensive stance; they felt it too.

"Okay," he said, trying to project confidence. "We'll stay here for now. In the meantime, I'll call for help."

He didn't relish admitting he was locked in an abandoned mansion with two teenage ghost hunters, but the time for saving face had long passed. Who to call? Not Lambert. Definitely not Lambert. Thomas? Good lord, his mother? He settled on Raven and dialed her number.

Nothing.

"Must be an outage," he said.

Liz shook her head. "The ghosts won't let us use our phones."

"Come on. You're jumping to conclusions."

"LeVar," Scout said, "what if we're not alone?"

He peered around the room, worried she was right.

"Stick close. We got each other's back, no matter what."

The glow of his flashlight revealed the peeling wallpaper and the decrepit bed. They weren't safe, and the only escape was straight down. Out of the top-floor window, like Virginia Radford.

A gust of wind whipped through the room, causing the drapes to flutter. Both girls screamed in terror, clutching each other. LeVar spun around, searching for the cause of the disturbance.

"Keep calm, y'all," he said. "It's just the wind."

"Wind? From where?"

He was losing control of the situation.

"Old houses are drafty."

As he studied the bed's headboard, he noticed something that hadn't been there before. A message scrawled in the dust, beckoning him to read it.

Liz was too frightened to approach. Scout stayed by her side.

"What does it say?" Scout asked.

He leaned in closer, squinting to make out the words. A shock ran through his bones.

"It says, *Daddy pushed me.*"

"It's Virginia. She's communicating with us."

The girls burst into tears as the enormity of the situation took hold. He reached out and pulled them away from the bed, his arms encircling them as he tried to offer comfort.

"Hey, it's gonna be okay."

"Virginia's father killed her. We just solved a century-old mystery."

"We can't stay here," Liz whispered, her breath hitching with every sob. "This is getting too real."

LeVar agreed. "Grab your gear and contact Virginia's ghost. Maybe she can unlock the damn door."

Once they had the spirit box set up, he hesitated for a moment before addressing the empty room.

"Virginia Radford, if you're here with us, can you please communicate through this device? We saw your message. Is there another way out of this corridor?"

The static from the spirit box provided a chilling soundtrack to their mounting hopelessness. They asked questions about the message, about her father, and any connection to the strange occurrences in the house, but there was no reply.

"Maybe she doesn't want to talk to us," Liz said.

"Or maybe something's keeping her from speaking," Scout said.

LeVar frowned. "Or she told us all she wanted to say."

Did he believe in the supernatural now? He swore the message on the headboard hadn't been there before, but it was possible he'd overlooked it. Anyone could have written the message—Lambert, kids pulling a prank.

So why were their phones inoperative? Perhaps a cell tower had failed.

"Pack up the equipment," he said. "We're leaving. Now."

Liz stared. "But how? The door is locked."

"Then I'll break it down, no matter how long it takes."

Wasting no time, they tossed their devices into the bags. No one wanted to spend another second in the dead girl's bedroom.

At the end of the corridor, he studied the locked door. Was it jammed? He stepped forward, prepared to break down the door.

"Stand back," he warned as adrenaline surged through his body.

The girls moved away. He braced himself, preparing for impact.

But as he reached out to push against the door, it swung open with a creak, revealing nothing but darkness beyond.

"Wasn't this locked just a moment ago?" Liz whispered.

"Something's not right here."

Scout switched the bag to her other shoulder. "Don't ask questions. Just go through."

No sooner did they start down the hallway than his phone rang. Impossible. It wasn't working in the bedroom. He checked the caller ID and saw Thomas's name.

"LeVar, it's me," Thomas said. "I need you to listen. Claire Brookins has gone missing."

"Missing? But how? When?"

The girls looked at him in question, but he held up a hand.

"All I know is she disappeared after leaving work. I could use your help."

"Give me time to take Scout and Liz home."

"Wait, you're still inside Radford Mansion? It's three in the morning."

It was? He swiped the back of his hand across his lips.

"I'll explain later."

"Just get to the office, LeVar. I need all hands on deck."

LeVar led Scout and Liz down the staircase. Though he watched the shadows for hidden dangers, nothing prevented them from leaving. No unexplained sounds, no strange lights.

The girls questioned him about Thomas's call as they crossed the lower floor.

"I'll tell you everything in the car. Right now, all I want is to get out of here."

43

Claire's head throbbed as consciousness returned, her eyes fluttering open to pitch darkness. She tried to move, only to realize she was lying on her side in a cramped space, reeking of stale air and gasoline. As her hands explored the rough fabric beneath her body, she recognized the texture.

Panic surged through her as she remembered the bone carvings she'd studied for the sheriff's department. The Carver. Had the serial killer abducted her?

She screamed, her voice muffled by the confines of the trunk. Where was she? The rumble of the tires over the road gave her no clue.

The car struck a bump, and the momentum tossed her body upward. Her head struck the top. She crashed down on her spine. Her breathing grew labored as terror clawed at her chest. She needed to find a way out or a weapon to defend herself with.

Her fingers fumbled through the darkness, searching for anything that she could turn into a makeshift weapon. But all she found were the grooves in the carpet, a plastic ice scraper, and a sense of growing despair.

Every breath came harder than the last. The thought of sharing the same fate as the Carver's victims sent her into a frenzy—her limbs would be removed one by one, the bones carved into tiny sculptures and mailed to the sheriff.

Such thoughts wouldn't help her escape this mess. If she wanted any chance of surviving this nightmare, she needed to calm herself.

Her fingers brushed against the ice scraper again. It wasn't much of a weapon, but it would have to do. She realized her phone and keys were missing. The kidnapper had taken everything. Her frustration grew as she searched the trunk.

The car's engine roared as it sped around a curve. The vehicle swerved around corners, jolting Claire back and forth in the cramped space. She pressed her hands against the sides of the trunk, trying to steady herself.

Straining to hear sounds beyond the car, all she could make out was the relentless hum of the engine and tires rolling over the macadam. No way to tell if she was in the village or the country. As the car sped along, Claire envisioned the route they were taking. But every twist and turn seemed unfamiliar, leaving her with no sign of where the psycho was taking her.

The erratic journey continued as they weaved through the darkness. She wondered if he was doubling back so she wouldn't know their location. The engine revved louder, and her stomach churned as the car raced through what felt like a tunnel, the echo of the engine amplifying the danger.

She tried to recall leaving the county coroner's building after the box fell from the shelf and spooked her. But the memories seemed distant and unreachable, lost amid her growing dread. Had the killer been inside the building while she worked?

The car sped along, carrying her farther from the life she'd known and deeper into the terrifying unknown. Then the driver slammed the brakes and brought them to an abrupt halt. Time seemed to freeze. Seconds later, the trunk popped open, and the frigid night air rushed in.

As she squinted against the sudden brightness of the moon and stars, she saw him—the shadowy figure standing beside the car. Her muscles tensed. Adrenaline surged through her veins. She wouldn't succumb to torture without fighting.

"Get out," he said, his voice cold and emotionless.

As he grabbed her, she swung the ice scraper and clipped his head. He wrestled the weapon from her grip and tossed it aside. She lunged at the man and raked her nails at his eyes, but he sidestepped her attack. Undeterred, she attacked again, trying to bite his hand as it reached out to grab her.

"Nice try," he snarled, grabbing a fistful of her hair and wrenching her head back. Pain shot through Claire's skull. She gritted her teeth and spat in his face. "You're not going anywhere."

"Let me go!"

"Quiet," he said, slamming her head against the car.

Stars exploded across her vision as she struggled to remain conscious, her thoughts becoming disjointed. She threw an elbow into his ribs, but his grip on her hair was unrelenting. Again, he threw her head against the car. Her body went slack as he lifted her like a child's doll.

No one was coming to save her—not Sheriff Shepherd, not her friends, not her family. She was alone and at the mercy of a man who would slice her into pieces. The night air slid over her skin, making her tremble. He carried her through the darkness. Somewhere ahead, a light shone. Her eyelids kept fluttering shut, but she forced them open long enough to recognize they were outside a country house with no neighbors in sight.

The attacker's pace quickened as she regained enough

strength to struggle, her legs flailing. She knew it was futile, but she refused to give him the satisfaction of seeing her defeated.

"Where are you taking me?" she asked as she fought for breath. "Who are you?"

"Quiet," he said, his tone brooking no further argument. They approached the house, its windows staring down at her like malevolent eyes.

He kicked open the door and carried her across the threshold. Images of the gruesome carvings flashed in her memory.

She prayed her life wouldn't end like the other victims.

44

The moon tracked lower in the sky as LeVar pulled into Scout's driveway. He stared at the dashboard clock and winced; it was almost 4 a.m. Naomi would be fuming over their late arrival, but all that mattered was seeing Liz and Scout safely inside.

"Thanks for the ride, LeVar," Liz said, her voice soft with exhaustion. "I hope you find your friend."

"Stay safe. We'll find Claire."

Scout wanted to help, but he would have none of it.

He stayed in the car, watching as they entered the house. As soon as the door closed, he shifted into reverse and parked outside the A-frame. He raced back to the guesthouse, shedding his civilian clothes and donning his uniform with haste. When a friend was in danger, every minute counted. The investigation into the Carver had become personal.

Upon arriving at the sheriff's department, he found Aguilar, Chelsey, Raven, and Darren already inside, their faces tense and drawn. They huddled around a table littered with maps and notes, the weight of their task clear in their tired eyes.

"Thanks for coming, LeVar," Chelsey said, forcing a smile that didn't reach her eyes.

"Any updates?" he asked, not wasting any time.

"Nothing yet," Raven said, worry creasing her forehead.

"Thomas is waiting for you in his office," Aguilar informed him, nodding toward the door. "He's been pacing nonstop since he got here."

"Has anyone spoken to Naomi?" LeVar asked, unable to keep the concern from his voice.

"Scout spoke to her," Chelsey answered. "She was worried, but she understands. Sounds like you'll have a helluva story to tell after this nightmare ends."

"Time to find Claire."

"LeVar," Darren said, clapping a hand on his shoulder. "With everyone working together, we can't fail."

"Hope you're right, dawg," LeVar said, offering a tight-lipped smile before heading towards Thomas's office.

As he walked, he thought of Claire's life hanging in the balance and the monster holding her captive. He entered Thomas's office, pure adrenaline masking his fatigue. The only source of light came from a desk lamp. He found Thomas walking from one wall to the next, rubbing his forehead as if trying to massage away the stress.

"Thomas," LeVar said quietly, not wanting to startle him. "We're all here for you, man."

"I don't know where to start," Thomas said, shaking his head. His anxiety radiated off him in waves, flooding the office. "I can't see the pattern yet. If he cuts her up like he did the others—"

"Thomas, I'll help you find her. We're going to bring her home safe, I promise."

"God, I hope so." Thomas stared at the wall. "He gave me a clue, LeVar. The Carver. He left a pair of dissecting scissors for me to find at the Coral Lake gala, and I didn't put two and two together."

"Come out of your office and join the others. If you stay in here, you'll drive yourself insane."

"But I need to concentrate."

"No, you need to brainstorm. Let's go."

After LeVar coaxed Thomas out of the room, the desk phone rang; the sudden noise made everyone jump. Thomas answered the call, his face pale with anticipation. Before anyone could ask who was on the line, Thomas put the caller on speakerphone.

The voice on the other end was distorted, scratchy and muffled as if filtered through a faulty connection.

"Who is this?" Thomas said. "No more games."

"Sheriff Shepherd, do you remember me?" the voice taunted. As the connection cleared, sickness settled in LeVar's stomach. "The last time we spoke, I gave you a chance to dance with me, and you failed."

"The Carver." Thomas choked on the name as if it were poison.

"Very good, Sheriff. You always were a quick study. The clock is ticking, and your precious Claire won't stay intact forever."

"Where is she?"

"That's for you to find out. You have until midnight to find her. That's less than twenty hours. If you fail, don't worry. I'll send her back to you. In a box."

The room fell silent as a chilling sound pierced the air—Claire's screams. Her voice was hoarse and full of agony, echoing through the speaker and making LeVar's blood run cold.

"Who are you?"

"So impatient. Remember, you have until midnight tomorrow to find Claire. Fail, and I'll send you a fresh carving."

Thomas looked at LeVar and Aguilar in desperation. "Why are you doing this to us?"

"Payback, Sheriff. For the way you treated my family."

The line went dead, leaving only the ghostly echo of Claire's screams in the room. Thomas slammed the phone and stared at the maps and notes scattered across the table.

"For what I did to whose family?" Thomas asked the room. Chelsey's mouth fell open, but no answer came forth. "I told you this was personal."

The others gathered around the table, their expressions serious. Laid out before them was a map with pins stuck at different points.

"You placed pins on the Coral Lake gala and the coroner's building," LeVar said. "What do you see, Shep?"

Thomas noticed patterns and connections the others couldn't see, piecing together clues like a computer.

The sheriff didn't answer. He scratched behind his ear with uncertainty.

"Tell us, Thomas," Chelsey said, taking his hand. "I see the wheels turning in your head."

"The coroner's building doesn't have security cameras, but there's a digital log of when people come and go. Claire walked out the door twenty-eight minutes after I encountered the man in the raven's mask at the gala."

"You remember the time you bumped into someone?" Raven asked, agape.

"Don't you remember times when something unusual occurs?" They all gave him blank looks. "After he passed me the raven figurine, he escaped the gala. I assume he parked close to the entrance so he could leave in a hurry. Even so, it took him two minutes to weave through the dancers, cross the floor, and reach his vehicle."

"Two minutes," Darren said, rubbing his chin. "How did you ... never mind."

"This guy is intelligent. He wouldn't speed and risk the

police pulling him over. But that's not all. He needed time to hide his vehicle so Claire wouldn't see him. Let's say six minutes."

"If you say so."

"Predatory serial killers who hunt in one region don't wander far from their homes. If we assume the gala and coroner's building are each within a thirty-minute drive from his house, we can draw overlapping circles." Thomas drew two radii and jabbed a forefinger at the intersection. "That leaves us an area approximately twelve miles tall and wide."

"But twelve miles north and south," Raven said. "That has to be more than—"

"Yes, it's 144 square miles."

LeVar arched an eyebrow. "Shep Dawg, how are we supposed to search 144 square miles in twenty hours?"

"We can narrow the area by focusing on the missing person's list," Chelsey said, snapping her fingers in understanding.

"Now you're getting it," Thomas said. "By sticking to the people who vanished inside the overlap, you can whittle down the missing people to focus on. There's a pattern. We just have to identify it."

The others leaned in, following his train of thought.

"Maybe he's trying to recreate something from his past," Darren said.

"Or he's using the geography of the area to his advantage," Aguilar said, studying the topography of the map.

Thomas shook his head. "No. He's out for revenge, and I'm the target."

45

The old house groaned beneath the weight of its own decay, as if it were some ancient beast struggling for breath. Floorboards creaked under each tentative step, whispering secrets lost to time. It wasn't so much a home as a place for pain and killing.

Claire struggled against the ropes that held her to a wooden chair in the center of this decaying tomb. Her heart pounded against her ribcage, a desperate drumbeat that echoed through her body. Bloodstains marred the floor and walls. This was where the Carver carried out his unspeakable acts.

The room smelled of damp, rotting wood mingled with the unmistakable metallic tang of blood. She was not the first person to occupy this chair, and she would breathe her last breath here if she couldn't find a way out.

She had spent countless hours studying the gruesome relics sent by the Carver, attempting to piece together the puzzle. Now she was a part of it, another unwilling participant.

As she scanned the room, she noticed a glint of light reflecting off something on the far side. It was a small mirror, cracked and clouded with age. With a jolt of panic, she realized the killer had placed it there so she could watch herself screaming while he tore her to pieces.

In this place, where so many had met their end, she would either find the strength to survive or succumb to the same fate that had befallen the psychopath's victims.

The groan of a floorboard made her breath catch in her throat. She turned her head as far as the restraints would allow, but she only caught glimpses of the figure emerging from the shadows. He was tall and broad-shouldered, his weight causing the old floor beneath him to protest. His clothes were dark, nondescript, and stained with what must be the blood of his previous victims. On a wooden table lay a raven's mask.

"Dr. Brookins," he said. "I've been looking forward to our little meeting."

He stepped into the light, and Claire felt a shiver of terror run down her spine. The Carver's eyes were pools of darkness. They glinted in the weak light as if they alone held all the malice and cruelty of which this man was capable.

"Why me?"

A grin spread across his face. "You've become something of an expert on my work, haven't you? And I can't have someone like you snooping around, uncovering my secrets. Besides, I want to make your sheriff friend suffer. Imagine his screams when I send your body parts to him. Fine art can't wait. Let's get started, shall we?"

From the shadows, he produced a bone saw, its serrated teeth marred with blood. He gave it a quick flick, and the metal sang in response, a dreadful sound that sent chills down Claire's spine.

"First, your arms," he said, as if discussing the weather. "Then your legs. I'll take my time so you can fully appreciate my work. Any last words before I begin?" the Carver asked, bringing the saw closer to her flesh.

"Go to hell."

"Interesting choice," he said, his dark eyes dancing with madness. "But hell will have to wait. Justice first."

He raised the saw, its teeth poised to bite into her tender flesh. As the blade descended, she braced herself for the pain.

"Wait! Don't do this. There must be another way."

The Carver paused, the bone saw hovering above her skin. He tilted his head, studying her tear-streaked face. "You think your pleas will save you?" he asked, his tone mocking. "Pleas never saved my family."

"I want to understand," she said, trying to appeal to any shred of humanity that might still exist within him.

"Understand? You've been studying my artistry, haven't you? You see beauty in my creation, yet here you are, begging for mercy. How very . . . contradictory."

"What do you gain from this?"

"Ah, the curious mind of a scientist," he taunted. "Very well. I'll indulge your curiosity before I take a limb. You see, my dear Claire, my art is not simply about the act of carving. It's an expression of power. Through the figurines, you will live forever. As I carve, I imbue their bones with my own desires, forever marking them as mine."

Claire shuddered. She couldn't reason with him; he was too far gone, lost in his own madness. But why was he using her to get to Thomas? Who was this man?

"Your studies intrigue me. No one has ever shown such interest in my work, such dedication to unlocking its secrets." He withdrew a scalpel from his pocket and held it up, letting the light catch the tip. "You see too much. I think I'll start with your eyes."

"What do you want with Thomas? What did he ever do to you?"

"You don't remember, do you? Of course not. That idiot

Virgil Harbaugh preceded you. The sheriff won't be able to save you this time. It's just you and me."

She spied a loose floorboard near her feet, and an idea formed. She shifted her foot, trying to maneuver it beneath the board. If she could somehow use it to free herself, even partially, it might be enough.

The scalpel loomed before her eye.

"The sheriff will make you pay for this. He'll put the pieces together. He always does."

"By then, you'll be my personal jigsaw puzzle. But please, continue to entertain me with your futile hope."

As the scalpel inched closer, Claire's foot found purchase under the floorboard. With a surge of desperation, she pushed up, sending the board flying into the air.

The end slammed against his leg and drove a rusty nail into his flesh. Seizing her chance, she threw her weight against the chair, toppling it to the side and avoiding the swipe of the scalpel. As he shouted in pain, she kicked out. The heel of her foot struck his leg and tripped him.

The scalpel fell to the floor as her bindings unraveled from the broken chair. His eyes widened as he saw what she intended.

Her hand clasped around the scalpel before he could stop her. She lashed out, slicing the wicked blade across his arm. Blood splattered. He screamed.

His arms trembling, the madman reached for a knife. The instant before their weapons met flesh, the room seemed to freeze, leaving both predator and prey suspended in the fragile balance between life and death.

46

Exhaustion tugged at Thomas. Except for two hours of uncomfortable sleep in his office chair, he'd worked from sunup until sundown. His team had fared no better. Almost twenty-four hours of following up on leads and examining the Coral Lake gala guest list had yielded no results.

As darkness spread over Nightshade County, he loomed over the table, his eyes locked on a map marked with pins and strings. The impending deadline bore down on him as midnight drew closer. Nervous silence filled the room, broken only by the occasional shuffling of papers or the rattle of the heating system.

Determined expressions marked the faces of each member of the team: Aguilar, the seasoned deputy who had seen too many lives lost during her time on the force; LeVar, the young deputy who had left his life as a gang member behind to protect and serve; Chelsey, an expert private investigator; Darren, the former police officer turned forest ranger who donated his time whenever it was needed; and Raven, LeVar's sister, whose intelligence and tenacity made her an invaluable asset.

Chelsey paged through the reports as he tapped a forefinger

over two overlapping circles between the gala and the county coroner's building.

Urgency made Thomas's throat constrict. His connection to Claire Brookins, Nightshade County's first female medical examiner, made this case even more personal. She was one of them, part of their close-knit community, and Thomas couldn't bear the thought of losing her.

"Keep going through the missing persons list," Thomas said. "There has to be a connection we're missing."

Darren's eyes flicked from one report to another, his stubbled face creased with concentration. "What about the gala? Does anyone on the guest list stand out as a suspect?"

"Chelsey and Raven are cross-referencing the list as we speak."

"Maybe it's time we consider other avenues," Aguilar said.

"Like what?"

"Like past investigations. You say the killer is making this personal."

"I went through the high-profile arrest records. Everyone who is still alive is in prison." His attention returned to the map, searching for a pattern he'd overlooked. "Everyone, keep pushing. Claire's life depends on us."

"I counted nine missing persons in the target area over the past year." He could see the wheels turning in her mind as she continued. "It's like they vanished into thin air. No connections between them, no real patterns. Men, women, varying age brackets."

"Chelsey," Thomas said, "cross-reference the missing persons list with the guest list from the Coral Lake gala. Target guests who live within twenty miles of a missing person."

"Got it," Chelsey replied, her fingers drumming against the keyboard. "I'll look for any overlap. It might not be much, but it's a start."

As Chelsey worked, the team exchanged uneasy glances.

"Still nine potential suspects," LeVar muttered, rubbing his temples. "We gotta narrow this down somehow."

"Let's focus on those with known criminal histories or any connection to Claire," Raven said.

"Good idea," Thomas agreed, doing his best to hold on to hope. "Keep digging. We're running out of time."

Chelsey's eyes flicked between the two lists, searching for any correlation that could provide the crucial clue they needed. The clock ticked in the background, reminding them of the impending midnight deadline. "Here's one. Maybe it's our break?"

Darren leaned forward, his fingers tapping on the table as he studied the name. "Gresham Thompson lived inside the overlapping radii of both the gala and the county coroner's office. He's been missing for three weeks now, and his house was within twenty miles of eight people on the guest list. He was last seen just two blocks away from the coroner's office. Your deputies discovered his car abandoned in an alley. No sign of foul play."

Thomas nodded. "I remember the car. Let's call Thompson's family. See if he had any enemies."

Aguilar grabbed the phone and dialed the number, placing the conversation on speakerphone. As they waited, LeVar paced.

"Hello?" a woman's voice answered on the other end of the line.

"Mrs. Thompson? This is Deputy Aguilar from the Wolf Lake Sheriff's Department. We're investigating your husband's disappearance, and we were hoping you could help us with some information."

"What do you need to know?"

"Did your husband have any enemies? Anyone you can think of who would want to harm him?"

The team listened, each member holding a breath, waiting

for a piece of information that might lead them closer to finding Claire and the killer.

"Gresham was a good man. He didn't have any enemies. He had a few arguments with some coworkers, but nothing that would lead to ... well, you know."

Another two minutes of questioning led them nowhere.

"Thank you for your help, Mrs. Thompson," Aguilar said. "We'll be in touch if we have any further questions."

"Please find Gresham," the woman said, sobbing.

Thomas' eyes darted from the clock to his team members. Eight o'clock. Four hours until the Carver sent him the first body part.

"We need a fresh approach," Thomas said. "Go through the missing persons list again. Look for patterns, similarities, anything that could connect them to Claire or the gala."

Raven typed away on a computer, cross-referencing the guest list with the missing persons database, while Chelsey combed through news articles and police reports for any overlooked details.

"Hey, Thomas," LeVar called out. "I found something interesting. There's a note here about one of the missing women. She had an argument with someone who attended the Coral Lake gala just before she disappeared."

"Good catch, LeVar," Thomas replied, his interest piqued. "What's the name of the woman?"

"Melissa Chambers," LeVar said, scanning the report. "It doesn't say much about the argument, only that it happened."

"Who was the gala attendee?"

LeVar's face fell. "Dead end. A seventy-two-year-old lady name Connie Blankenship. I don't think Mrs. Blankenship is the Carver. Sorry for getting your hopes up."

"Keep that train of thought, LeVar. You'll find something."

Thomas expected the phone to ring with another taunt from

the killer. Nothing since last night. Gresham Thompson fit as a potential victim. He was a male who fell into the age bracket Claire had estimated after studying the crow figurine. How long had the killer watched the medical examiner before striking?

An enemy from Thomas's past had returned, seeking revenge.

47

"Chelsey, focus your efforts on everyone living within twenty miles of the coroner's office and the Coral Lake gala who went missing in the last seven days. The killer is escalating."

"Got it, Thomas," Chelsey said. She swiveled back to her computer and ran another query.

Thomas chewed the inside of his cheek. What if they were too late? What if the killer murdered Claire before the deadline?

"Thomas," Lambert said, his buzz cut bristling beneath the lights, "we've got a list of names here. People who lived close to the coroner's office and attended the gala."

Lambert had just arrived and was working for his eighth straight day without a break, but he didn't mind. He assisted Chelsey and fed information to the other team members.

"Good work, folks," Thomas said.

"Lambert is right," said Chelsey. "There are three names that match the criteria you gave me."

"Let's see them." Thomas leaned over her shoulder and studied the screen. "Gather all the information you can on these people. We'll split up and investigate each lead."

"Understood. Here's one name that sticks out: Parry Bonner. He went missing earlier this week after leaving Kane Grove Builders. That's within our search radius, and the store is open twenty-four hours a day."

The clock read 9:15 p.m. Time was slipping through their fingers. He called up the missing person's report and scanned the details. Yes, Bonner fit his criteria. Like Gresham Thompson, he was male and the right age. Had one of Bonner's bones adorned his desk?

"I'm convinced. Keep working while we check it out." He beckoned to Aguilar and LeVar, who had been waiting for further instructions. "You two are with me. We need to find out if anyone saw something unusual the night Bonner disappeared."

Twenty minutes later, they arrived at Kane Grove Builders. The store's lights were blinding beneath the black sky. Thomas led the way inside.

"Excuse me," Thomas said to a manager. "We're looking for information about Parry Bonner. He was here the night he disappeared. Is there anything you can tell us?"

"I wasn't around, but Pete was." The manager pointed at a gangling man stocking the shelves. "He and Parry are close."

"Appreciate it."

They approached Pete, who set a boxed ceiling fan on the upper shelf.

"Pete? I'm Sheriff Thomas Shepherd. We're looking for information about Parry Bonner's disappearance."

"Sure thing, Sheriff," the employee replied, dusting off his hands. "I was working that night. Everyone loves Parry. Nice guy, always the first to lend a hand. You're gonna find him, aren't you?"

"That's my intention. Did you notice anyone bothering Parry or acting strange?"

"Acting strange? Kinda," Pete said, shaking his head. "There was a guy asking about some pretty odd stuff."

LeVar tilted his head. "What kind of odd stuff?"

"He wanted a saw sharp enough to cut through bone. Parry figured the man was joking. People say weird stuff to get a laugh."

"Did you get a look at this guy?" Aguilar asked.

"Sorta. His back was to me most of the time. Big dude, muscular arms and shoulders. Dark hair."

"Age?"

"Didn't get a good look at his face. Hey, we're a regional chain, so this place has tons of security cameras. I'd check with the manager."

"Thank you," Thomas said, exchanging a glance with Aguilar and LeVar. They'd found another piece of the puzzle. "If you remember anything else, please contact the sheriff's department."

Outside the manager's office, Thomas leaned against the wall, deep in thought. Aguilar and LeVar stood beside him, waiting for the manager to return.

"Parry Bonner could be our victim," Thomas said. "We need to find whoever was asking about those saws."

"I have a sick feeling the stranger is our killer," LeVar said.

"Could be," Thomas said. "But we won't know for sure until we figure out who he is."

The whirring of saws and the pounding of hammers filled the air as they stood outside the manager's office. The scent of freshly cut wood mingled with the metallic tang of sharpened tools.

A minute later, the manager rushed back to them, wiping his hands on his pants.

"Sorry, Sheriff. I'm always putting out fires."

"It's all right, sir," Thomas said, nodding. "You've been very helpful. Can we look at your security footage from the night Parry Bonner disappeared?"

"I don't see why not," the manager said, leading them to an office in the back.

The room was cramped and filled with monitors displaying various angles of the store. The clock on the wall ticked, echoing the heartbeat in Thomas's chest. He knew they were close to uncovering the truth, but they only had a little over two hours.

"Here," the manager said, rewinding the footage to the night in question. "This should be the correct time frame."

As the video played, Thomas, Aguilar, and LeVar watched, searching for any sign of their suspect. And there he was, talking to Parry Bonner by the saws. The camera angle obscured his face, leaving them with nothing but a vague description.

"Ain't helping," LeVar muttered under his breath.

"Keep looking," Thomas said. "There has to be something we can use."

They continued combing through the footage, growing more desperate as the minutes ticked away. But despite their determination, they couldn't find anything that revealed the stranger's identity.

"Let's check neighboring businesses," Thomas said, his eyes still glued to the screen. "There must be footage that can give us a clearer picture. If we're lucky, we'll catch him driving out of the parking lot."

"Smart idea," Aguilar agreed, pulling up a list of establishments in the area.

As they sifted through their options, LeVar suggested they focus on a gas station across the street from Kane Grove Builders. "It's open twenty-four hours," he pointed out. "And it has a clear view of the parking lot."

"Perfect. Let's see what they've got," Thomas said.

The boy working behind the register gulped when he saw

the sheriff and two deputies striding into the store. He gave the officers anything they wanted, allowing them to sift through the recording.

In another tiny room, Thomas fast-forwarded through the gas station's security footage, scanning the screen for any sign of Parry Bonner or the stranger. Then, as if by divine intervention, they spotted a car ramming Bonner from behind.

"Stop," said LeVar. "Wind it back and play it at normal speed."

On the screen, they watched the car pull into the frame moments after Bonner left the store. The man had been waiting for his target. The car idled for a beat, then raced up behind Bonner's vehicle.

"Gotcha," Aguilar smiled.

"Can we get a license plate?" Thomas asked, knowing the answer might be their key to finding Claire.

"Let me zoom in," LeVar said. He isolated the vehicle, but the resulting image remained blurry.

"Send it to the lab. They can clean it up enough to read."

"Will do."

It was now 10 p.m. Two hours until the killer made good on his promise. If only they had another hour to work with.

48

Claire's eyes fluttered open, her vision blurred and spinning. From her scalp to her aching legs, every inch of her body screamed in pain. She recalled the struggle—the way she'd sliced the murderer's arm with the scalpel. Ultimately, he'd overpowered her, tied her up once more, and left her in this room. He hadn't shown himself since, and Claire knew she must have hurt him.

As she focused on her surroundings, her ears picked up a disturbing sound. A whistling tune resonated through the house, distant yet clear. It was a haunting melody, the volume ebbing and flowing as if the source moved through the halls. Her captor was somewhere nearby.

She checked the ropes holding her wrists against the chair arms. They were loose, as he'd tied her in a hurry, intent on stopping his blood loss. She couldn't shake the dizziness fogging her mind; it clung to her body with filthy fingers, making it difficult to think straight.

The pitch-black outside the window told her midnight was approaching. Almost out of time.

The whistling echoed through the halls, each note a chilling reminder of the Carver's brutality and sadism. As the tune danced through the air, her fear intensified. He would return soon, and when he did, he would inflict unthinkable pain.

Had to focus. Had to escape the bindings before the clock struck midnight.

The scent of blood was unmistakable, a coppery stench that polluted the air. Her eyes darted around the room, taking in the gruesome tableau. Blood splatters marred the walls and floor, a macabre testament to the killer's cruelty. As she shifted in her chair, she felt a sticky sensation beneath her feet. The very floor was saturated with the lifeblood of past victims.

Nausea rose inside her. She focused on steadying her breath, working to keep the bile from surging its way up her throat. She couldn't end up like the others.

As desperation sent her into a frenzy, Claire spotted something glinting in the corner—a knife, its blade reflecting the light. Hope raced through her veins. She realized the killer meant to use the knife on her, yet it lay tantalizingly close, a potential lifeline against her fate. Had he lost it in the struggle and forgotten?

Her eyes fixed on the weapon. She had to reach it somehow, but her bound hands made it impossible.

Grinding her teeth, she rocked the chair from side to side, pushing herself to the point of collapse. With a grunt of effort, she knocked the chair over, the impact jarring her body. Ignoring the pain, she wriggled her wrists against the ropes.

Had he heard? The whistling continued.

Sweat beaded on her brow. Inch by inch, she felt the ropes give way until her hands slipped free.

She crawled toward the knife as quickly as her weakened body allowed. Her fingers wrapped around the handle, a surge of hope coursing through her.

Battling another wave of vertigo, she clutched the knife. In the muddy light, the blade seemed to take on a life of its own, reflecting distorted shapes and shadows on the blood-spattered walls.

She glimpsed a figure in the reflection. A tall, broad-shouldered man, his face contorted by a sinister grin.

The Carver had returned.

He approached her from behind, unaware that she saw him. In his gloved hand, he held a bone saw.

When he was inches away, she spun around, slashing the knife through the air. It plunged into the killer's shoulder, sinking into his flesh with a tearing sound. He recoiled, a pained grunt escaping his lips.

The madman stumbled back, his hands clutching the wound. His breath came in ragged gasps, and he stared at Claire with a mix of shock and rage. The bone saw clattered to the floor.

Then he smiled.

She threw herself out of the way as he lunged. His body collided with the table and sent more weapons toppling to the floor. Her feet skidded against the bloody floorboards.

As he bellowed, she staggered out of the room.

49

The ring of the desk phone sent a flare of hope through Thomas. At the sheriff's department, he had a task force ready to rescue Claire and stop the Carver, but not until the lab cleaned up the video footage.

"Thomas," the IT specialist on the line said, "we cleaned up the image and identified the license plate. It belongs to a New York driver named Jack Kemper."

"Kemper." Thomas snapped his fingers and pointed at Aguilar, who tossed him a pen.

He tried to remember if he had heard that name before, but his mind drew a blank. Who was Jack Kemper, and why was he seeking revenge on the sheriff's department?

Chelsey spoke up. "Jack Kemper attended the gala."

"Kemper has to be our guy. Give me everything you have on him."

"He owns two pieces of real estate—a mansion in Coral Lake and a house in the woods."

"If he's our killer, then I'll bet anything he took her to the forest. He needs privacy."

"That house is located five miles from the county coroner's building."

Thomas grabbed his jacket. "Lambert and LeVar, you'll accompany me to the first location. We'll coordinate with the state troopers."

"Be careful," Chelsey said, touching his arm before she stepped back.

The responsibility settled on his shoulders. He couldn't let anything happen to Claire, not when they were so close to finding her.

He gathered the team.

"We have reason to believe that Jack Kemper is the Carver and that Claire Brookins is being held at his house in the woods. We'll work with the state troopers to execute a swift operation. Deputy Lambert, you'll run point."

"Got it, Thomas," Lambert said.

"All right. I want three deputies to head to Kemper's Coral Lake address as a precaution," Thomas instructed as he studied the digital map on the computer screen. "Aguilar, what can you tell me about his house in the woods?"

"Isolated," Aguilar said, zooming in on the map. "No close neighbors, which makes it an ideal spot for torturing victims without drawing attention."

"That has to be the place. Let's move out."

As Aguilar contacted the state police to inform them of the operation, Thomas led Lambert and LeVar to the cruiser. The night air chilled his skin.

"Stay sharp," he said as they climbed in. "We don't know Kemper's background or why he's doing this."

"Understood," said LeVar, his dreadlocks swaying as he nodded. The former gang member had come a long way, and Thomas couldn't be prouder to have LeVar by his side.

Lambert called out from the driver's seat. "You know we'll do everything we can to get her back, right?"

"I know," Thomas said, his eyes meeting Lambert's. "I trust you both."

The drive to the rendezvous point with the state troopers was tense, each passing mile bringing them closer to the unknown.

"Thomas," LeVar said, breaking the silence. "You really think Kemper is the Carver? Why would he go after you?"

"Everything we've found points to him. But we won't know what his motivations are until we take him down."

"And we'll take him down hard. He's a killer and a sadist, and anyone who crosses my friends pays a steep price."

As they neared the rendezvous point, Thomas allowed himself a moment of introspection. Saving Claire and catching the Carver was all that mattered now, and he knew the upcoming operation would test the limits of their teamwork. But as he looked at Lambert and LeVar, he remembered the strength they possessed when everyone stood together.

"What you said, LeVar. We'll take him down hard."

"That's the badass Shep I know and love."

The dashboard clock read 11:45 p.m. when they pulled up to the rendezvous point, a desolate stretch of road outside Wolf Lake. As Thomas killed the engine, his fists clenched at the thought of his friend bound and terrified. He whispered a quiet prayer for her safety.

LeVar unbuckled his seatbelt. "Fitzgerald's crew is already here." He pointed to a cluster of state trooper vehicles parked nearby, their red and blue lights spinning over the surrounding woods.

"Let's not keep them waiting." Thomas stepped out of the truck. The air stung his cheeks, but he welcomed the jolt, steeling himself for the task ahead.

State Trooper Fitzgerald, a tall man with black hair that wasn't much longer than Lambert's, approached him with an outstretched hand. "Thomas, Aguilar briefed us on the situation. Let's get down to business."

"We believe Kemper is holding Claire at his house on Morning Star Lane, five miles from the county coroner's building. Our priority is getting her out alive."

"What's the plan?"

"His property is isolated, which means we can't risk alerting him with a frontal assault." They all looked at Thomas for direction. "We need to approach from multiple directions, using the cover of the woods to get as close as possible before making our move."

"Sounds like a solid plan," Fitzgerald said. "My team will follow your lead."

"One problem. We're racing against the clock."

"Midnight, right?"

"The deadline is approaching. Once the clock strikes twelve, the time for discretion ends."

The state trooper tapped his holster. "My pleasure."

"Good. Lambert and LeVar, we'll attack from the east. Fitzgerald, you take two of your troopers and approach from the west. The rest of your team comes in through the back door."

"Got it. Let's synchronize our watches."

As they prepared for the operation, Thomas felt a knot of anxiety twist in his stomach. The stakes had never been higher. He drew strength from the unwavering support of his team.

"Remember," he told them, "our priority is Claire's safety. Stay focused and stay sharp."

"Roger that," Lambert said.

LeVar nodded in agreement, his eyes burning with intensity.

"Good luck, gentlemen," Fitzgerald added, his voice steady and confident. "We'll see you on the other side."

Full dark smothered the landscape, leaving only the cold glow of the moon to guide them as they drove through the woods.

Thomas focused on the narrow winding road. "We need to approach Kemper's house without alerting him."

"Considering the isolated location, I suggest we park our vehicles out of view of the house and continue on foot," Lambert said. "That should minimize our chances of being detected."

LeVar chimed in: "And if we use the cover of the trees, we can get even closer before he spots us. Taking the topography into account, there seems to be a small creek just north of the property. We could follow it until we're within striking distance of the house." LeVar showed Lambert a meandering blue line on the map.

They parked the cruiser in a spot where it would be hidden by the shadows of the towering trees. As they disembarked, Thomas checked his gun.

With each step toward Kemper's house, tension grew like an electric current, humming beneath the surface of their quiet determination. The outline of the house appeared through the trees. He gave a last nod to his team before they disappeared into the darkness.

50

Claire's legs trembled beneath her. The muscles in her thighs strained with her effort to remain upright. Her vision blurred, making it difficult to discern the dark shapes of the unfamiliar rooms. Each step was a painful endeavor. Her ankle throbbed from the fall she had taken earlier.

In the shadows, the Carver watched her struggle, his sadistic grin hidden behind the crusted blood covering half of his face. His right hand clutched his shoulder where the knife had pierced him, but his determination to catch Claire overrode the pain.

Where the hell was the exit? Mud filled her brain. She couldn't recognize one room from the next. Whatever he'd injected her with clouded her mind and suppressed her instincts. Some kind of drug.

"I'm coming, Claire."

The killer's voice reverberated behind her. His footsteps grew closer, each sending tremors of terror through her. But where was he?

"I'm going to chop you into pieces."

His laughter echoed through the house, coming from everywhere at once. Her eyes dropped to the floor, and she spotted blood droplets. He'd come this way. Was she walking in circles?

She stumbled forward. Her shoulder collided with the wall, and she fought the urge to vomit as the room spun.

Her vision blurry, she limped through the hallway while a plan hatched in her mind.

"Can't find your way out?"

It sounded like he was right behind her. She swung her head around, but an empty corridor revealed two rooms she swore she'd passed twice.

Had to keep moving. Where was the exit? The house couldn't be this large; the drugs were playing tricks with her sense of direction. She forced herself to keep moving.

As she turned a corner, the gleam of metal caught her eye. A breaker box lay against the wall, its gray surface scratched and worn with age. It presented her with a desperate chance for survival.

Claire stumbled toward the box, her fingers grasping for the handle as she struggled to ignore the pain in her bones. His footsteps echoed through the hallway. He had to be right behind her.

She was too confused to locate the door, but it wouldn't matter if he couldn't see her.

Her fingers found purchase on the cold metal handle. With a moan, she yanked open the breaker box door, revealing a row of switches inside. A flick of her wrist switched off the main breaker, plunging the house into total blackness.

His footsteps stopped; he had been startled by the sudden darkness.

Claire held her breath, listening for the killer. She had bought herself a little time. It was enough. In the darkness, he would be just as blind as her. She'd leveled the playing field.

Feeling for the wall, she dropped to her hands and knees. The darkness was absolute, like a heavy blanket smothering her senses.

"Where are you, Claire?"

She started crawling.

"I'll find you. And when I do, I'll chop you into pieces so small they'll never be able to put you back together."

She shuddered, her fingers digging into the floor as she blindly crawled, trying to keep her progress quiet. She felt the rough edges of splintered wood, the jagged remnants of furniture destroyed by the man who now hunted her.

An unmistakable creak echoed through the house, and Claire realized the killer must have stepped on a loose floorboard. In that instant, she decided. Fight or flight. She couldn't run anymore.

She hesitated, her trembling hands hovering above the floor, searching for something she could use as a weapon. All she found was broken glass, shattered picture frames, and debris from their deadly game of cat and mouse. She tucked a shard into her palm.

"Tick-tock, Claire. Where's your precious sheriff?"

As the sound of his steps grew louder, she braced herself for the confrontation. She might not have a weapon, but she had her wits. In the darkness, perhaps that would be enough.

Her hands sank into the thick layer of dust on the floor. And something sticky. His blood, or that of his victims? The footsteps stopped again, and for a moment there was only silence. She strained to catch any sign of his movements.

Then it came. The rustle of fabric against skin, and she knew he was close. Too close.

The floor groaned beneath his weight. Amid the all-encompassing black, she knew where he was. Two steps behind her.

As soon as she heard his breath, she turned and lashed out

with the glass shard, raking it across his face. He screamed and stumbled against the wall.

She leaped to her feet and dragged her injured ankle behind her. The drugs were wearing off. Her senses returned as he ambled after her.

A chill touched her flesh, and this time it wasn't fear. Outside air.

The door was close.

51

Through the dense woods, Thomas led LeVar and Lambert across the snowy landscape. The deputies scanned the area, their hands resting on their guns.

Lambert trailed them. He moved like an experienced soldier, which was no surprise given his time in the army. He removed the gun from its holster, ready for the unexpected.

The state-trooper siege team approached from the opposite side of the woods, their equipment rustling as they moved through the snow-covered underbrush. Each member wore tactical gear and carried firearms suited to the task at hand.

They were almost to Kemper's property line when the radio crackled.

"Thomas, it's Aguilar." Her voice trembled. "I have information on Jack Kemper. He's Justice Thorin's half-brother. I repeat, he's Justin Thorin's half-brother."

Terror shot through Thomas as he remembered the subterranean prison where Justice Thorin had held Aguilar captive.

"Copy that, Aguilar," Thomas said, maintaining outward calm despite the turmoil inside him. "Now we know why he's out for revenge."

LeVar looked at Thomas. "Ready to take this guy down like we did his brother?"

"I'm ready."

They needed to act with caution. One wrong move could cost them Claire's life.

"All right, let's keep moving," Lambert said, checking the chamber of his gun. "We need to put an end to this."

Thomas crouched behind a tree, his breath visible in the air. His watch said nine minutes and thirty seconds until midnight. Time was running out.

"Trooper Fitzgerald," Thomas said into his radio, maintaining a low profile. "Is your team in position?"

"Ready, Thomas."

"On my signal, we go."

"Copy that."

"We'll breach simultaneously. Lambert will go in first, followed by me and LeVar. Your team will hit the residence through the front door. We don't know what Kemper's capable of, so stay sharp."

"Understood. We're ready."

Thomas surveyed the darkened house, noting how quiet it was. The lights were off. Had Kemper lost power, or was he trying to lure them into a trap? The uncertainty gnawed at him as he double-checked his sidearm, ensuring it was loaded and ready.

"LeVar," he said, turning to his deputy. "We have at least one prisoner in the house and the lights are off. Double-check your target before you pull the trigger. We can't afford any mistakes."

"Gotcha, boss," LeVar said, his eyes focused on the house. Lambert nodded silently.

"Remember, we don't know what's waiting for us. Kemper could have booby-trapped the place, or there might be multiple hostages. Whatever happens, keep your wits about you. We need to end this tonight."

The wind sliced through the air, biting at exposed skin and seeping into their bones. Snowflakes danced around them as they approached the darkened house. Thomas led the team from one side of the property, while the state troopers formed a second line on the opposite end. The two groups moved in unison, their weapons at the ready.

"Fitzgerald, take the front door and windows," Thomas commanded through his radio. "We'll cover the back entrance and side windows. Expect anything."

The teams fanned out, each member taking up their assigned position with practiced efficiency.

The only sound was the intake of breath. Despite the cold, sweat beaded on Thomas's forehead.

As they settled into position, he ran his eyes over his deputies. His team members' lives, as well as the potential hostages inside, rested in his hands. But he couldn't afford to let that pressure affect him now.

The wind picked up, scattering snowflakes as if they were restless spirits in the night. A gust whipped snow into his face, and he crouched behind a bush. He scanned the dark windows of Kemper's house but saw no movement.

A blood-curdling scream tore through the night, echoing from within the house. Thomas knew it was Claire.

He lifted the radio. "That's it. We're moving in now. Go!"

As the team surged forward, the cold rushed through his clothes. Lambert was the most experienced at leading sieges, and Thomas allowed him to take the lead.

"Breaching!" Lambert called out as he kicked in the back door, the sound of splintered wood reverberating through the night.

Thomas followed, his weapon raised and ready. The darkness in the house seemed to swallow them whole as they entered. Shadows seemed to dance and shift, playing tricks on his eyes. The metallic scents of blood and death assailed his senses, making him want to retch.

Another scream pierced the quiet, followed by a guttural, animalistic growl. Thomas's blood curdled. Claire was somewhere in the house with Kemper chasing her. But where?

As they neared the end of the hallway, Thomas glimpsed something moving in the shadows. A figure appeared in a window, its features obscured by the darkness. Kemper or Claire?

"Hold your fire," he said, but before he could react, the figure vanished, swallowed by the darkness.

The team raced forward, and Thomas couldn't shake the feeling that they were rushing into a trap. But with Claire's life hanging in the balance, turning back wasn't an option.

52

The pitch-black house seemed to breathe with a sinister life of its own, the shadows coiling around Claire in tendrils. The Carver's footsteps thundered through the darkness as he stumbled and groped for the walls. A floorboard creaked beneath his weight, and Claire knew he was getting closer.

"Where are you, my dear?"

The chilling breeze she was following brushed against her skin with a whisper of hope. It must be coming from the door, her one chance for escape. This monster would not claim her as his victim. She would survive.

The sudden crack of splintering wood shattered the silence, followed by a dull thud. Someone had kicked the door in.

"Breaching!" someone shouted from the back of the house. Lambert?

A vice-like grip encircled her throat from behind. The Carver had found her.

He hissed against her neck, his breath hot and fetid. His fingers squeezed, and she gasped for air, desperate for a lifeline.

The footsteps in the house grew closer, coming from multiple directions. Help had arrived.

Too late. He was strangling her. As her vision blurred at the edges, she raised her hands and clawed at the arm that held her captive.

Claire's breath wheezed from her ribs to her throat. She wouldn't die. Not like this. Not with rescue steps away.

Her strength waned. With desperation, she turned and raked her nails across Kemper's eyes, tearing at the delicate skin and drawing blood.

The Carver screeched in pain, releasing his grip and staggering back. She stumbled and fell to her knees, gulping in air as her vision cleared.

His hands flew to his injured eye. Blood seeped through his fingers, but the murderous intent remained undiminished in his remaining eye.

"You're nothing," she said, wiping the sweat from her brow with a shaking hand.

He crouched and reached for a weapon on the floor. The bone saw. Serrated teeth hungered to chew through her flesh.

As he shuffled forward, a shout came from behind her.

"Stand aside!"

Thomas's voice.

She dove to the side.

"Drop the weapon," Lambert said, joining Thomas as an army of state troopers closed in from the opposite end of the hallway.

Kemper ignored the commands. He raised the saw above his head as blood poured from a hollow eye socket.

Thomas pulled the trigger, three shots ringing out in quick succession. Kemper's body jerked back as the bullets tore into his chest, the force of the impacts sending him to the floor.

The room fell silent, save for Claire's breathing and the

distant wail of the sirens. She collapsed to her knees and sobbed.

～

THE ROOM WAS a portrait of chaos, the air thick with death and the scent of gunfire. Claire's body trembled as she slumped against Thomas. Kemper's lifeless form lay on the floor, the blood pooling around him, staining the wooden boards a dark crimson.

"Are you all right?" he asked.

"A few cuts and bruises," she said. "Would have been a lot worse if you hadn't arrived when you did."

The lights flicked on, blinding Thomas.

"Someone turned off the power," Lambert said, holstering his weapon and surveying the scene.

She raised a hand. "I did that. Wanted to make it harder for him to find me."

"Intelligent woman."

The other deputies and state troopers filed into the room, their faces a mix of shock and grim satisfaction.

"Why me?"

Thomas's eyes held hers. "Because he wanted to get to me. His name is Jack Kemper."

"Should I know that name?"

"No. According to Deputy Aguilar, Kemper is Justice Thorin's half-brother."

She stared at the wall, seeing another time and place. Claire had joined the former medical examiner Virgil Harbough in examining the underground prisons. She'd handled the autopsies of Thorin's victims. Understanding seemed to drain the energy from her body.

"It's over," a state trooper said, clapping Thomas on the shoulder.

Thomas nodded, but his focus remained on Claire. He could see the exhaustion in her eyes, the psychological scars.

"Let's get you out of here," he told her, offering her a supportive arm. She hesitated for a moment before accepting his help, then climbed to her feet. As they made their way out of the house, the assembled law enforcement officers began the somber task of processing the crime scene, taking photographs and collecting evidence.

"Thank you," Claire whispered as they stepped outside, the night air a balm on their battered bodies and souls.

"I'm always here for you." There was a depth to his words, a promise that went beyond a mere response to her gratitude.

As the two of them stood there, surrounded by the flashing lights of police cars and the distant murmur of conversation, the gravity of what she'd faced sank in. She had confronted evil and survived. He knew in his heart the other victims were dead, though there was no sign of the bodies.

"I'll ride with you to the hospital," Thomas said.

She opened her mouth to argue that she didn't need to see a doctor, and in that moment he knew she was just as fearless and stubborn as Chelsey, LeVar, and Lambert. And him.

Her grip on his arm tightened as they walked toward the waiting paramedics.

And as the sirens wailed and the darkness of the night enveloped them, a strange sense of resolution settled over him. The book on Justice Thorin was finally closed.

Forever.

53

The ambulance's siren wailed, fading into the distance as it carried Claire away. Thomas stood motionless. He scrubbed a hand down his face as the red taillights disappeared around the bend. Kemper had used Claire to get to him.

Lambert placed a hand on his shoulder. "Boss man, the inside of Kemper's house is like nothing I've ever seen before. LeVar and I can handle the job."

"No, I'm all right."

"You sure?"

"This is my responsibility. It was me he was after."

They entered the house, its shadowed interior reeking of blood and decay. Thomas screwed up his face as they stepped over broken furniture, shattered glass, and the remnants of the once-imposing man's grisly deeds. Claire had almost shared the same fate.

"Look at this place," Lambert whispered, his voice hoarse. "He must've killed so many people."

As they searched the rooms, their flashlights revealed walls stained with blood, floors littered with bits of bone, and a world of dread and horror. The silence echoed the dead, punctuated only by the creaks and groans of the old house and their own labored breathing.

"Over here," Lambert called from one room, his voice tense.

In the center of the room, a large table bore the remnants of Kemper's work. Tools lay strewn about—saws, knives, and hammers, all crusted with blood. The stench was overpowering.

"God," Thomas whispered, his stomach churning. "I can't believe this."

"Jack Kemper was worth two million big ones," Lambert said. "Who would have believed he was a murderer in disguise?"

"Let's gather the evidence. The sooner we're done, the better."

LeVar stood in a corner with a hand over his nose. He'd left one haunted house and entered another.

The horror of Kemper's actions pervaded every corner of the house. Thomas felt as though the walls were closing in on him, suffocating him. So many had suffered and died because of him.

"Thomas, are you all right?" asked Lambert.

"Don't worry about me."

He stepped into Kemper's living room to find the air heavy with dread. Blood smeared the walls and floor in a macabre display, making Lambert cover his mouth.

"So many victims," Thomas said, trying to keep his emotions in check. "But where are they?"

He ventured further into the house.

"And where are Bonner and Thompson?" Lambert asked.

"I don't know." A trail of fresh blood led toward the back door. "But we need to follow this. It looks like someone made a run for it."

"With a missing leg?"

"If you were in Bonner or Thompson's place, wouldn't you drag yourself to safety to escape?"

Lambert didn't need to answer. Tracks in the snow drew their attention.

"I'll send Fitzgerald's team to follow the footprints," Lambert said.

"Tell them to get the bloodhounds. We might have a lost victim."

Lambert rushed off, leaving Thomas and LeVar to continue investigating the house. One room to go. It stood at the end of the hallway. The closed door grew larger with each step, as though it were a gateway to hell.

"Here goes nothing," LeVar muttered as he pushed the door open, revealing an abattoir of horrors.

In the room, a single hanging light bulb cast sickly shadows on the walls. It was here that Kemper had performed his gruesome work. Piles of dismembered limbs lay strewn about the floor like discarded toys, and the smell of decay colored the air.

"Dear lord," LeVar whispered.

"Be careful where you step."

"Look at the bones." LeVar pointed to a corner of the room. Kemper had used them to create grotesque sculptures, mockeries of humanity's form. It seemed Kemper had taken pleasure in his work.

"Evil knows no bounds."

That was the last thing he remembered saying before the room went black.

"Thomas!" LeVar grabbed his arm as he swayed. "You okay?"

It took a moment for the light to return, and he needed to crouch to keep his head from spinning.

"Almost fainted. Thank you for catching me."

"That's why you pay me the big bucks," LeVar said, struggling to inject humor into the situation. "Shep, you don't have to carry this alone. Why don't you go outside and breathe for a while?"

"We're almost finished."

Cameras clicked as two forensic investigators moved down the hallway. Thomas had to get his deputies out of the house so the forensic team could do their work.

"Bloodhounds are on the way," Lambert said as he stepped into the room.

No sooner did the senior deputy take in the horror than he clenched his mouth shut to keep from regurgitating. Thomas's eyes watered as he fought his body's instinct to gag. LeVar and Lambert moved forward, boots sticking to the congealed gore that coated the floor.

"Sheriff." A woman's voice. A forensic investigator. "You'd better look at this."

They followed the voice to the kitchen. A woman with golden hair stood beside an ancient-looking freezer. The door was slightly ajar, releasing cold tendrils of air into the room.

"Open it," Thomas said, bracing himself for whatever madness awaited them.

She pulled the freezer door open. Inside, wrapped in plastic, were rows of severed limbs. He swallowed hard.

"Catalog everything," he ordered. "We need to identify the victims."

LeVar snapped photos with grim resolve.

Thomas didn't argue when the forensic team's lead investigator ordered him to exit the house. Thompson and Bonner were dead. Were their body parts included in this gruesome collection?

The nightmare was over. But as in the dilapidated interior of Radford Mansion, the ghosts would stay.

54

The sun peeked through the curtains, casting a warm glow on the room as Thomas stirred awake. Outside the bedroom window, water dripped from an icicle. As impossible as it seemed, spring wasn't far away. He turned on his side and took a breath, appreciating Chelsey's presence beside him. Her wavy dark hair splayed across the pillow, and he smiled at how peaceful she looked.

"Morning, love," Chelsey murmured without opening her eyes. She reached out to place a gentle hand on his cheek before pulling the covers up to her chin.

He slipped out of bed, trying not to disturb her. As soon as his feet touched the wooden floor, Jack leaped out from beneath the covers, tail wagging with enthusiasm. He ruffled Jack's fur, feeling a sense of comfort in being surrounded by his loved ones.

"Come on, boy," he said, leading Jack out of the bedroom and down the stairs.

Though it was a bright morning, Thomas couldn't unsee last night's horrors.

"Hey," Chelsey said as she entered the kitchen, her green Honda Civic keys jingling in her hand. "Was it that bad?"

"The worst. I'm thankful you didn't see it."

"Sit down. Talk to me." She pulled a chair out for him.

He complied and took a seat, rubbing his temples as he tried to find the words.

"I feel so guilty about Claire. Kemper used her to get to me, and I missed an obvious clue at the gala."

"Thomas, you can't blame yourself for everything. You're a good man, and you do everything in your power to protect the people of Nightshade County. Sometimes things happen that are beyond our control."

"I need to be better. For Claire, for everyone."

"Promise me you'll talk about these feelings, okay?" Her eyes searched his. "Don't keep it all bottled up inside. It's not healthy."

"I promise I'll stay open. As soon as I get back, I'll call Dr. Mandal and schedule an appointment."

"Get back? Please tell me you aren't going into work today."

"No, I'm not, but I want to check on Claire. If you had seen that house, Chelsey..."

"It's okay. You don't have to pull yourself back to the moment."

After a quiet breakfast, Thomas slipped on his jacket and headed out to his truck. The morning air was crisp, but an unexpected earthy scent met his nostrils. The snow was melting. He climbed into the driver's seat and started the engine, letting the purr of the motor settle over him like a familiar blanket.

Ten minutes later, the sight of Claire's modest home came into view. He pulled into her driveway, noticing the toppled mailbox lying in a freshly carved tire track. He stepped out of the truck.

"About time you got here," she said with a smirk, leaning against her porch railing. He took a moment to assess her condition. Her russet hair was pulled back into a loose ponytail, revealing bandages wrapped around her neck and shoulder. A faint bruise lingered at the edge of her jawline, and a roadmap of lacerations trailed down her arms.

"Someone took the turn too fast again last night and ran over my mailbox," she said, shaking her head. "Can you believe it?"

"Third time this month," he said, sharing her smile. "Don't worry, I'll put it up before I leave."

"I can do it."

"I know you can, but I want to help."

"Thank you."

As they walked inside, the levity faded.

"Listen, Claire," he began, "I wanted to talk to you about everything that happened . . . with Kemper."

She sighed and lowered herself onto the couch, wincing as she adjusted her injured shoulder. "What's left to say?"

"It's my fault he targeted you. If I had been more careful, if I had understood the clue he left for me—"

"Thomas," she said, stopping him mid-sentence. "This isn't just on you. I should have been more cautious after leaving work. We can't keep blaming ourselves."

"I could have done more to protect you."

"Look at me. We can't change what happened. But we can learn from it and move forward."

"I know you're right, but I can't help feeling responsible."

"Is it your fault Justice Thorin abducted Aguilar and tried to kill her?"

"I guess not."

"And could you have known the Carver was Thorin's half-brother?"

"Kemper made it personal. That should have tipped me off."

"I worked on the Thorin case, remember? And yet it never occurred to me that the bone carvings had anything to do with a deceased killer. Let's make a pact. From now on, we both promise to look out for Nightshade County and never blame ourselves when we don't foresee every eventuality."

"Deal," he said, a smile tugging at the corners of his mouth. "Speaking of vigilance, I've been thinking about the coroner's office security. I think it would be wise to install a security camera."

She raised an eyebrow, considering the idea. "That's not a bad thought. It's just a matter of getting the funds."

"Would you be willing to petition Nightshade County?"

"If it'll help keep us all safer, I'll do whatever it takes. I have to look out for Kalifa too. I'm sure the county board will see the need after what happened."

"Good. I'll do my best to assist you in securing the funds. We can't let something like this happen again."

"It means a lot to me that you're dedicated to our safety."

"Hey, it's the least I can do," he said, a hint of self-deprecation in his tone.

They sat in companionable silence for a moment, lost in their own thoughts. Sunrays shone through the trees, melting the winter landscape one drop at a time. The glow seemed to envelop them in a protective barrier, a quiet symbol of their united front.

"All right," Thomas said, standing up and stretching his legs. "Let's fix that mailbox of yours. After that, I have to talk to LeVar about his ghost hunt at Radford Mansion with Scout and Liz."

"Sounds . . . interesting." Claire smirked. "Good luck with that."

In the shed behind her house, he found a new post and a toolbox.

"Darn drivers always taking that turn too fast," she said while he went to work, her hands shoved into the pockets of her jeans.

"Maybe we should install a speed bump," he said, plunging a spade into the frozen earth. "Or those reflective poles."

"Wouldn't be a terrible idea." She leaned against a tree, watching him work. "You know, I appreciate you doing this. I feel useless standing around while you sweat."

"Anytime, Claire," he replied, setting the post upright. After securing the mailbox, he stepped back to admire his handiwork. "This should last at least twenty-four hours."

"Until the next daredevil comes around the corner. Thank you for coming to see me. It helped."

"Always here for you." He wiped his hands on a rag. "Now, I better go have that talk with LeVar."

"Tell everyone I said hello. I'll see you around, Thomas."

"See you, Claire."

As Thomas climbed into his truck, he replayed their conversation in his head. The events with the Carver were still fresh, and he knew they both needed time to heal. But there was something about their bond, their shared determination to protect each other and those around them that reassured him.

He lived by a simple credo: Treat family like friends and friends like family.

And his family grew every day.

55

Icicles dripping outside the window portended the end of winter. Spring was weeks away, but the sun provided hope that the cold wouldn't last forever.

Scout watched from the bed as Liz packed her clothes after the sleepover. The girl stuffed clothes into her bag with a haste that was unlike her. Her shoulders slumped, and she remained unusually quiet.

"Hey, Liz," Scout said, leaning forward to get a better look at her friend, "you've been acting kind of strange all morning. Did I do something that upset you?"

Liz hesitated, her hands pausing over the clothes she had yet to pack, before letting out a groan. She sat on the edge of the bed, her posture betraying a lack of confidence, and turned her face away. The silence that followed contained unspoken thoughts.

"Liz, you can tell me anything; you know that. If I said something out of place, I'm sorry."

Liz's words were halting and unsure. "It's just . . . I don't know, Scout. I guess I've been feeling lonely lately, and LeVar has been . . . nice to me."

As the girl spoke, she fidgeted with the hem of her shirt. Scout reached out and placed a comforting hand on Liz's shoulder.

"All this stuff with LeVar seems sudden. Where did it come from?"

"Something about him just makes me feel safe, I guess. I like knowing that he'll always be around."

Scout nodded, understanding dawning inside her. "I get it. We're growing up, and things are changing."

Liz's fingers twisted together, knuckles turning white. She stared down at her hands.

"I don't want to be alone."

Scout studied Liz's face, piecing together the puzzle. It wasn't just about LeVar; it was something deeper. A fear of what the future might hold for their friendship.

"Is this about me leaving for college early?"

Liz met her eyes for a moment before looking away again, a small nod confirming Scout's suspicions.

"Hey," Scout said, reaching out to gently lift Liz's chin so they could look each other in the eye. "I haven't made any decisions. I'm still considering my options."

Liz's lower lip trembled. "It's just hard because we became best friends so quickly, and now everything is ending."

"Nothing is ending. No matter what happens, we'll make it work. We won't let distance keep us apart."

"Do you really mean it? I wouldn't blame you for making new friends at college and forgetting about Wolf Lake High."

Scout watched the sunlight filtering through the blinds, casting stripes of light and shadow across Liz's face.

"Remember when I was at my lowest, back when I thought no one would speak to me after I learned to walk again? You accepted me, even when I couldn't accept myself."

"Of course. You're my best friend."

"And you're mine. Nothing will ever change that, not college or distance or anything else. We'll always be friends, Liz."

A genuine smile spread across her face. "Thank you, Scout."

"Besides," Scout added, a playful grin forming on her lips, "we can't let your little crush on LeVar go to waste, now can we?"

Liz blushed, her hands flying up to cover her face. "Oh God, don't remind me. It's so silly, isn't it? He's like four years older than me."

Scout chuckled, nudging her friend with her elbow. "Hey, age is just a number. And you have to admit, he's pretty attractive."

"Ugh, fine," Liz conceded, dropping her hands and joining Scout in laughter. "Yeah, he's totally gorgeous. But I acted like such a jerk around him."

Together, the girls finished packing Liz's belongings, their laughter filling the room as they shared memories and jokes. As they zipped up the last bag, their eyes drifted to Scout's laptop. The Radford Mansion footage played on the screen, revealing the chilling secrets that lay within its walls. They had captured something special.

"Can you believe it?" Liz asked. "We actually did it. This is huge."

Their hard work had paid off, and the result was right there on the screen—undeniable proof of the mansion's dark history. It was a breakthrough that would send shivers down anyone's spine.

"The YouTube footage got a hundred-thousand hits. New York Ghost Patrol must be shaking in their boots."

"Oh my goodness, yes. I won't be surprised if they cancel their trip to Wolf Lake and go somewhere else."

"They should totally cancel. We captured everything."

"Has LeVar seen how well the footage turned out?"

"Nope."

"Then we should show him."

Scout arched an eyebrow. "You just want an excuse to check him out again."

"That too."

"Then what are we waiting for?"

56

LeVar huddled with Liz and Scout around the computer screen in the guesthouse's front room, bathed in the soft glow of the display. The icy lake stretched like a frosted mirror beyond the window, reflecting the blue winter sky. As the girls scrolled through articles about the Radford mansion tragedy, a sense of relief washed over him. Liz had finally stopped flirting. He could be friends with both her and Scout with no awkwardness.

"Look at this," Scout said, pointing to an old newspaper article on the screen. "The police never found any solid evidence back then, but people still believed it was murder. It took over a century for us to prove everyone's suspicions."

"Seems like that ghost we talked to wanted to get the past off her chest," LeVar mused, scratching his chin.

The sound of the door opening drew their attention away from the computer. Thomas stepped into the room, his sandy hair ruffled by the wind, and his blue-green eyes scanning the scene with surprise. He widened his eyes at LeVar. Thomas had warned him to be careful about spending time alone with Scout, and here he was with two teenage girls in his home.

"Hey, Thomas," he said, trying to suppress the defensive edge in his voice. "We were just researching the Radford mansion tragedy. We think it might have actually been a murder. Remember those ghosts we told you about? They hinted at it too."

Thomas' expression softened. "Ghosts, huh? Well, that's certainly a new angle on the legend."

"Trust me, if you'd seen what we saw, you'd believe in them too."

Liz chimed in, her eyes wide with excitement. "It was so creepy. I've never experienced anything like it before."

"Neither have I," Scout said, cleaning her glasses with the hem of her shirt. "Virginia Radford's ghost left a message on her headboard. It said that her father had pushed her."

Thomas' eyes widened at the revelation.

LeVar shifted in his seat. Part of him still believed Lambert was behind everything, that ghosts weren't real.

"Really?" Thomas asked. "You guys actually saw this?"

"Sure did," LeVar said. "I never thought I'd be one to believe in supernatural stuff, but after what we experienced, what can I say? The girls convinced me."

Thomas chuckled. "Well, I never thought I'd see the day when you'd believe in ghosts."

"Hey, man, sometimes you gotta adapt your beliefs based on the evidence. Besides, you're the one who's gonna have a tough time arresting a spirit and bringing the deceased father to justice."

"Ha! You're right about that," Thomas laughed, shaking his head. "I guess we'll just have to settle for solving the mystery as best we can, without relying on spectral witnesses."

The space heater breathed warmth through the room, mingling with the aroma of hot cocoa that Liz had made earlier. The cozy atmosphere contrasted with the icy lake outside the window. Liz was already scrolling through her phone, searching for their next ghost hunt location.

"Hey, what do you think about the old Thatcher House? There have been reports of hauntings there too," Liz suggested.

"Sounds interesting," Scout said, pulling up information about the abandoned house. "It says here that it used to be a hospital during the Civil War and then became an insane asylum for a short time."

"Creepy," said LeVar, peering over Scout's shoulder. "You're really going all-in with this ghost hunting thing, huh?"

"Absolutely. We'll need to upgrade our equipment. I'm thinking 4K-infrared cameras, extra-sensitive EVP recorders, and maybe even a new spirit box."

"Let's not forget extra EMF meters," Liz said. "And we should probably invest in better walkie-talkies so we can communicate during our investigations, just in case we lose each other in the dark. Plus, LeVar will need his own."

LeVar's jaw dropped. "Uh, who said I was down for more ghost hunts? One was enough for me."

"Now, now," Thomas said. "I won't let the girls investigate abandoned locations without a deputy to keep them safe. You won't stand in the way of their adventures, will you?"

"What's wrong with sending Aguilar or Lambert? Yeah, send Lambert."

"But you're an official member of our team, LeVar," Scout said.

"Am I? I don't remember pulling an official membership out of a cereal box."

"And we can't stop now," Liz said, turning her attention back to her phone, "Our Radford Mansion footage is blowing up online. We've already got hundreds of comments."

Scout blew out a breath. "That's way more than I expected."

"Same here," LeVar admitted, scratching his head. "I guess

people are really into this kind of stuff. Who knows? Maybe we'll become famous ghost hunters someday."

"Dude, we're already famous," said Liz.

Scout chuckled, shaking her head at the thought. "Let's not get ahead of ourselves. For now, we'll just keep investigating and see where it takes us."

"But I've got a feeling we're onto something big here."

Thomas leaned against the wall, arms crossed over his chest.

"Scout, how do you plan on handling school, your internship at Wolf Lake Consulting, running this amateur investigator's club with LeVar, Chelsey, Raven, and Darren, and now ghost hunting? You've got a lot on your plate."

She pursed her lips before answering, "It's a lot, but I can manage. I'll just have to prioritize my time better."

"You're already staying up late working on cases, and now you want to add ghost hunting to the mix? What about your schoolwork and your internship? You don't want to stretch yourself thin."

"Thomas has a point," LeVar said. "We don't want you to burn out."

Liz laughed. "You just agree with Thomas so you can chicken out of the ghost hunts."

"Can't blame a guy for trying."

LeVar grinned. When Scout set her mind to something, she was unstoppable.

57

Snowflakes drifted outside the floor-to-ceiling windows of the A-frame dining room, melting on impact with the thawing ground. The house radiated comfort, with its rich wood tones and soft, golden light cascading from the overhead chandelier. The scent of pine filled the interior, carrying with it the promise of memories yet to be made.

Inside, Thomas stood at the head of the table, his hair tousled from the heat of the kitchen. He bustled about, putting the finishing touches on the meal. Chelsey sat beside him, and LeVar leaned against the wall, his black dreadlocks swaying with each nod of approval for the food. Claire sipped from a glass of wine, while Aguilar passed around a tray of sourdough bread.

He had spent the afternoon preparing this feast using fresh organic ingredients he had picked up from the farmer's market. He'd chopped tomatoes, aromatic basil, and onions with precision, his knife gliding smoothly through each ingredient. The vegetables were gently sauteed in olive oil, their flavors melding together over the dancing flame. Then he'd seared tender cuts of steak, seasoning them with a blend of herbs and spices before adding a red wine reduction. The aroma wafting from the stovetop was tantalizing, guaranteeing a meal that would not soon be forgotten.

"Thomas, this smells absolutely amazing," Chelsey said, her eyes lighting up as she caught sight of the plates being set before her.

"Thank you," he said, dishing out more food and giving LeVar an extra helping. "I just hope it tastes as good as it smells."

"Knowing you, I'm sure it will," LeVar said, patting him on the back.

As everyone settled into their seats and savored the fruits of Thomas's labor, the air became thick with conversation and camaraderie. Each bite seemed to strengthen their bonds, further solidifying their connections to one another. The snow continued to fall outside, but within the walls of this A-frame sanctuary, all was warm and bright.

After everyone enjoyed the meal, Chelsey suggested they move to the living room and unwind by the fireplace. She led the way, her laughter echoing through the downstairs. The hearth dominated one wall of the space, and the chairs formed an arc before the couch so everyone could face each other.

"Nothing like a fire on a snowy night," she said, gathering a few logs from the stack beside the fireplace. The wood was oak, known for its slow-burning properties and pleasant aroma. Carefully arranging the logs atop the grate, she struck a match and held it to the kindling nestled beneath the larger pieces. Since the events on Laurel Mountain, she'd become an expert at starting fires. The blaze caught, filling the room with a comforting crackle.

As the flames grew, Jack and Tigger sauntered into the living room. Jack wagged his tail, making his way around the group and nudging each person's hand for a scratch behind the ears. The cat leaped onto the back of the couch and strutted along the cushions, purring as he rubbed against anyone within reach.

"Jack, you big goofball," LeVar chuckled, scratching the dog's head. "You always make yourself the center of attention."

Claire reached out to stroke Tigger's fur. "These two are quite the pair."

"Speaking of pairs," Thomas said, smirking at Chelsey, "I heard a rumor that you and Raven had quite the dance competition after I closed the investigation."

"Who told you that?" Chelsey asked, feigning shock but unable to hide her amusement.

"Guilty as charged," Aguilar admitted, raising her hand with a grin. "But in my defense, it was one of the most entertaining spectacles I've ever witnessed."

"Entertaining? I think 'legendary' is more like it. I can't remember the last time I laughed so hard. I nearly broke my ankle trying to keep up with Raven."

"My sister claims she won," LeVar said.

"Not gonna lie. She whipped me."

"You ought to know better. You let her choose C+C Music Factory? She becomes a woman possessed when they hit the speaker."

"True enough." Chelsey laughed as she recalled their antics. "But next time, I'm choosing the music. Let's see how well she moves to The Cure."

LeVar raised an imaginary glass in toast. "To good friends, outstanding food, ridiculous dance moves, and Raven getting her comeuppance."

"Cheers!" everyone chorused, their laughter mingling with the soothing sounds of the fire.

Thomas watched Claire, noting the subtle changes that signaled her growing comfort. She leaned back, her eyes creasing at the corners as a genuine laugh escaped her lips. It was a sight he hadn't seen since before the Kemper abduction. She'd found solace in the company of friends.

Tigger stretched across the back of the couch, eyeing the group with feline indifference.

"Hey," Aguilar said, leaning closer to Claire and lowering her voice. "I just want you to know, if you ever need anything—someone to talk to, whatever—I'm here for you."

"Thank you," Claire whispered, her eyes glistening with gratitude. "That means a lot."

It comforted Thomas to see the unearthing of Justice Thorin's specter hadn't affected Aguilar. Even better, she could support Claire. He felt a deep sense of appreciation for his friends. They were family, bound by shared experiences and unwavering support. And as he watched Claire laugh and smile, her pain momentarily forgotten, he wished this night could last forever.

At ten o'clock, the party broke up. Thomas and LeVar stepped outside with Claire and Aguilar, everyone shivering in the frosty air. The glow of the porch light reflected the flurries and turned them into fireflies, a hint of the steamy summer that would arrive before they knew it. The yard, blanketed by melting snow, glistened under the moonlit sky. Silhouettes of barren trees loomed at the edge of the property, swaying in the breeze.

"Thanks for joining us tonight," Thomas said. "It was amazing to see everyone together."

"Thank you for the invitation," Claire said, rubbing her arms as they walked. "If this sheriff thing doesn't work out, you should open a restaurant."

"Come on. It wasn't that good."

"Are you kidding?" Aguilar asked. "I ate more than LeVar."

"She did," LeVar said, shaking his head. "Won't happen again."

As they approached the vehicles, LeVar opened the door for Aguilar, who chuckled and waved him off.

"Dawg, I appreciate the chivalry, but I can handle opening my own door."

"*Aight.* Just wanted to make sure you were all set."

Thomas rapped his knuckles on the hood of Claire's car when she started the engine. These wonderful people had come together to support one another during a time of hardship.

"Drive safe, everyone," LeVar called out as Claire and Aguilar pulled out.

"See you tomorrow," Thomas said, waving as the vehicles drove away.

As he stood beside LeVar in the crisp winter night, both men wore expressions of contentment. The laughter and camaraderie they'd shared still resonated, a reminder of the strength of their bonds. And as they turned back toward the house, their steps leaving fresh tracks in the snow, they knew they were part of something greater—a blessed light that would guide them through the darkest nights.

GET A FREE BOOK!

I'm a pretty nice guy once you look past the grisly images in my head. Most of all, I love connecting with awesome readers like you.

Join my VIP Reader Group and get a FREE serial killer thriller for your Kindle.

Get My Free Book

www.danpadavona.com/thriller-readers-vip-group/

SUPPORT YOUR FAVORITE AUTHORS

Did you enjoy this book? If so, please let other thriller fans know by leaving a short review. Positive reviews help spread the word about independent authors and their novels. Thank you.

Copyright Information

Published by Dan Padavona

Visit my website at www.danpadavona.com

Copyright © 2023 by Dan Padavona

Artwork copyright © 2023 by Dan Padavona

Cover Design by Caroline Teagle Johnson

All Rights Reserved

Although some of the locations in this book are actual places, the characters and setting are wholly of the author's imagination. Any resemblance between the people in this book and people in the real world is purely coincidental and unintended.

❦ Created with Vellum

ACKNOWLEDGMENTS

No writer journeys alone. Special thanks are in order to my editor, C.B. Moore, for providing invaluable feedback, catching errors, and making my story shine. I also wish to thank my brilliant cover designer, Caroline Teagle Johnson. Your artwork never ceases to amaze me. I owe so much of my success to your hard work. Shout outs to my advance readers Marcia Campbell and Mary Arnold for catching those final pesky typos and plot holes. Most of all, thank you to my readers for your loyalty and support. You changed my life, and I am forever grateful.

ABOUT THE AUTHOR

Dan Padavona is the author of The Wolf Lake series, The Thomas Shepherd series, The Logan and Scarlett series, The Darkwater Cove series, The Scarlett Bell thriller series, *Her Shallow Grave*, and The Dark Vanishings series. He lives in upstate New York with his beautiful wife, Terri, and their children, Joe, and Julia. Dan is a meteorologist with NOAA's National Weather Service. Besides writing, he enjoys visiting amusement parks, beach vacations, Renaissance fairs, gardening, playing with the family dogs, and eating too much ice cream.

Visit Dan at: www.danpadavona.com